It was pitch-black when Anwen woke again.

had woken her. There was a smell nearby like leather and sandalwood.

She opened her eyes. He was so close she thought the blackness of his eyes was simply the darkness of the room. Then the heat of his gaze touched her and she realised this blackness was alive. A feeling of quietude entered her. The one who'd comforted her in the night had returned.

'You've come back,' she said, trying to smile.

He did not reply, but his eyes held hers. She couldn't look away.

Nicole Locke discovered her first romance novels in her grandmother's closet, where they were secretly hidden. Convinced that books that were hidden must be better than those that weren't, Nicole greedily read them. It was only natural for her to start writing them—but now not so secretly. She lives in London with her two children and her husband—her happily-ever-after.

Books by Nicole Locke

Mills & Boon Historical Romance

Lovers and Legends

The Knight's Broken Promise
Her Enemy Highlander
The Highland Laird's Bride
In Debt to the Enemy Lord

Visit the Author Profile page at millsandboon.co.uk.

IN DEBT TO THE ENEMY LORD

Nicole Locke

Published in Great Britain 2016
by Mills & Boon, an imprint of HarperCollins*Publishers*
1 London Bridge Street, London, SE1 9GF

© 2016 Nicole Locke

ISBN: 978-0-263-91742-0

Our policy is to use papers that are natural, renewable and
recyclable products and made from wood grown in sustainable
forests. The logging and manufacturing processes conform to the
legal environmental regulations of the country of origin.

Printed and bound in Spain
by CPI, Barcelona

IN DEBT TO THE
ENEMY LORD

To Mary,

Look, oh, look. I finally finished this story! The one
I started so many years ago; the one you patiently read
as I turned sentences around and repeated paragraphs.

Please look at this book, this wonderful,
dreadful book. The one I never finished
while you were still here.

Oh, it's not the book I want you to see,
but your family, your grandchildren,
their red hair so similar to yours.

I so wish you'd look, oh, look and see how much
we miss you.

Prologue

Helplessly, he stood beside her in the early morning light. He stood partly in darkness, but she knelt on the cold stone floor at the entrance of the fortress and the sun's light cut like spears across her huddled form.

She wept.

Tears streamed from swollen eyes and fell to clenched hands. Her fine grey gown gathered around her like shadows and her black hair, tangled, writhed to the floor. She pulled her head back, suddenly, like a wounded animal showing its jugular to its killer and the cruel light slashed across muscles strained with sobbing. She opened her mouth, but the only sound that came out was a guttural crackling deep in her throat. Then silence. Then with a sound he would never forget, he heard her scream a name he would never allow to be spoken again in his presence.

'William!' Her body contorted upwards, her

face raised in an effort to throw her voice. The name whipped around him as her breath came in small pants.

Teague watched his mother weeping. Watched, as she tore at her dress and as the deep jagged sounds shuddered and tore through her body. He watched and could do nothing to change the truth. No matter how long she cried for him, his father could not hear his mother's call. His father was dead. He had been standing by his mother's side when the messenger delivered the news.

Now, he stood behind a pillar and clenched his fists against his sides. He did not grieve. His pain came from a much deeper and darker emotion. Anger. The anger he'd felt since he heard his mother and his aunt arguing a fortnight ago.

Their voices had been soft, but discordant, and he had hidden behind the green-linen wall coverings to hear them. It did not matter that he was only a child. He had understood then, in their rushed accusations, his father was never coming back. His father was dead, but he paid no heed to the news. To Teague, his father had died when he had forgotten his son and forsaken his wife.

He did not mourn his father's death, but he was helpless at the sight of his mother's grief. She wept, when he could not. She loved him still, when he would not. They were both unwanted. They'd been betrayed. Yet, he could hear the love she felt when she screamed his father's name. Teague stepped out from behind the pillar and placed his arms around his mother's neck. He held her for only a moment before she suddenly stilled and let out a new sound. One hand clutched her heavily swollen stomach, while the other clenched his hands.

'Teague! Teague, get help!' she gasped.

Beneath his mother's knees the stones darkened with water and rivulets of red. The foreboding liquid pooled and streamed towards his feet before he let go. As he raced to find some help, Teague made his heart a promise.

Chapter One

Wales—1290

'**I**'m going to die,' Anwen of Brynmor muttered. 'And why would that be? Because I climbed a tree and plunged to my death. That's why.'

She circled the giant oak again. The thick lower branches could easily hold her weight. But it wasn't the lowest branches terrifying her. No, it was the thinnest sprays of green at the top where she needed to go. She could no longer see her hunting goshawk tangled in the highest branches, but she could hear his screeching.

'Oh, now you need me, do you? It would have been useful if you heeded me when you broke your creance and flew into Dameg Forest.'

She jumped, reached but missed the lowest branch. Her great blue gown billowed heavily around her legs. She quickly began unlacing the bodice.

'No, I called and called and you just flapped your little wings, trailing your leather jesses behind you. You care now, don't you? Now your jesses are tangled.'

Finished unlacing, she shrugged her shoulders until the gown pooled at her feet. Shivering, teeth chattering, she stepped out of the material. It was too cold to be in the forest, certainly too cold to be shedding any layers of clothing. At least it was also too cold for many people to be in the forest at this time of morning so there was no one to protest her lack of modesty. Shaking out any mud or wrinkles, she laid the gown gently on a fallen tree. It was her best dress despite the worn hem and hole in the sleeve.

'I'd leave you if I could, Gully. But we have England's fine King, and Gwalchdu's arrogant lord, who'd order a hand chopping for losing you.'

The tiny hawk let out a wild screech.

'Oh, you're for the death punishment as well, are you? It won't be me who will be punished, it will be Melun. That kind old falconer never hurt you one day in his life. So I'll fetch you for his sake, not for your stringy neck.'

Stepping closer to the trunk, she crouched low and leapt. She was rewarded with shredding her hands against the bark and falling on her backside in cold, partially frozen mud.

'Owwww!'

She sat catching her breath, but not able to catch her anger which bloomed up out of her. Punching the mud, she vented her frustration. 'Why couldn't I simply go home peacefully? You know I loathe visiting Gwalchdu village with all its perfectly thatched houses and perfectly cleaned streets.'

Thinking of Gwalchdu angered her more. She sprang up and threw mud at the tree trunk. 'Then you fly off, making more work for me. And now I'm ranting, you rotten bird!'

Jumping, she grabbed the branch with her lacerated hands. Pain knifed through her arms, but she wouldn't let go. Swinging her legs, she pushed her feet on to the roughened bark. Her grip slipped and fury arced through her.

It was bad enough losing her pride and yelling at a bird. It was worse yet wanting to sulk. And for what? Only so she could compare Brynmor with Gwalchdu? Her home was superior to Gwalchdu and it always would be.

She bit her fingers deep into the bark. She refused to slip. Strongly Welsh, Brynmor had fought to the end of the war against the English and so would she. Pulling up with all her might, she screamed.

'Did you hear that?' Teague, Lord of Gwalchdu, halted his horse.

'There is nothing here in Dameg's Forest but

the beasts, the trees and the icicles clinging to my stirrups.' Rhain shuddered. 'In fact, I can think of little reason to be this deep in God's forgotten forest this early in the morning.'

'Silence.'

Rhain snorted, but pulled his horse closer.

Teague forced his ears to listen for any sounds above the frozen ground crunching beneath the horses' hooves. The late autumn air was heavy with the smells of pine and damp earth and the fluttering sounds of small creatures. If there was someone in the forest, they weren't nearby.

Dismissing the sound as a bird's cry, he growled. 'You know why we are here. It's the only place left to hide.'

'We hold no chance of finding anyone here,' Rhain said. 'It's been hours since we received the threat and the enemy is gone by now. We search for only a trace.'

Teague's frustration mounted as he urged his horse forward. 'Then we search for a trace.'

It was too early in the morning for this search and too cold with a storm threatening. If the enemy was in the forest, they were more foolish than he thought. But it had to be a fool who threatened a Marcher Lord. One who retained and gained more power and land through the wars between Wales and England over a decade ago. One who could request aid from King Edward himself.

But Teague didn't want aid, didn't want to call attention to what threatened his home. So he and his brother searched alone. But so far had found no trace of an enemy. An enemy who, without provocation, left him hostile messages.

At first, he dismissed the messages. After all, he'd never been liked by his own countrymen, the Welsh, and certainly not by the English. Still, he earned the right to both sides' respect. Though his countrymen continued to roll with hatred toward the English, the war was over. It was just a matter of the Welsh accepting their fate. He'd certainly accepted his fate as a traitor when he sided with the English. When he helped win King Edward's war and kept Gwalchdu as his home.

No, he wasn't well liked by his countrymen and he could dismiss petty threats. However, now the messages no longer just threatened his own life, but those of Gwalchdu's inhabitants. When the enemy attached bloodied carcasses of animals he protected within Gwalchdu's stone walls and showed that his fortress's defences could be breached, Teague could no longer dismiss the threats.

He didn't understand why the messages began so long after the war and didn't understand the purpose of them, since the enemy demanded nothing. But Teague understood that he would put an end to them.

'It's uncannily quiet here.' Rhain slowed his horse to follow him through the narrow passages between the trees. 'What I wonder, dear brother, is why you are risking your precious neck for this purpose? If your enemy hides here, you disadvantage yourself by going blindly into his lair.'

Teague leaned to avoid a branch. The skittish horse sidestepped and he pulled the reins sharply to avoid slicing his leg against bark. 'The coward will not show his face to me, but by God's breath, I will find him.'

He would find the enemy, and when he did… But it would not happen with words. And it would not happen while he discussed his safety with his brother. 'I have no patience for this conversation. We will separate until the sun reaches midday.'

His sword ready and hidden by dense foliage, Teague stood awestruck. At any moment Rhain could rejoin him, but he couldn't clear his thoughts. His blood, coursing hotly through his body, pooled lower. Whatever he was expecting when he heard the harsh creaking of shaken branches, this woodland nymph was not it.

She stood on the branch of an enormous oak tree. Her back was to him and her arms were wrapped around the trunk. Her blonde loose hair fell far down her back as she gazed upwards.

But it was not her standing in a tree that riveted

him. It was the fact she was almost…naked. The grey chemise she wore was so threadbare he could see the rosiness of her rear and the large holes gave him glimpses of pure soft skin underneath.

She pulled herself over a higher branch and straddled it. When she grasped it between her hands, her chemise pulled tight and the position outlined the generous curves of her body.

By necessity, he leaned forward to get a better view. It was not enough; he stepped forward. He was less quiet, less hidden, but he did not care. She wore the most tantalising outfit ever conjured in his fantasies.

'And there I'll be, trapped in purgatory!'

He paused mid-step and adjusted his sword. Her husky voice was not that of a woodland nymph, but a vengeful harpy. Someone was with her. And that cracked through his desire like the tip of a cold sword pricking his neck.

'If it wasn't for the food you hunt…' she stood clumsily, her feet and hands finding little purchase until she braced herself against the tree '…food we desperately need, I might risk my hand with the false King Edward.'

Crouching back into the shadows, but not out of sight, Teague listened to her treasonous talk.

Her movements were abrupt, shaky, as she pulled herself up to the next branch. 'It's the Traitor's fault I'm climbing this tree.'

Whoever was with her remained silent. She not only spoke of treason, she talked like his enemy. Higher and higher she climbed, to the slenderest branches, and still she did not stop.

'All I wanted to do was give you a little training, purchase some fine jesses and return home.' Adjusting her weight, she stretched out far from the trunk and the branch creaked loudly until she grabbed one above her. 'I didn't want to get stuck in this rotten forest. And I certainly didn't want to have to purchase your jesses from my tanner that the Traitor stole.'

He edged closer, now confident she was alone. It was then he saw her goal: a bird caught by the leather straps around its legs. She talked to the bird and was spouting foolhardy words he was sure she'd want no one to hear.

Especially him.

'Just like the Traitor stole everything else when he sided with the English vermin.' Her hands sliding above her, she shuffled away from the trunk until she stood beneath the bird's branch. With one hand she tore at the thin strips of leather until the bird rose free. 'Wales should have won the war. Would have, too, if the almighty Lord of Gwalchdu hadn't switched sides. And why? So he could feed his fat belly!'

His enemy was here. And not a man, but a mere woman, who was neatly trapped in a tree.

Teague slashed the brown dried undergrowth with his sword and strode out underneath the oak's branches.

Startled, the woman's hand slipped off the upper limb of the tree. The thin branch she stood on swayed as it took her entire weight. 'You!'

Even from this distance, he saw her incredulity, then recognition, then a look so full of venom, he knew it mirrored his own.

'Yes, me.' Teague's satisfaction was so complete, he felt like a fox sinking fangs deep into prey. 'And you will come down to pay your due.'

'My due?' she spat, her body tight with ferocity. '*My* due!' she repeated, as the branch she stood on protested with sickening snaps.

She spun towards the trunk. Too late.

'Catch me!' she demanded as the branch cracked. Surging out from the broken tumbling limb, she swung her arms wildly, but it was not enough.

Her arm, her body, her *head* glanced against unforgiving branches before her landing in his arms forced the breath from his lungs. Then he couldn't breathe at all when he lowered her seemingly lifeless form to the ground.

She breathed, but blood coursed from her left temple. He laid her down, tore a strip off his outer tunic and wrapped the fabric around her head. Avoiding the deep gashes on her arms and legs, he felt for broken bones. She was intact, but for her head, and she desperately needed a healer.

She was his enemy, but she was alone. Her golden hair was matting with blood. With her paling complexion, she looked ready for the grave. If he left her here she would die.

Cradling her head within the crook of his arm, he lifted her to his chest and whistled for his horse. It would take precious time to reach Gwalchdu on foot, but he could not risk jarring her head.

This wasn't how he felled his enemies. His enemies died by his own hand, not by some tree.

'What has happened?'

Teague veered to his right. With several miles to go before he reached Gwalchdu, he hadn't expected to see anyone. It took a moment to realise his brother's presence did not represent a threat.

'Where the hell have you been?' Teague demanded.

Rhain dismounted. 'The way you ordered me away, I would not have guessed my presence was so desired. I could have told you how wasteful it was to separate for our search. If I didn't know better, I would think you thought little of my sword skills.'

'I have no time to mend your hurt feelings. She is wounded.'

'Let me help you mount and then I'll go ahead to notify Sister Ffion.'

'She's not dead!'

Rhain stretched out his arms. 'I can see that, dear brother. Ffion may have the necessary herbs to help heal her.'

Teague placed the woman in Rhain's arms, before mounting his own horse and gathering her close to him again. Edward's wars trained them well in handling the injured. But this was no soldier's body, heavy with armour. This was a woman: one so slight it was like holding nothing at all.

'Ffion will not be pleased that you bring someone home at this time,' Rhain said.

Ffion would not be pleased when she knew *whom* he brought home. 'When has our aunt ever been pleased? It appears her God was not listening when He deemed me this woman's only protection.'

'You could always leave her with one of the villagers.'

'No!' Teague said, surprised at his reaction. He did not want to leave her in the care of someone else. 'We waste time. Ready my room.'

Teague didn't wait to see his brother go. His attention was pulled to the woman in his arms. Limp, she moulded against him and he could feel each shallow breath filling her body. His white tunic wrapped around her head was soaked bright red with blood, her hair was tangled with leaves and bark and her face was almost translucent. He had the horse but even so, the journey to his home would be slow.

He only hoped he wouldn't be too late.

Chapter Two

'**W**ho is she?' Rhain spoke in an undertone, more for privacy than for courtesy.

Teague didn't look away from the woman lying on his bed. 'I don't know,' he answered. 'But I have my suspicions.' The servants had worked quickly and now a warm fire blazed in the grate, hot water steamed in buckets, and Ffion was mixing healing herbs.

'And you brought her here to Gwalchdu, to your room?'

'Yes.' Teague crossed his arms. He watched Greta, one of his most trusted servants, bathe the head wound. The woman's eyes fluttered, but they did not open. She could die despite the care given.

'Yes?' Rhain repeated. '"Yes" is a very interesting word, dear brother. Very interesting indeed.' He turned to leave the room. 'I'll be in the Hall, eating.'

Teague watched Rhain close the door behind

him. He knew he should go. He would need to explain what had occurred in the forest.

There was no reason for him to stay. No need for him to watch Greta gently pat around the wound to dry it. He needed to bathe before eating, as he was still covered in sweat and blood. *Her* blood.

She looked so different now to how he'd seen her in the forest. There she had moved, without grace, but with an unexpected strength. Now, but for the steady rising of her chest, he'd think her dead.

Her head wound needed stitching. He watched as Greta plaited the woman's hair to keep it out of the way. It was a menial task, one he had never seen before, but simple enough. Yet he stood transfixed as Greta's thick fingers wound to the very end and secured the plait.

He remembered how the long golden strands shimmered when the sunlight touched it. Bound, her hair lay as limp as she did.

He quickly dismissed the feeling of loss and left his room.

After his bath, Teague entered the Great Hall. The evening meal was over and his footsteps rang in the vast emptiness of the space. Rhain sat on a large high-backed chair before a low fire crackling in the smallest hearth.

'What happened in the forest?' Rhain asked.

Teague poured the wine left on the table and drunk deeply before grimacing.

Rhain chuckled. 'The wine has been watered. You may not be so observant, but you know how Ffion is when it comes to the wine.'

'Remind me to have a word with my steward about keeping a closer eye on my personal supplies.' Sitting on the other great chair, Teague explained what he had seen and heard from the woman in the forest.

'It doesn't make sense. Why would she be in the forest by herself? Especially so deep and so close to Gwalchdu,' Rhain said, after Teague recounted all the facts.

'She is the enemy.'

'Are you so sure?'

'She spoke against me and the King.'

'We are on the border of Wales. What villager hasn't spoken against you or the King? I worry your insurmountable patience is thinning and you are jumping to conclusions.' Rhain stopped and tented his fingers against his lips. 'Why don't you blame me?' he asked.

Teague's eyebrows raised. 'For what? You were not on watch last night when the message was left.'

'The threats didn't start until I returned to Gwalchdu.'

Teague flashed him a look of irritation. 'You're not the enemy.'

'You trust too easily; that could be your undoing.'

'I trust no one.' Teague swirled his goblet in both hands. 'And I don't know why I am encouraging this conversation.'

'Because you are no fool,' Rhain argued. 'The facts easily point to me. I came home last summer after being separated from you since childhood. The messages began a month after I arrived. Those messages are specific threats against your life and brought to you in your own keep, yet you cannot find who is behind the messages.'

'It isn't you,' Teague said.

'Who is to gain from your death? I am. Who can move freely to leave those messages? I can. Who can get close enough to kill you? I can.'

'Enough,' he growled.

'Why are you so sure?' Rhain pressed.

'You are my brother.'

'You are mad.' Rhain chuckled. 'Or perhaps you feel my more reasonable influence and you realise it would be foolish for me to threaten my own home.'

'Or maybe I realise you talk too much to hold any secrets.'

Rhain reached for the wine. 'Then why have

you so quickly concluded this woman is the enemy? Because she is silent?'

Teague peered into the depths of his cup. The colour of the wine looked black in the low light and he could not see the bottom.

'Why was she so near my keep?' He took a draught of wine. 'Her coming here, albeit by my hand, is too convenient. If she is not the enemy, then maybe she's a trap.'

Rhain rubbed his hands against his knees. 'She is no trap. She almost died falling from that tree. She needs our trust.'

Teague had expected his brother's open nature to surface. 'And you call me mad?'

'Well, it's your nature to mistrust. It's my nature to trust. You are still stubborn, while I am as flex-ible as water. Why should now be any different?'

'Perhaps because our home is being attacked by an unknown enemy?' Teague said.

'And you think that injured woman in your bed is the enemy?'

'Yes, I do. It's better to approach this situation with caution, rather than to be knifed in the back.'

Rhain arched one golden eyebrow. 'That *situa-tion* lying in your bed was brought into this home by you. And she can hardly keep awake, let alone wield a knife.' He stood and stretched. 'No, I am curious about her. I believe once she is well, I will simply ask her for answers.'

* * *

It was late at night, the keep was quiet and Teague found himself returning to his chambers. The woman was not alone. Greta slept in a chair in the corner, her great chin resting on her chest.

Compelled, he crouched by the woman's bedside so his face was closer to hers. He could not get her out of his mind: her climbing the tree, her hair swinging with the movements of her legs and arms.

Then, in that moment when the branch broke… his powerlessness; her demanding that he catch her. He knew she was his enemy, he knew he could not help her, but still he had held out his arms. Though hatred was etched across her every feature, she fell towards him.

Before he could stop himself, Teague placed his hand upon her head and brushed his fingers across her hair. Her eyelids fluttered, but she did not wake. He was…grateful. Somehow, this caress quieted him. Made him less restless…less alone. The feeling was as foreign to him as the other feelings she had inadvertently inspired in him.

Hope. She'd given him hope. With his arms outstretched, she had leapt towards him as if she could make it.

Hope. A ridiculous emotion that served no purpose.

He stood and walked away. He must be tired. It

was not in his nature to be open. He'd been alone most of his life, as he would continue to be. His people trusted him to protect them.

A woman could be as deadly as any man, or even more so. It was the reason he'd not lain with a woman since the threats began. In these times, hope had no place. Their very lives depended upon it.

Drifting on something soft, warm and comfortable, Anwen was half-asleep when the door creaked.

She opened her eyes. In the now-opened doorway was a small boy shaking mightily from the weight of a water bucket.

'Oh!' He dropped the bucket. 'You're awake!'

Her head throbbing relentlessly, she could not reply.

The boy straightened the bucket. 'I have your washing water, my lady. But you're awake! The house must be told.' He fled, but she could not move her head as she stared at the empty doorway.

Her vision cleared as a man filled the door frame. He was the most beautiful man Anwen had ever seen.

He was golden. From his head to his feet, he had the look of pure gold in sunlight. His eyes, the colour of warm amber, were brilliant against a square jaw and aquiline nose.

Then he smiled. She knew that smile would make many a maiden faint, but not her. Not under these circumstances.

'Where…where am I?' She forced the words out.

'You don't know?' Grabbing a stool, he stepped closer. 'Do you remember anything?'

Pain, her head full of knives. 'No.' Blackness hovered, threatening to take her again, but she couldn't let it. *'No.'*

The man placed a cloth to her face. Welcoming the cool moisture, she closed her eyes. Images flashed through her mind: someone taking care of her, a deep voice, a gentle, callused touch. Was it this man?

'Who are you?' she asked.

'My name is Rhain. Be easy.' He grabbed a cup of something and cradled her head so she could drink.

Struggling to swallow the diluted wine, she tried to concentrate on his words. 'My head feels… tight.'

'You've hurt it. The tightness is the dressing there.' Rhain sat down, put out a hand and stilled hers. 'No, do not touch it. Your wound is still too fresh.'

'But how did I—?' She stopped. There had been someone. Under a tree. Someone…

The door swung open and in walked a god or

a demon—no, it was a man, but he was no ordinary man. Where Rhain was golden, this man was dark. His hair, his eyes, his sun-darkened skin all reminded her of the night. But it was more than his colouring, it was the man himself. *He* was dark. Wariness overcame her, but she would not take her eyes off him.

He was familiar, like someone she'd seen in the darkness, but it could not be him. She remembered the person who had soothed her when the blackness overcame her, when the pain worsened. This man did not soothe, he cut.

'She wakes?' he asked, his eyes never leaving hers.

Rhain's eyes narrowed as he took in the dark man's mood. 'Is this necessary?'

'More than ever.'

Anwen's eyes burned as she strained to keep them open. The closer he got to her, the more she wanted to protect herself against the great waves of tightly controlled anger emanating from him. Power and authority were etched in every curve of his face. It was clear he wanted something from her and if she didn't give it, he would take it. Pain slashed across her head as her body tensed.

'She is not well. Leave her in peace.' Rhain stood and pushed the stool aside to let the other man stand closer to her.

'She is awake; she can speak.'

She could not speak. Her heart beat too fast and sweat covered her. Her stomach churned as she took in great gulps of air.

'Brother,' Rhain warned.

The rolling in her stomach would not subside, her head was spinning. Great waves of nausea drowned out whatever else was around her.

'I am—' she tried to say. The dark one leaned closer to her. 'I am—'

Anwen pushed herself up and retched over the breeches of Lord Teague of Gwalchdu.

'By Gwyn!' he exclaimed, before she blacked out again. It was a moment before the two men reacted to the considerable mess Anwen had made.

'Well, that was a first, I must admit.' Rhain's droll tone was not lost on Teague, who shot him a look. 'Oh, Teague, she did it not on purpose.' He took the cloth from the bucket of cooled water and wiped Anwen's mouth and face.

'I did not think her so weak.' Teague grabbed another towel and dipped it into the bucket to wipe his front.

'Ah, yes, weakness. I forgot what an unforgivable trait that can be. But she is a woman and even God allowed them a softer side, regardless of whether you acknowledge such a terrible flaw.'

'I am no beast. I know she is a woman. It's only—' Teague remembered her determination in climbing the tree and her quick thinking when she flung herself away and towards him. She was not like most females of his acquaintance.

'She surprised me,' he finished.

Rhain's mouth pursed in amusement, his gaze pointed at Teague's wet front. 'Yes, well, I can see that, but I differ with you regarding her weakness. She is not weak. Only strength of will could have pulled her out of such an injury.'

'She's weak now and useless to me asleep.'

'Why the need for interrogation? Have you heard from Robert at Brynmor?' Rhain asked.

'Yes, he sent me a missive. It appears they are missing a woman. An Anwen.'

'Now the question is if this is Anwen.'

'And if she is the threat,' Teague said. The woman's face had softened now she was sleeping. But her hands were still curled into fists, lending her an air of determination at a moment in which she should have been most vulnerable.

Teague remembered she had not cried out in fear when she fell. To see her this fragile went against everything he knew of her. Frustration rushed through him. He didn't know her at all; he needed answers.

'I must get clean.' Teague dropped the soiled rag into the bucket. 'Make sure she receives care,' he ordered before he left the room.

It was pitch-black when Anwen woke again. This time she didn't move her head. Her throat was sore and her stomach was filled with acid. Sleep was blessed, but something woke her. There was a smell nearby like leather and sandalwood.

She opened her eyes. He was so close, she thought the blackness of his eyes was simply the darkness of the room. Then the heat of his gaze touched her and she realised this blackness was alive. A feeling of quietude entered her. The one who'd comforted her in the night had returned.

'You've returned,' she said, trying to smile.

He did not reply, but his eyes held hers. She couldn't look away. If she could look long enough, she'd see—

Pain!

It slashed across her head and exploded behind her eyes. Moments of agony, subsiding only when she became aware of her gasping breaths, and a warm hand holding hers. She concentrated on the warmth and gentleness of his hand. It was a while more before her breathing eased and she was left with a dull ache weighing her down.

'I didn't mean to wake you.' His voice was deep, soft and vibrated through her.

They were such simple words, but she could hear…something…some meaning. The hand holding hers belonged to this voice. If her head didn't hurt, she'd be able to understand. Maybe it was concern? No, it sounded more like pain, like loneliness, but that was more confusing. She was here and he wasn't alone.

It didn't matter if she couldn't understand. She felt the need to *do* something for him, but she couldn't seem to open her eyes and blackness was seizing her again. He was being so kind. She didn't want him to feel pain.

'I'm here,' she whispered, her voice slowing as gentle waves of sleep took her.

A mad desire to keep her awake plaguing him, Teague watched the woman return to sleep. Looking at her hand still in his, he listened to the gentle rhythm of her breathing. It was almost enough to keep his restlessness at bay.

It was time to go. There was no logical reason for him to watch over her. The ravages of her fever were far from over and while she could suffer a relapse, she was regaining consciousness. Despite the pain, she was recovering. Soon, he would be forced to decide what to do with her.

Teague scrutinised the room. Since he'd brought her to his bed four nights ago, the sole change to the room was Ffion's mortar and pestle and some herbs littered on a table. Yet it felt foreign to him.

Gently placing her hand on the bed, he walked to the windows and opened the thick shutters to look into the courtyard below. The lit torches dotted across the dark stone walls and the full moon made it easy for him to watch his soldiers on patrol. He tried to put a name to the feeling of longing in him as he watched them.

Envy. His soldiers understood their tasks. They had a purpose in the night. He felt envy, too, that they had companionship as they went about their tasks. For him, although he was busy during the days, he was alone during the nights. His brother was here now, but Rhain had too many female admirers to be much company. His solitary nature had never bothered him before…but now he felt a longing that couldn't be fulfilled.

With the threats on his life, companionship was a luxury he could ill afford. Still it did not stop the conflict between his wanting and denying.

He turned from the courtyard and leaned against the window frame. There was no reason in any of this madness. It must be tiredness making him ache. Without sparing a glance at the sleeping woman, Teague left the room.

Chapter Three

Anwen woke to puffs of air brushing across her cheek. Two cloudy grey eyes, surrounded by folds of papery wrinkles and topped with hair the colour of snow, were mere centimetres from her face.

The old woman gave a delighted giggle. '*Ooooh*, you're awake. My name is Edith. Are you feeling a mite better? We knew you would wake today. You tried so hard yesterday though the blackies would get you again and of course you got awful sick. Almost undid all my hard work!'

Anwen blinked. She tried to make sense of Edith's words, but it was like listening to wind through trees and she felt, rather than understood, the words.

'Today, I said that little child would live.' Edith grabbed a wet cloth and gently wiped Anwen's face with cool water. 'You still have a mite of fever, I feel. Nothing like you had, though. You nigh had us scared witless when he carried you in five days ago silent as a kitchen rat.'

Anwen turned her head with some effort. 'Five days?' she asked. 'Where am I?'

The bright light pouring through the many narrow tall windows hurt her eyes, yet she could still make out the dark, intricately carved bed she lay in and its cream-coloured coverlet bordered with rich red which was repeated in the linens covering two walls to give warmth. The rest of the room was decorated with deerskin rugs, carved tables and chairs, and a chest with locked brass fastenings.

The room belonged to someone of great wealth and she didn't recognise a thing.

'Ooh, you can talk. Oh, yes, m'lady. Well, maybe a wee bit more than five days.' Edith grabbed some pillows and carefully stuffed them behind Anwen's back. 'You're probably starving, you poor thing.'

With confusion setting in, Anwen shouldn't be tempted by food, but the small bread loaf and flagon smelling of wine on the table next to her resembled a feast.

'Nothing but broth for days.' Edith tore off pieces of bread and fed them to Anwen. 'How does it taste? Good? Too much?'

She couldn't answer around the bread in her mouth.

'Now what was I saying? Oh! Though you've been asleep, you've had the house in an uproar, what with him always asking how you fared, and if the answer wasn't satisfactory, he'd check on you. Never saw anything like it.'

Edith kept stuffing bread in her mouth, but Anwen wanted to ask questions. Such as where she was and who Edith kept talking about, and who, for that matter, was Edith?

'Him?' she finally managed to say.

'Did you say "him"? Don't you remember anything at all?' Edith shook her head. 'That's one question answered for us. We had a bet, you see— not exactly we and not exactly a bet, because I don't do those sort of things—but there are some in the kitchens who have been wondering, heavily, whether you went into the sleep because of your head wound or because of him. But you see, since you didn't know about him, then that answers the question for us.'

With a flash of a practically toothless grin, Edith turned around and faced the door. 'I need the towels by the bucket, Greta. She doesn't know about him.'

A large woman with big beefy hands carried linens into the room. She didn't say anything, but her face was open and her brown eyes danced as she gave a wide friendly grin.

'Who is he?' Anwen could feel a headache beginning because of the kind of commotion no ancient old woman the size of a rinse bucket should make.

'Why, he is the lord, of course, m'lady.' Edith rolled down the covers. 'Dear me, that head wound must make you suffer some. I'll need to cool you with water while you lie still.'

Edith pushed Anwen's chemise up to bare her legs. 'You must be weak as a fawn.'

Anwen inspected her chemise. The weave was too fine and too white. It was not hers. 'What happened? Where am I?'

Edith sighed. 'Oh, very well. I'll not be saying much that you couldn't find out by looking out of a window. Just outside the walls is Dameg Forest. You have heard of Dameg Forest?'

'Yes, I live near Dameg Forest, but where am I now?'

'Well,' Edith started, 'we're by the forest, too.'

Anwen looked to Greta for a clearer answer, but the other woman simply wrung a cloth in her hands. The worry on their faces turned her confusion to panic.

Flashes of memory. Brynmor. Gwalchdu. Gully flying into the forest.

Anwen's heart lurched as she remembered the sickening crunch of the breaking branch. There was a man under the tree. She was angry. No, that didn't make sense. Why would she be angry if he was there to catch her? She was safe. The man made her feel safe. But who was he?

She contemplated the fine furnishings of the room, the thick stone walls, the rich wall coverings and an awful thought filled her head.

'Who is the lord of this place?' she asked.

Edith was suddenly all of a flutter. 'Don't you mind me none. Got no manners and don't know my place. I know that, by goodness I do. Going on like I did and you hurt and all. Why I could be causing you more harm than good.' Edith bent to wring the water from the cloth.

And that's when the answer to her question entered her room. Framed by the doorway, he was dressed in partial chainmail as if for a joust. But this was not the type of man to do mock battle. His black eyes were too harsh, his face too hardened and, despite the daylight, shadows emanated from him. This was not a man to play at things, but to take and take by force.

'Are you well?' he asked, his voice deep and resonating around the room.

Vaguely aware of Edith and Greta, both of whom were now standing at the far end of the room, she stared at the man walking towards her.

'Did you eat? Can you hear me?' he repeated.

He was the dark man to the golden man's light. He was anger to any kindness. He was the man who had watched her for days and at night had held her hand. He was the man beneath the tree and the man who had saved her life. In one incredulous moment, she knew who he was.

He was Teague, Devil of Gwalchdu and the Traitor. He was a legend with the sword, a Marcher Lord of King Edward and her sworn enemy. And here she was lying in his bed. But she was no coward.

'Yes, I hear you,' she answered.

He nodded, before his eyes skimmed down to her legs.

Her bare legs.

Before she could cover herself, Teague closed the distance between them and tossed the covers roughly over her. When he did not step back from the bed, she was forced to look up.

'You should not move,' he ordered. 'Are you well?'

Teague of Gwalchdu stood before her. Why hadn't she recognised it immediately when Edith was the only one in the room, when there might have been a chance to escape? How could she have been such a fool? But how could she have imagined she'd ever be brought to hell?

Without turning, he addressed Edith and Greta. 'Leave us.'

Frustration swamping her, she watched as Edith and Greta closed the door behind them. She was alone with the man who had torn her family apart and had brought the ruination of Brynmor. She had dreamed of meeting him face to face, but not when she was so weak she could barely sit up.

He narrowed his eyes, assessing her. 'No, you're not. You're far too pale and that bruise is likely to continue spreading before you are healed. Does it hurt?'

'Do you care?'

He ignored her. 'Who are you?'

'Is it important?'

He lowered his arms to his sides. It was clear he wanted an answer.

She didn't feel like giving him one. He didn't know who she was, or more specifically where she came from. It was no secret Brynmor and Gwalchdu were enemies. If she could keep her identity from him for long enough, perhaps she could escape.

'If you don't provide me with a name, I will give you one of my own.'

'Anwen,' she bit out.

'Anwen?' he asked and his tone implied he expected more.

'Yes, Anwen,' she said, repeating her name slowly as if he didn't understand her.

'Have I missed anything?'

It was this man's brother, the golden one, who opened the door. He looked so different to Teague. His reputation was different, too. This man had been too young to fight in the Welsh wars. To him she would be civil.

'Rhain?' Anwen said.

'Yes!' Rhain grabbed a stool and a chair and set both by her bedside.

'Do you remember anything else?' Rhain asked, sitting on the stool.

She shook her head once. It was safer to pretend.

'No one has told you of this place?' Teague did not take his eyes from hers.

'No,' she answered.

'You would want to know who we are and where you are, I imagine.' Teague's voice had grown silky, his mouth shaped into a mock of a smile. 'How rude of me not to introduce myself, especially since you have supplied so much information to me.'

He sat on the chair Rhain had placed near the bed. He was now so close she could see the growth of his beard, the deep furrows around his mouth. His lips held an odd curve, making them full, soft, yet harshly masculine at the same time. Without releasing her gaze, he answered, 'I am Teague, Lord of Gwalchdu.'

She could say nothing as her worst suspicion was confirmed. She lay in the bed of Gwalchdu's lord. 'Gwalchdu' meant 'black hawk' and there was no more evil a bird in all of Welsh myth. The name fit this place and the traitor who now sat before her.

'So you have heard,' he said, gauging her reaction.

'I have heard, but have seen nothing.' She tried to keep her eyes unreadable. She had hated this man all her life. She would not back down now, despite the pounding in her head.

He gave a curt nod. 'You are wise to be blind. But it seems you watch now.'

This was no word game he played with her. This was no pastime of a bored nobleman and there was no false smile on his face.

Anwen tensed and immediately regretted it as her body protested. It would take all her resources to escape. But she had herself. That had proven enough in the past and it would prove enough now.

'I don't watch so much.' Anwen tried to get her thoughts together as pain slashed across her left temple. 'I'll watch even less once you let me go.'

Rhain stood. 'We should go. It is clear you are unwell and have need of rest.'

Rhain glanced at Teague, but the lord's gaze locked with Anwen's. For a moment she didn't think he would answer.

'She needs time, Teague,' Rhain argued.

'Call for Ffion.' Teague's voice was low, but not soft.

* * *

Anwen did not breathe again until the two men closed the door. She was trapped. Trapped by a huge giant of a man with eyes as dark as obsidian. Eyes she knew matched his soul. She knew his name, as a person knows the name of evil. At Brynmor, the people did not even whisper his name aloud without crossing themselves and he had sat so close to her she'd noticed the slight shadows under his eyes.

Why would she notice he was tired? He was the Traitor. Dear God, she was beholden to the Traitor of Gwalchdu! It was clear he had saved her life by bringing her here. But now she recognised him, she wondered at his motive. She doubted it was kindness or gentleness. She'd seen his eyes caressing her bare legs; his motive could not be kindness.

The pain was increasing, but she must fight it. She put a hand to her head, the thick dressing holding its shape; if only the dizziness didn't increase, as well. The Traitor wanted something from her and she had no intention of staying to find out what. Anwen pushed until she was able to sit up. For a moment she thought she would make it, then the room spun, and blackness overcame her.

'Well, at least we know she is innocent of any treachery,' Rhain whispered before they reached the bottom stair.

'Do we?' Teague walked through the entrance into the rare winter sunlight. He headed towards the gardens. It was wash day and the shrubbery was covered in linens.

Rhain followed. 'She called herself Anwen. Since we know Brynmor is missing someone by that name, we know she belongs to them. Now it will be simply a matter of letting her rest until we can return her.'

Teague sat on a bench and stretched his legs. He admired the newly tilled and almost bare garden, knowing his winter larder was full. 'But she didn't say she was from Brynmor.'

'She didn't?' Rhain thought for a moment, then shrugged. 'So?'

'So, she could have been given that information.'

'What significance can it have? All manors have sworn allegiance to Edward.' Rhain sat, and adjusted the dagger at his waist.

'All manors have, but not all the people.'

'You think that woman is a threat?'

'Yes. When she practises deception and tells us nothing.'

Rhain shrugged. 'Does it matter since we know her identity and her home?'

'It matters that she deliberately hides facts. What else is she hiding?'

Rhain fingered his dagger's hilt. 'She suffered

a severe head wound and could have mistaken your questioning.'

'No, I saw her eyes on me when I entered the room. She knew who I was. She is hiding something.'

Rhain pursed his lips before answering. 'She has been deeply hurt, Teague. Let her go. She can have no knowledge of what plagues us here.'

Teague scuffed his foot through the rough dark dirt. Many razed stalks were bare, but protected by compost. Come spring, he was sure the herbs would be flavouring his meals. Yet he wasn't sure of the woman in his bed. He couldn't take a chance on her innocence. 'Like hell I will.'

It was the time of night that was almost day, but despite the hour, she could feel he was there. She was too tired to fight and didn't open her eyes. 'Why are you here?'

Teague watched Anwen fall asleep, watched as her breathing slowed, and her eyelids ceased their fluttering. 'I don't know,' he said, even though she could not hear him.

He shouldn't be here. Now that she was conscious, it was time to stay away from her. He might know her identity, but he still did not know her motivations and those would take time and distance to discover. But still he lingered idly by her side like some besotted troubadour.

No, this wasn't an idle feeling, but a deep churning in his blood.

When he entered his chamber, the sight of her had been like the flat of a sword to his gut. She had lain in his bed, propped up with his pillows, her legs bared as if waiting for him. As if she belonged. He was ill-prepared for the lust which had assailed him.

When he tried to find some semblance of control, she refused to answer his questions. Weak as she was, she defied him. She might have been truthful in giving her name, but she withheld something. He could feel it. She had known he wondered where she lived, but had avoided answering him. She'd asked where she was, even though she already knew.

Teague averted his gaze from her sleeping face. It was wrong for him to be here, but she was wrong in hiding something. She could not be allowed secrets. He had an enemy threatening his home. He would discover what she hid from him. He had to. For all their sakes.

Chapter Four

'You have overexerted yourself, I see.' With long strides, an older woman, wearing voluminous black robes, approached the foot of Anwen's bed. 'Take care, girl. I am Sister Ffion and I don't have time to cater to you and do my duties here.'

Biting her lip to keep from snapping at a woman of God, Anwen watched Ffion pull herbs from her satchel and place them in the mortar on the nearby table.

'You took a blow to your head.' Ffion lifted and swirled the matching pitcher before pouring the dark liquid on top of the herbs and mashing them more. 'I'll do the best I can, but it is in God's hands.'

As Ffion ground the concoction, the air turned foul. Anwen's eyes watered.

'I'll have none of your complaints.' Ffion set the pitcher down and came to her side. 'You about undid all of my healing. For days this poultice has been placed on your head to help heal your wound.'

Anwen tried to breathe through her mouth, as she lifted her head and concentrated on Ffion's cold hand supporting her neck. 'You have been here?'

'From the beginning.' Ffion unbound the wrappings. 'Dear Rhain notified me immediately of your arrival. He knew of my healing abilities. Why, if it wasn't for him, you would have died.'

Ffion dropped the bandages in a bucket. 'It's quite a miracle you pulled through. Rhain was right in notifying me immediately. I was able to prepare the herbs in time for them to take.'

Anwen patted the side of her head. 'Wasn't... wasn't Lord Teague under the tree? Didn't he save—?'

Ffion seized Anwen's wrist; her cold fingers dug like claws into her skin. 'Gwalchdu's lord saves nothing!'

Anwen jerked her wrist free and Ffion's lips pursed before she shook her head. 'I only meant it is better if you don't touch the wound. You may harm my healing.'

Anwen rubbed her wrist and quickly damped her anger. Ffion was trying to help her. 'How bad is my wound?' she asked.

'You'll scar.' Ffion began to clean the wound and the water brought both pain and relief. 'It'll be permanent, too. Most likely a disfigurement so no man would have you. But that is probably for the best.'

Ffion slowly rinsed the linen in a bowl, as Anwen processed the Sister's almost gleeful words. Despite her Welsh-born accent, Anwen knew Ffion would be no ally.

'But your disfigurement does not seem to keep some men away now, does it?' Ffion dabbed at the wound. 'However, the wound is healing according to God's wishes. You must still be chaste.'

Anwen didn't want to think about all of Ffion's words, but she needed to clarify something. 'It's healing?' she asked.

'Yes. In His great wisdom, God gave me gifts and knowledge of the healing arts. I suspect your healing to take at least another sennight.'

'Surely it won't be that long.' The poultice stung.

'A few days ago, we didn't think you'd live. You are staying here for a sennight so you will not undo all my work.'

'I didn't mean to stay as long as I have.' Demanding woman of God or not, Anwen had no intention of staying. She was needed at Brynmor. And not only for Melun's sake. She wondered if Alinore, her sister, was alive; if Urien, Lord of Brynmor, had hurt her again. It hurt to think of them. She needed a distraction from knowing she wasn't there to protect either of them now.

'Have you been here long?'

'Almost all my life.' A look of pain crossed Ffion's face as she added, 'Many years.'

'You've known the family that long?'

'I *am* the family. I am the sister of Teague's mother and Rhain's aunt.'

Edith opened the door, her hobbling-and-hopping gait shaking the bread and pitcher on the tray she was carrying.

Ffion's frown increased. 'I had requested Greta bring food for you. Pity, for Greta would be better for your healing.'

There was a loud rattle as Edith set the tray on the table at the far end of the room.

Gathering her mortar, pestle and satchel, Ffion said, 'It will do you well to remember the seventh commandment. Now go with God.'

Edith continued to arrange the tray until the door closed behind Ffion. 'Go with God, she says. As if *that* woman walks with the Maker himself! Her lecturing you not to commit adultery, when you're having trouble eating!'

Edith opened the door and stuck her head through it.

'But surely she means no harm,' Anwen said.

'Oh, don't mind me, dearie.' Edith gave her a smile over her shoulder. 'Don't mind me. I'm an old woman and tend to talk when I shouldn't.'

Anwen thought about furthering the conversation when the smell of food wafted in. Edith stepped away from the door and Greta carried a large tray of dried meat and cheeses into her bedroom.

'Thank you.' She smiled at Greta, who was setting the tray across the bed.

'Oh, don't mind Greta none,' Edith began, as she checked the fireplace, then straightened the window shutters. 'Speechies took her voice away a long time ago, but you'll never find a smarter soul than our Greta.' Edith paused, then said more reflectively, 'Maybe the lord and his brother, but certainly nobody kinder.' For all her small stature, Edith moved and talked like a whirl of dust in a storm. Shaking her head, she added, 'Simply look her way when you speak, and she'll get your intention sure enough. Hearing's good.'

Looking at Edith and Greta, Anwen wondered at the one-sided conversations these two women must have had over the years.

She looked back at Greta. 'Thank you, again.'

Greta's smile lit up her brown eyes.

Anwen chose a piece of cheese. When it stayed down, she felt a faint glimmer of hope. Despite everything, she was healing. Soon, she could return home and everything would be set aright again.

'I thought I'd find you here.' Rhain climbed the last two stairs to the top of the outer bailey tower.

Despite the cold, Teague stood just beyond the torches' flames so he could remain in the shadows. It was easier to watch his men this way. It was also easier to hide that he stood alone while they walked the cold night in camaraderie. He had long become accustomed to being a voyeur to the life they led.

'Ffion says Anwen is recovering, but she still needs to stay a sennight,' Rhain said.

News of the woman again, who was as obscure to him as the darkened forest beyond the courtyard. Was it she who made him aware of his solitary life?

'Well?' Rhain prompted.

'Let Ffion have her say in this.'

'It may be easier, but I wonder.' Rhain shrugged. 'Ffion is not as she was.'

'You left when you were a child,' Teague reminded him.

'True. But what about tonight's episode during dinner. Has it happened before?'

Ffion's episodes, as well as her anger and unintelligible murmurings, were worsening since his brother's return. He worried for her. 'Yes, it has happened before, but tonight it was mild.' Teague pulled his cloak tighter around him. The ground was already hardening with frost, his breath gusted out in front of him. He hadn't been aware of the cold until his brother arrived.

'It was as if something upset her.'

'Christmas approaches. Though Ffion is fierce on celebrating Christ's birth, there are those who celebrate more than the Christian traditions. It is a battle she doesn't like to lose.'

'You once wrote to me about the Mari Lwyd. Is she still arguing about that?'

'Every year,' Teague said. 'Ffion insists the decorated horse skull with white linen is to celebrate the Virgin Mary and should come at the end of the Christmas season in January.'

'But the villagers...'

'Still bring it out at the end of harvest on Martinmas. When we slaughter the animals for winter, there's always celebration.'

'Wassailing? I could see how that would worsen her condition.'

'It does.' Teague nodded. 'Since Martinmas approaches, I am glad you are here.'

'For all her faults, at least her stubbornness proves she's family.'

Ffion had shown Teague only stubbornness and animosity. Though he never doubted she was family, it wasn't what secured her home at Gwalchdu. It wasn't the reason why he protected her, when her episodes became noticeable, and the Church made enquiries.

No, it didn't matter if his aunt hated him, most people did. He would protect her; he would pay off the Church and their damning enquiries because he would be for ever in his aunt's debt.

'Stubbornness is no doubt what gives her strength,' he said.

'Well, the battle of winter traditions will certainly make for an interesting Christmas,' Rhain said.

No one ever won, but Teague ensured Ffion's wishes were obeyed and that the villagers hid their pagan ritual. It was the least he could do for his aunt.

He'd been a mere boy when his mother gave birth to Rhain and, as a result, he was barred from her birthing chamber. But Ffion had been by her side, tending to her in those last hours. Knowing what he knew of Ffion's skill now, he had no doubt she'd waged war to save his mother's life.

'It seems as if her condition worsens.' Rhain sighed raggedly, his breath visible in front of him. 'I knew she wasn't well when she approached the table. I could see the whites of her eyes and she was sweating profusely.' Rhain wrapped his arms around him and patted his sides as if beating off the cold. 'But her prayer! I couldn't understand a word she said.'

When Teague had paid his respects to his mother, he hadn't known what to expect. He'd been but five years old and within hours witnessed his mother's heart breaking and heard her pain-filled labour. Yet when he saw her lying there in the bed all he saw was peace.

Ffion had given his mother peace in the last moments of her life.

'Tonight, you had a calming effect on Ffion.' Teague tilted his head. 'When it happened before, I stepped in, but her rage worsened and she was dragged out of the Hall.'

There was a part of him that still believed as the child did, that Ffion, in order to give her sister peace, had taken the grief and pain as her own. For ever after, Ffion was never the same. Her countenance was lit with some wrathful vengeance he couldn't understand.

But he didn't need to understand everything. He understood what mattered most. That he owed his aunt a debt he wished he could pay. And he hated that she suffered.

'It's almost unbearable to see her so altered,' Rhain said.

Teague couldn't disagree. Ffion was the only family they had left. Over the years her episodes continued and so did her demands for control and order.

Just like the demands she made now when it came to Anwen of Brynmor. He stamped his feet against the cold seeping into his shoes. Instead of ruminating on the past, and freezing his toes in the process, he should be searching for Gwalchdu's weakness and the enemy.

He should be scanning the forest beyond for a fire. If Anwen wasn't his enemy, or was only an accomplice, the main perpetrator would still be nearby. On a cold night such as this, a fire would be necessary.

But the darkness beyond Gwalchdu's walls was complete. So Teague turned his attention to the barbican. There were two guards above the gate and two standing next to the closed portcullis. Such manpower was excessive, but the threats could not continue.

And though his aunt's demand for Anwen to stay had been made with the greatest disdain, it was a simple request to agree to. In fact, he wouldn't want it any other way.

'Let the woman stay the sennight,' Teague said. 'But I want a guard at her door.'

Rhain glanced at Teague. 'A guard at Anwen's door? I wonder you do not apply this to all passages.'

Teague shot him a look.

Rhain shrugged. 'She won't like it, but it would do more harm to move her and no harm will come of her staying.'

Teague's mouth twitched. 'No harm? What of the threats and the fact she is not from Gwalchdu, but an enemy's manor?'

'We haven't received any messages attached to a slaughtered animal since the day we brought her here.'

'There were weeks between messages before and the villain still won't show himself.'

'It is all very odd. The messages never demand anything, neither money, nor horses, nor services. There's never a pattern to their appearance. Everything we've been taught about an enemy doesn't apply, except the slaughtered animals and the threat of your death, which is always there.'

Teague leaned over the rampart to feel the burst of cold night wind. Everything Rhain said was true. The enemy didn't follow any normal pattern. He couldn't negotiate to stop the threats when he didn't even know who to negotiate with. Until the enemy revealed himself, Teague was a warrior in a ghostly war. His sword and training were useless because he could not see or strike his enemy. A lord with no power to protect was no lord at all.

'How?' Teague hit the rampart. There was not the usual talking amongst the soldiers as would be expected this time of night. All the men had been notified that there would be a great reward for any information or capture of the enemy. 'How is he coming in? How is he getting to the livestock or my falcons?'

'He's not getting in; he's already here.' Rhain

gestured in front of him. 'Look at this place. There are torches lit at night, when we expect no visitors; extra soldiers at the entrances, when the gates and portcullises are closed.'

Teague shook his head. 'The threat is too recent. The people here are loyal and this is their home.'

'I think we need to stop asking how it is happening, but why.'

Teague hid his impatience. 'I thought the messages made it clear.'

'Yes, someone doesn't like you, but why now? Why these threats, but no action?'

'The enemy waits for fear to seep in before they strike. It's just as we did in Dolwyddelan. Fear, ultimately, is the conqueror.'

'And is there fear here?'

'By God or Gwyn, no,' Teague growled. 'Never.'

'Exactly.'

He turned to Rhain. 'Exactly what? The enemy doesn't want me afraid?'

'No, it means it's something else.'

'Or it could mean the enemy miscalculated,' Teague said. 'We'll know who is right when the next message comes.'

'Are we so sure it is but one person?' Rhain asked. 'It would seem, given the wide dispersal of the messages, that it could be at least two.'

'No, it has to be one. I'll not question Gwalchdu's defences that much. They're too tight for two or more people to go unnoticed.' Teague paused, before his tone turned lethal. 'But one man or twenty, I will end this ghostly battle.'

'When you are like this, I do not wonder why you are known as the Devil of Gwalchdu. No wonder the King trusts you so well with such a strategic castle.'

'Gwalchdu belonged to our family long before Edward's Welsh Wars or his campaign against Scotland. He would need to be a hundred kings before he could wrest its governing to someone else.'

'Have you told Edward about the threats?' Rhain asked. 'I am sure he would not appreciate games here.'

Teague shook his head. 'He is spread too thin with the Scots. He barely responds to correspondence regarding our positioning in Wales; I could not bother him with private matters.'

'Perhaps he's distracted by his worry of Eleanor, who has been sickly.'

Teague could never understand Edward's obsession over his wife. The time he spent with her could be used to solve the problems in Scotland, to tighten his reign in Wales. Instead, the King was almost…devoted to her.

He remembered his parents' relationship. They, too, had seemed devoted to each other. But it had been all a lie. His father had abandoned his family, his pregnant wife, for another woman. And with grief racking her body, his mother had begun an early, bloody and heartbroken labour.

'The King's affection for Eleanor seeps the strength from him,' Teague said. 'She bore him enough sons for a dozen monarchies. He wastes his time on petty worries.'

Rhain slapped Teague on the back. 'It's love, Teague, not simply affection, and some would disagree with you and say their love strengthens Edward for all his trials.'

Teague knew better. Love had sapped the strength from his mother just when she needed it most to bring Rhain into this world and it had killed her.

'Love? What use is love?'

Chapter Five

'I trust you are well today?' Ffion entered Anwen's room without knocking.

Anwen didn't turn from her seat in the window. The courtyard was full of market wagons, kitchen maids with arms of laundry and soldiers training.

'Your situation will not end simply because you ignore it,' Ffion continued.

'I did not know prisoners were allowed any benefits.'

'You are hardly a prisoner,' Ffion admonished as she went to the table to make her poultice.

'I have been well for three days. Well enough to return to my home, yet a guard is at my door and he will not let me leave this room.' Anwen unwound the bandages from her head. Ffion had taken the stitches out a few days before, but the poultice and the wrapping of her head continued.

'As you know, the guards have explicit instructions you are to remain here for a sennight. Need I remind you that if it were not for me and the hospitality of Gwalchdu, you would be dead?'

Ffion never failed to remind Anwen who tended her.

Anwen tilted her head so the older woman could apply the paste. 'If you'd let me have a mirror, which must exist here, I could put this on myself.'

'Of course we have a mirror, we have several, but I believe you need these visits.' Ffion pressed her hand to secure the bandages so she could wrap them. 'There is much sin in this keep and many lecherous thoughts. We need God and prayer to purge us. Have you been practising your lessons of chastity, obedience, poverty?'

'I am a Christian, Sister,' Anwen said, 'and do my prayers as often as time will allow.'

'At Gwalchdu I expect prayers to be six times per day. Now you are better, perhaps it will be time for you to join us.' Ffion raised her finger in the air. 'Remember: community—'

'Prayer, study and service,' she interrupted. 'But I am not staying at Gwalchdu and you cannot keep me here.'

Ffion opened the door, and stepped across the threshold. 'It seems we will both have to await God's answer to your fate. In the meantime, I will expect you to pray with us. The bells will tell you when.'

Anwen turned her attention to outside her window. She had no intention of following Ffion's directives and she had no intention of staying here.

From what she could see, she was in an inner tower that was surrounded by a low wall. Directly underneath her, there were no gardens with flowers and benches. Without any ornamentation, the grey stone walls jutted out forcefully from the hard-packed ground. It was as if the castle stood in defiance of nature. Very much like the lord who governed it.

She had not spoken to Teague since the day he had asked for her name. Then she had still been so weak and sick, she could only feel the darkness and tightly coiled anger surrounding him.

But at night, Teague had been almost reluctantly kind. There was such a difference between the man at night and the man at day, she wondered whether she had dreamed the night. It had probably been Greta or Edith. There could be no kindness in the Traitor of Gwalchdu.

The cold reality of daytime should prove that to her. She was kept a prisoner here no matter what Ffion said. She doubted the lord kept her here because Brynmor was her home. If he knew she was from Brynmor, all he had to do was inform Sir Robert and ask for a boon. Teague was Marcher Lord and consequently had power over Brynmor. He also had power over her.

She rested her head upon her knees and stared out the window. If she was counting the days correctly, she had been here over a sennight. It was long enough for either someone to rescue her, or to think her dead.

She could endure whatever the Traitor expected of her, but there were people who needed her at Brynmor. Melun, who had raised her like a father, was losing his sight and depended upon her to care for the birds. The falconer had probably already been punished for losing a goshawk. And fragile, gentle Alinore needed protection from her father, Lord Urien of Brynmor, and his spitting rages.

Feeling trapped and restless, Anwen fisted the rich green gown they'd given her. She was as unused to this inactivity as she was to long gowns, but it was easy to spot the man responsible for her imprisonment. For days she'd been watching Teague. His tall frame, dark hair and movements were now as familiar to her as a hawk's flight.

He was training his men in hand-to-hand in the lists. A circle of men surrounded both Teague and a red-haired man. Both of them were crouched, their arms stretched and angled in front of them. Even in the cold heavy mist, they were similarly garbed—bare, except for loose braies that bunched at the waist and fell above the knee.

But it was Teague she watched. On him, the

braies didn't look so much like they were worn as much as they hugged a tight waist that supported a wide defined chest, broad shoulders and arms and legs rigid with muscle.

He was often hardly clothed, yet each time she saw it, it was as if his body presented some new facet for her to watch. He held a savage beauty, like a peregrine's wings arching back only to pound the air in a fluid rhythm.

His eyes never left his opponent and his arms remained steady, but she saw the almost imperceptive movement of his great thigh muscles when he launched. With one arm sweeping around his opponent's neck, he forced him to the ground.

Then each of them stood. Teague gave a satisfied grin as the man re-entered the crowd.

Anwen's breath caught in her chest. It was a strange breathlessness that had occurred to her more than once in the days she watched him. His face did not hold the perfect symmetrical beauty of his brother's; his features were masculine, hardened, and his cheeks, brow and jaw looked as if they were fragments of Gwalchdu's stone. One did not call him beautiful as one does not call a cliff that jaggedly slashes downward to crashing waves beautiful, but both held a magnificence that could not be denied. And when he smiled, his eyes flashing victory, Teague was truly magnificent.

Even having won, he did not rest, but pointed

to another man, who entered the circle. Teague pushed his long dark locks over his shoulders before crouching in the almost ritualistic stance. It would continue for hours until Teague was satisfied and it seemed he was never satisfied.

He pushed his men as she had seen no man train before. Teague would not call a halt until muscles visibly shook from strain, and sweat built upon sweat and dirt upon dirt. There were times he would get hurt, by a misstep, or a flawed arc to a sword, but never did she see him lose.

Through it all, he still held the air of a leader. Day after day, soldiers and servants came to him. He either directed or simply listened, but she would never see or hear a complaint or an argument against his direction. It seemed everyone obeyed Gwalchdu's lord out of respect and admiration.

For many days she had watched the Traitor, yet in all this time of trying to find a weakness so she could escape she had found only one. What she knew of Teague now conflicted greatly with her earlier knowledge. His arrogance and power were there, and a few servants crossed themselves on his approach as if warding him away, but he was also a fair leader and generous caregiver. No, Teague of Gwalchdu wasn't only the Traitor, yet that facet would always exist.

She had seen the consequences of him siding

with the English for Brynmor and even now, he kept her a prisoner. For those facts alone, she could not trust him.

It was hours later when Greta and Edith barged in carrying full water buckets. More servants followed with a large hip tub and more buckets.

'The kind Sister thought you could use a bath.' Edith set the buckets near the tub.

There were more important things for Anwen than a bath, but the steam from the buckets was intoxicating. 'Thank you. But you shouldn't be cross with Sister Ffion if she wanted me to have one.'

'Oh, I'm not cross with Her Mightiness about the bath.' Edith helped Greta pour the water into the tub after the other servants discreetly left. 'I'm cross because she had to decide when. I knew I shouldn't have asked for one days ago.' Edith gestured with her arms. 'Why don't you come here then and let me help with your clothing?'

Anwen, who had never been mothered a day in her life, couldn't get used to the coddling, yet she bent as Edith stripped her clothes and bandages.

When the bandages were gone, Anwen did something she had wanted to do for days.

She approached the tub, leaned over and without touching the smooth water, she scrutinised her reflection. She saw, as she expected, a stranger.

The woman looking back at her was gaunt, with cheekbones pronounced. Her hair fell lank around her down-tilted face, but it was the left side of her face that caused her to gasp.

Ffion was right—despite the stitches and poultice, the wound would scar. The raised jaggedness covered her entire left temple, but it wasn't so wide, or it would have affected her eyesight. Tentatively, she placed the tips of her fingers over the wound.

She could almost imagine it didn't exist. But it did and would for ever. Quickly standing, she immersed herself into the bath, causing waves to crash against the surface.

The steaming scent of lavender and sage immediately surrounded her and she rested her head against the back of the tub to simply enjoy it. Which she did, for about two drips of a candle; then Edith was there to assist.

'You can't rest now. Why, what if you go to sleep before we can get you clean? Help me here, Greta, get her up a bit, I've got to get to that hair and I can't do it proper and not affect the healing, as well.'

Anwen's thoughts of a lovely leisurely bath were dashed long before Edith began work on her back and arms. The woman cleaned her with a determination paralleling her speech. The only grace was that it was quickly finished.

Edith beamed and Greta swiftly cleaned around the tub. 'You look like an angel now.'

She grimaced. 'Thank you, but only if the angel had tripped and ripped the left side of her face.'

'Give it time,' the older woman said.

Greta patted Edith's arm before she poured another bucket of hot water into the tub.

'Oh, yes,' Edith said. 'Greta thinks we should leave you in peace for a bit now.'

Greta, with a wad of dirty cloths under one arm, grabbed Edith with the other.

'We'll be back, child,' Edith warned, walking as fast as she could with Greta dragging her. 'Don't go tiring yourself, just when you're on the mend.'

'I won't move a muscle.' Anwen smiled.

Knowing Edith and Greta would be back, Anwen didn't open her eyes when she heard the door open.

'Can you talk?'

Teague stood a few steps from her tub. He came straight from the lists and still wore nothing but braies. His wide torso was textured by scars, bruises and the line of black hair that ran down his abdomen. His bare chest gleamed and sweat ran in rivulets following the curves of his rigid muscles and dampening his waistband. Blood showed bright from cuts on his arms. His stance was one of a conqueror; his arms folded across his chest, feet apart.

She felt her heart thumping harder inside her as she took in the smells of sweat, heat and maleness. His black gaze held hers just as steadily, just as transfixed, then he slowly lowered his eyes…to her breasts not quite covered by the water.

Gasping, she stood and quickly turned to grab a cloth. The movement cost her. Swaying, grabbing the side of the tub for support, she wrapped the material around her. He didn't offer to help, didn't move at all, but she heard his sharp inhalation.

When the dizziness faded, a slow anger built inside her. For days he'd visited her when she was too sick to defend herself, then he ignored and imprisoned her. Now he didn't show her courtesy for her modesty. When she turned to face him, she'd lost a handle on her caution.

'Yes, I can talk and I ask, can you not see? Because if you could, you would know I wish for privacy. Leave.' Outraged, Anwen wanted to point to the door, but the saturated cloth needed both her hands.

His expression hardened. 'You are commanding me to leave?'

'Yes, now. This is not right. This is rude.'

'Rude.' He regarded the room. 'You sleep in my bed, you have worn my clothes and now I am rude?'

'You want my thanks for your type of hospitality? You, who take advantage of me and keep me prisoner?'

He needed to leave. Now. The longer Teague stared at her, she could feel her precarious position. She could see the light in his eyes, that he, too, recognised her predicament.

'Take advantage of whom, I wonder.' He tilted his head. 'From my position, it could be you taking advantage of me.'

The air changed with his words. Making a slow perusal of her wet hair and her bare shoulders, he took a step closer. If he continued to close the distance between them, she could do nothing to stop him. The moment she stepped out of the tub, she'd only expose more of herself. She was stuck. Ire, frustration and something close to rage ran up her spine. She hated men who prayed on those who were weaker.

'How could I take advantage of you? When it is you who have afforded me no courtesy, made me well, but allowed me no freedom, you who have provided food for me, but not the open air?'

He tilted his head. 'Are you that innocent? I wonder. When I first saw you in the forest with your hair swinging and your paltry chemise giving me glimpses of your skin underneath, I couldn't take my eyes from you.'

He took another step so that his feet almost

touched the tub. 'Then you were so sick, I thought you dead,' he continued. 'Ffion and my servants took care of your body, but still I watched, unable to leave you. I *watched* you, Anwen.'

She could not speak, could not breathe, her anger changing into something else. So she hadn't been dreaming or mistaken.

'It *was* you at night,' she whispered, when she knew she should accuse him instead. How could it have been this man, this traitor, who comforted her?

'Yes, it was me at night, *my* hand you held, *my* touch you sought when the pain was bad. While you recovered, I knew I could no longer simply watch you. So I stayed away.'

His eyes roved over her body until she blushed with heat. Until she was acutely aware of the cooling water, the brush of cold air in the room.

When he spoke next, his voice was like velvet. 'You asked whether I can see your present state of undress. Oh, yes, I can see. I can see that although you cover yourself, in my mind you are still laid bare to me.'

Anwen's blood turned to ice, then to flame; her skin prickled and flushed. The Traitor had comforted her, imprisoned her and now he was doing something else. Something that affected her body more than her anger, more than his care and capture.

His eyes gleamed black mercury as he continued, 'You clamp your hands to your breasts, thinking that cloth covers you, but instead it outlines. Your breasts are like perfect globes waiting to be touched, silky wet from the water beading on them, just right for the heat of a man's mouth. My mouth.'

She had no weapons against these words of his. None at all. Her anger had disappeared, only to be replaced by something hotter, more liquid. She could fight his care and escape his capture, but she couldn't fight her own body's response to this.

His eyes returned to hers and he seemed to war with himself before he asked roughly, 'How can you take advantage of me, you ask?' The sensuousness of his voice was gone, anger surrounded him and when his eyes locked with hers, she could only see cold stone. 'That is what I intend to find out. Dress yourself and meet me in the Hall. I will have words with you.'

The door closed, but it took several more moments before she could react; her entire body was trembling. She didn't want to know if it was from her anger, embarrassment, or the heat of his words, so she got out of the tub and briskly dried herself.

Why had she challenged him? It wasn't as though she would ever win any battle with him. He was a man who commanded, not one to take commands. She was not usually so foolish.

What battle was it she wanted to win? She grabbed her clean clothes off the chair. It certainly wasn't the one he had challenged her to. His crude words shook her. She was not so innocent she didn't know what he was speaking of.

Yet, he hadn't touched her. He had obviously used the words as retribution to her commanding he leave. He'd meant to embarrass her, but the words only humiliated her at first. Then other images came unwittingly: the images of *his* mouth on her breasts, *his* dark hair caressing her skin.

Perhaps these images would not have been so real if she had not remembered his touch so acutely. Yet he had touched her, at night, when there was no one but him. She had taken comfort in his hand, concentrated on the gentleness and strength through her pain. Now she remembered how his calloused thumb had slowly rubbed circles in her inner palm and wrist. The fact she could so easily imagine his touch elsewhere should anger her, frighten her…but she could summon neither emotion. They were destroyed by his words.

She needed to escape.

Chapter Six

Swiftly entering the Great Hall, Teague strode to the two chairs set by the smaller fireplace. He needed solace and some wine, two flagons full, and not necessarily in that order.

He had not known Anwen was taking a bath or he would never have gone in the room, but once he'd entered, he'd been unable to leave.

He hadn't meant to make accusations, but her anger and the way she'd trembled as she stood overrode his better judgement. He didn't know whether to help her or to wrap her in his arms and kiss her. And he had wanted to kiss her, of that there was no doubt.

Teague shifted his position on the chair and rearranged his legs. Though she argued and spat words at him, the impulse to taste those luscious lips was overbearingly strong. Her lips, like forbidden fruit, had captivated him in the forest; now he was on fire to taste them.

'What has put you in such a mood?' Rhain asked, interrupting his thoughts.

He glanced at his brother. 'I'm surprised to see you alone.'

Grinning, Rhain gestured wide with his arms. 'Well, I cannot help that this dark and gloomy stone has been bereft of my presence for so long. Can you blame the girls for wanting to bask in my sunnier disposition?'

'I doubt Mary and Anne are there for your disposition,' Teague said.

Rhain crossed his arms and shook his head. 'Mary and Anne following me into the lists today isn't what has raised your ire. Indeed, you can hardly complain when my betterment of Peter, your captain, was extraordinary...as usual.' His eyes turned speculative. 'Has there been another message?'

Teague shook his head. 'I asked the woman to come down to speak.'

'You mean to question Anwen again?' Rhain's voice held a hint of amusement. 'Did you bring a change of clothes?'

'She is better.' Teague caught the eye of a passing servant and requested wine and food.

'You have spoken to her then?' Rhain sat in the other chair, stretched out his legs and crossed his ankles.

'Yes.' Teague wished he talked to her through

the door. He'd entered that room to confront her, but all thought had gone once he saw her. Her eyes had been closed, her head arched against the back of the tub, the mounds of her breasts glistening from the hot water. The water was deep, but the crests of her knees, thighs, legs, were shown sleekly. She was, as in the forest, revealed and yet concealed.

No, the feeling of lust was stronger this time. Because this time, *this time*, she was in his bedchamber. She had been so tangible to him in that instant, he had almost felt her, tasted her, sunk deep within her. Then she had opened her eyes and challenged him. Her trembling took whatever control he had over his lust and mingled it with his need to protect. He could not leave the room fast enough, but it hadn't helped the ache in his loins.

'That may explain your tenseness,' Rhain said. 'I find it curious she makes you prickly.'

'I do not get prickly.' Teague shifted in his seat. 'I do not know who she is and am wary.'

'The Devil of Gwalchdu is wary of a slip of a girl. Well, this place is certainly not dull. I will sit with you and await her arrival.'

Keeping close to the wall, Anwen carefully made her way down the stairs. At least her pace and the view from the stairs allowed her to take in the emptiness of the castle.

Gwalchdu's Great Hall's opulence, though it was expected, overwhelmed her. To be sure, she knew Edward and the Welsh Prince, Llewellyn, had visited Gwalchdu, but this Hall even outdid royalty's comfort.

Several large hunting tapestries covered the walls. Where there were no tapestries, thick opulent red-and-green-coloured linens hung and shimmered against the light. Standing candelabras and large sconces provided flickering light. Two fireplaces, of different sizes and opposite each other, brought warmth and ornamentation to the hall. In the middle, three long trestles were flanked by equally long benches. These trestles were intersected by another, which should have been placed on a dais to separate the lord from his soldiers, but it wasn't. It was level, indicating equality between the lord and his men. The sole indication of privilege at the high table was the ornate cushioned chairs and the huge fireplace behind the table. Both were used to provide the lord the greater heat and comfort.

At the other end of the hall was a smaller fireplace, and two large padded chairs occupied by men whose hair reflected dark and light in the firelight. Anwen strode forward.

Teague heard her first and stood, and Rhain rose after him. The setting sun filtering through the windows was weak, but the lights from the fires shone through her damp unbound tresses that curled like a halo of gold. As she walked, the white of her gown flowed angel-like around her small frame.

'My God.'

'What say you?' Teague's eyes did not leave Anwen.

'I thought you mad for bringing her here.' Rhain spoke low, his eyes riveted on the vision walking towards them. 'But now that I see her like this, as you must have seen her at first, I believe you the sanest man alive.'

With shuttered eyes, Anwen paused before them. She was still unwell. Her hands trembled and the pallor of her skin shone with exertion just from the small walk.

She had wide blue eyes, with eyelashes so pale they should have been unnoticeable, but instead, the golden colour made her eyes shine. *Shine?* He quickly rejected the frivolous thought.

'You came,' he said, his voice gruff.

'As you commanded,' she answered.

Teague looked much changed from when she had seen him earlier. Freshly washed, his hair was wet, and he was finely clothed in a dark blue tunic. The aesthetic affect was almost as unnerving as him standing bare-chested before her. Damp, his hair waved thickly and the tunic fitted his shoulders and skimmed over his chest and abdomen.

He was covered, but it did little to hide what was beneath.

'Do you always follow commands?' he asked.

'If they are not unfair.' Anwen would not curb her tongue.

Rhain coughed. 'It is good you have fared well.'

Anwen assessed the two men in front of her. From their colourings to their personalities, the contrast between them was stark. Both men were tall and their muscles were outlined even in their clothing, but there the similarities ended. Teague was dark from his hair to his eyes to his countenance. He looked every bit the devil, hewn from far below the earth's surface. Rhain, his golden handsomeness elegantly garbed in rich red fabrics, was powerfully built, but he was leaner and more graceful looking. He looked hewn from the sun's light, as if God himself had created a man-angel.

Anwen gave Rhain her most winning smile. She noticed out of the corner of her eye that Teague's frown deepened, but she paid him little heed. If he was an angel, perhaps she could appeal to Rhian's mercy. She would press any advantage he could give her. She must.

'Thank you,' she said. 'My headaches seem to be gone now and I have most of my strength. I fear I would not have fared so well had you not taken great care of me.'

Rhain returned her smile and gave a slight nod. 'I am glad, despite my desire for you not to be hurt at all. Would you care to sit?' Rhain indicated the chair he had been occupying.

She was weak, but sitting would increase the position of power Teague held over her. Still, she appreciated kindness, since she so rarely received it, so she gave him another smile.

'Rhain, Peter needs you in the stables,' Teague said.

The lord's brother's friendly face turned implacable as he gave her a nod. 'Of course, how discourteous of me to forget. If you'll excuse me?'

It was the mischievous twinkle in Rhain's eye, before he turned away, that worried Anwen more than Teague's frown. It was as if he knew a secret. But what? Teague had ordered him away. Demanded again as he was wont to do.

To be alone with her.

Whatever advantage she hoped to have with Rhain was gone. Only now it was replaced with an acute awareness of how alone she was with the Traitor.

His previous words still vibrated through her. In the bedchamber, had she revealed her body's treacherous response to him? She was dressed this time and prepared. Whatever happened then wouldn't happen to her again.

But Teague didn't speak and it still didn't matter. Something of his silence vibrated through her, too. She listened to Rhain's every step as he walked towards the Hall's doors, and every thump of her heart in her chest sounding like that of a captured bird. Then there was a creak of the door, a gust of unsympathetic wind brushing against her limbs and more of Teague's watchful silence.

She didn't want to sit, but her legs were weakening.

'Are you well enough to answer some questions?'

Ah, yes, he was too watchful. But her stubbornness and strength had been honed by men who flaunted their power and control over those who were weaker. How many times had she protected herself and Alinore against Urien's fists?

She might feel no anger from Teague now, but she felt his power, as she had since the first time she saw him. And somewhere deep in his silence and scrutiny she felt an insidious connection between them like a creance she'd snared herself on.

It didn't matter if it had started when he caught her under the tree, or comforted her in the night. It would end as soon as she returned to Brynmor. In the meantime, if her legs were weak and her head hurt, she merely needed to hurry along this encounter with the Traitor. 'Whether I answer yours depends on whether my question is answered.'

Teague's eyes narrowed on hers, but then he waved to the servants, who brought two flagons of wine and some fruit and bread and set them on the table between the chairs. 'Before we get to the questions, perhaps we should have some repast.'

Anwen did not take her eyes from the man who knew she wanted to rush this discussion. He understood it so fully, he was forcing her to wait.

Still, the food and repast gave her a reason to sit where he indicated, so she did. The plush chair immediately supported her just when her body needed it.

Now she wouldn't worry about fainting. She merely had to tolerate his scrutiny and match it with her own. Prepared, she wouldn't respond to him as she had standing naked before him. But when he took the opposite seat…something changed.

It was the deft way he picked up a green apple and cradled the ripe fruit in his sure hand. It was the way he bit into it and the way his eyes didn't leave hers as she watched the cords of his throat when he swallowed.

Her eyes went to his again. There was a different gleam there now. One which made her aware of the intimacy of them sharing a fire, a meal and a private conversation. His sudden predatory manner reminded her of their exchange upstairs. Despite her garments, despite the strength sitting gave her, she felt naked, exposed. Vulnerable. It was enough to shake her.

'Why am I a prisoner?' she asked.

'Is that what you think you are…a prisoner?' Teague bit into the apple again. This time she was prepared for whatever strange reaction she experienced before. Prepared, but no less affected. He was merely eating, but the way he did it… The smooth bite of his teeth, the sound of the crisp apple. The way he cradled the fruit.

She felt more like a prisoner than when she was locked in the room. Yet nothing kept her here except for his presence and the way she reacted to him.

'You're no prisoner. I merely provided a guard to give you some protection. Do you believe you have committed a wrongdoing to justify imprisonment?'

'How could I commit a wrongdoing when I was asleep for days?'

Teague tossed the apple into the fire, but her eyes remained on him, so she saw the smug curve of his lips as he continued. 'Perhaps it is what you were doing before you fell that we should be discussing.'

'What do you mean?' Her actions prior to her injury were none of his concern. If he didn't want people to come to his village, then he shouldn't have stolen the best tanner in the region.

'You are from Brynmor,' he said.

Anwen just managed to hide her surprise. 'Yes, it is my birthplace.' So it wasn't the tanner but her home that concerned him.

'So you admit to living in a Welsh minor prince's home?'

'I don't know what you mean. There have been no Welsh princes since Edward's wars. We are all English now.'

'But you do admit Brynmor was at one point an enemy manor?' he pressed.

'I believe that is a matter of perspective. Your home could just as easily be termed an enemy castle.'

'Are we enemies?' He stood and clasped his hands behind his back. He did it so suddenly, so restlessly, the move surprised her.

Anwen stood along with him, moved away from the chair, the repast and the warmth of the fire. She wasn't fooled by his friendly tone; she knew a trap was being laid. 'King Edward has declared we are not.'

'Then what were you doing in Dameg Forest so close to Gwalchdu?' Teague began circling her.

She felt like a hawk's prey and had a sudden instinct to move her head to follow him. Instead she stared straight ahead when she answered. 'My home is near yours and Dameg Forest. If we are not enemies, then there is no wrong in being in the forest.'

'You know Alinore, Lord Urien's daughter?'

'I am well acquainted with her.'

'And Robert?'

'One would hardly live at Brynmor without knowing its English-appointed Governor,' she answered through the tightness in her throat.

'What is your position at Brynmor?' he asked.

It was the question she dreaded. Her positions were many at Brynmor, and all of them would give anyone cause to question her veracity. It would hardly do to tell him the truth of who she was at Brynmor: bastard-born and unwanted. That Alinore was her half-sister and Lord Urien her father. But she could not avoid the question, so she chose one of her occupations.

'I am an astringer,' she answered.

Teague stopped in front of her. 'An astringer?'

She hated that incredulous smug tone. She was good as an astringer and people needed her. 'I work with hawks.'

'It's an unusual occupation for a woman,' he persisted.

'Any occupation is unusual for a woman, but that is what I do,' she said.

'There are other occupations that women do that are not quite so…unique.'

'How like a man to think bearing children is a woman's only occupation,' she retorted.

'It wasn't the bearing of children I had in mind.'

Anwen's face heated. She should have known he would turn their conversation to appeal to his lust. But whatever purpose he had in embarrassing her shouldn't matter. Her entire desire was to return to Brynmor and be done with the conversation.

'These are not questions I can provide answers to,' she retorted. 'You talk this way to embarrass me and I've little knowledge or care as to why. All I know is I am held here against my will and given no courtesy as to the reasons.' She wasn't worried about fainting or weakness or her head aching. Anger and frustration kept her strong now. 'You've now asked your questions, and I want mine answered. Can I go free?'

Further scrutiny, more feelings of vulnerability that angered her until he said, 'You are free...to walk around. You may not, however, leave Gwalchdu.'

'You can't keep me here!'

'I can,' he said. 'You see, I am in need of an astringer. I find you being here very convenient.'

Dark eyes stared at her intently, waiting for her to display weakness. She knew better than to show any vulnerability. 'I am not a very good one.'

'Not a very good one is better than none at all.'

Here was another trap, one where she'd have to

tell the truth. 'But I lost a bird in Dameg Forest. You would not want an astringer who loses birds.'

'You were training a bird this late in the season?'

His doubt stung her pride. It was late to be training Gully, but he'd hurt his wing early on. It was the only reason she travelled to Gwalchdu's village, to purchase better jesses. Yet, telling the Devil of Gwalchdu that she could, in fact, train birds late would defeat her purpose, so she shrugged. 'You now know the futility of keeping me for your own birds. You should let me go.'

'Losing a bird is serious,' Teague said. 'Is this the reason you request to leave Gwalchdu?'

He didn't exactly answer her questions, so she wouldn't exactly answer his. 'All hunting birds have some worth. This one has some consequence to persons at Brynmor if I don't find and return it.'

'What certain persons?'

'The falconer,' she said, which was all he needed to know.

'A falconer is of little worth.'

Only a man who cared for no one could say such a thing. Melun was everything to her. The man had taken her in, cared for her and was like a father to her. She had to return to Brynmor, but she could feel any advantage she hoped to obtain slipping away.

He spoke again. 'But it matters not. Your obligations are now here.'

'I told you I was no use to you and I have no obligations here.'

'There you are wrong,' he said. 'You do. You have a debt to pay. You owe me your life.'

Chapter Seven

'A debt, hmmm?' Rhain murmured after Teague recounted his conversation with Anwen. Despite the weight of their discussion, it hadn't taken long. It also hadn't taken long for Rhain to return to the Hall. In fact, Teague suspected his brother had been waiting and watching, for he arrived just as Teague glimpsed the last of Anwen's white gown trailing behind her when she ascended the stairs.

Teague sat and stretched his legs in front of him. 'It seemed efficient.'

'Not as efficient as simply tying and torturing her.'

'True, but she is still in a weakened state.'

'Ah, so it is your concern keeping her here against her will.' Rhain walked to the table and poured wine for them both. 'Maybe there is some good in you yet.'

Teague drank deeply and kept silent.

'Of course, the most efficient way would have been to simply tell her the truth.' Rhain shifted his stance and leaned against the stone wall heated by the fire's flames. 'For instance, you could have told her there are threats against your life and you believe she is connected.'

'So she could tell me the lies she concocted? No, we'll see what she does in her stay here, follow her around and when the line is long enough, I'll tighten the creance.'

'Have we established she is a liar so soon?'

Teague remembered her direct gaze despite the way she'd trembled. She was no coward. But he was certain she was hiding something. 'I do not have time to give her the chance.'

'You are usually not so quick to judge.'

Teague grabbed a handful of nuts. 'These are unusual times.'

'Why did you not mention the bird?' Rhain asked. 'She was most concerned for returning it.'

'Yes, but to where and to whom? To Brynmor only?' Teague's voice was laced with only a fraction of the impatience he felt. 'Do we truly know if she is the falconer's assistant? In his missive, Robert did not mention her station at Brynmor. Maybe she is an astringer, but then she could have been training the bird to relay messages. I find it most curious that she is a woman who works with birds. What lord would allow such a thing?'

'We know Urien's barely able to hold his precious Brynmor together.' Rhain swirled his wine. 'Perhaps it is not so strange. Robert is in charge and we know him to be lenient. Maybe it is the truth. Maybe she has pride in what she does, despite saying she wasn't any good.' Rhain shrugged, and took a drink. 'Interesting woman, wouldn't you say?'

Tired of his brother's attitude, Teague inspected each nut he ate. People were not always good. Betrayal could come when and where one least expect it. 'She is still not telling all. I know it.'

'There have been no messages, Teague, and it has been weeks. Perhaps they were simply the idle threats of a bored man.'

Teague brushed his hands against his legs. 'No, I know this is not over.'

'It is not the woman.'

'Perhaps.'

Rhain sighed and pushed off the wall. 'You know I am speaking the truth. You have hurt her somehow, which is the reason she lashes out at you.'

'And you have softened too much to a stranger.'

Rhain's set his cup down. 'I don't think it is I who has softened. I see how you watch her, and I know where you go at night.'

Teague shrugged. He owed Rhain no answers.

'I have no doubt Anwen would be lovely to

warm a bed at night. But as lovely as she is, we do not know her purpose. I do not believe she is the enemy, but I am concerned your thoughts are turned too far towards her and it takes your attention away from the real danger.'

'Do you worry for me?'

Rhain shook his head. 'Beware, Teague. I will not always be at your back.'

His mind full of wine, rapier words and lush curves, Teague watched his brother's retreating form. Rhain was right, there was danger creeping closer to him. It was a danger he could do nothing to stop and now he had added to his burden by bringing Anwen here.

She had stood weak before him, but her pride hadn't faltered, not in the face of her imprisonment, her injuries, even him. And that was the most perplexing of all. It was not that he thought himself invincible, but he knew other people thought him that way. He knew why and it wasn't solely based on his sword skills.

Devil's blood.

Most of his life he'd been plagued with the rumours that Devil's blood ran through his veins. But in truth it was his aunt who had suffered from the same rumours before him. It was her episodes that had started it.

Teague didn't wish for Ffion to ever suffer, so

when he could, he'd paid the Church well and his aunt had entered a convent. That stopped the rumours pointing to her, but they still existed. So he put them to use when he entered the battlefields and his enemies feared him even before he raised his sword. It was a simple solution.

The fact people saw him as tainted, whispered that he might have sold his soul, didn't bother him. He was a man who could defend himself. So he took responsibility for the rumour, and as the years went by, he ignored the way his people crossed themselves when he walked by.

At least Rhain was not treated the same. Maybe it was the difference in looks or temperament, or because he had sent Rhain away when he was a child. Whatever the reason, his brother's good nature and easy smiles were returned by his people and soldiers.

Teague frowned at the thought of those smiles. It seemed Anwen was not immune to Rhain's nature either. Even on such short acquaintance, she had differentiated between them.

Although he could shrug off his own people avoiding him, although he could shoulder the fact his countrymen thought him a Traitor and hated him, there was something inside him that wanted things to be different with Anwen.

These were useless, dangerous, thoughts. He didn't know her; she hid information when there was an enemy at Gwalchdu's doors. She could, in fact, be the enemy. An enemy who threatened everything he fought to protect. He'd given his life, the respect of his people and family, for Gwalchdu. No threatening message would take away this land and stone.

No mere woman, who affected him like no other, would make him falter in his protecting his home and those who lived here.

He'd known betrayal all his life. This stone, this land, his home was all he had; all he was ever meant to have.

Still, he didn't like that Anwen shared her smiles with his brother. Not when for him, her eyes were wary and shuttered. Except...when he bit into the apple. He'd seen something else. Something that echoed his own desires.

Crushing any feeling that thought brought, Teague refilled his cup. As Gwalchdu's lord, he couldn't afford his desire for Anwen.

So be it that Rhain was treated kindly. He was a good man, brave and second-born. He did not have the responsibility of this keep and its people. Teague would not change the circumstances for anything. Although he carried a great burden with the responsibilities of his keep, Teague also took great pride and pleasure in knowing its strength and efficiency. The people could keep fearing him. It had worked for him in the past and, once the mystery of Anwen was solved and the enemy killed, it would work again.

It did not go unnoticed in his own mind that he tried not linking Anwen with the threats against his life. She could be the enemy, could know the enemy, and yet the moment she had fallen into his arms he had been hit with emotions he hadn't experienced since he was a child.

Hope, fear, pride, possession. He didn't react to her as he had to any other woman in his life and even more puzzling was that she didn't react to him as expected either.

Instead of fearing him, she had trusted him. Instead of turning her eyes away as his own people did, she had grasped his hand. She did not cross herself, but challenged him. If she was the enemy, she was a surprisingly honest one. Every emotion played across her face: anger, frustration…desire.

Teague smiled satisfactorily into his cup. It hadn't been just when he bit into the apple when he saw her desire. It was there when she stood in the tub and her beauty wrenched his lust-filled words from him.

His words hit something within her and although she had been quick to hide it, he saw the flash of innocence and heat in her eyes. Oh, that he could afford to see where that heat would lead.

Teague inhaled deeply. His blood rushed

through him and he no longer smiled. His thoughts when it came to Anwen were too complicated, too unsolvable. It was going to be a long night.

Anwen paced the confines of her room. *His* room, she corrected herself. His massive bed, his fine furnishings, his bath, his wine, his food and his care when she could have died.

Her debt to pay.

There was no logical reason for keeping her here. She was almost well and he knew where she lived. She wasn't even asking him for an escort home. Yet, she sensed his antagonism from the beginning. At every moment, he tried to embarrass her.

She still did not know the purpose, but he was right. By saving her life, she owed him a debt.

Yet the Traitor of Gwalchdu did not save lives. The Devil did not save anything. And he was the Devil, of that she had no doubt.

She thought of escape, of open fields and the kind, gentle old falconer who needed her. She thought of Alinore, who couldn't hide from her father's rages. Who, even now, could have bruises from Lord Urien's fists. All her life she'd protected Alinore and now she was failing her.

She would pay whatever debt Teague of Gwalchdu believed she owed, but at the first opportunity she would escape. It was all she could do. It didn't matter how powerful he was. She had lives to worry about other than her own.

Chapter Eight

⁓⁓⁓⁓⁓

'What do you think she is doing?' Rhain gripped the horse's bridle.

Teague inspected the destrier's hoof for disease. The stable master, Henry, with a worried vein crossing his brow, stood beside him. The horses were not only expensive, but highly prized, and losing one would be costly.

Teague did not have to ask his brother who 'she' was. When Anwen entered the courtyard and disappeared behind a wall, awareness slid down his neck and, if he was honest, in other parts of his body, as well. He addressed Henry.

'What has been done for them so far?'

The stable master shifted his feet. 'Cleaning the hooves and stalls twice a day, sir. It was minor when it started and I thought to watch it a few days before coming to you.'

Teague patted the horse's neck. 'Your actions were sound, despite the worsening. Call in the blacksmith and seek Sister Ffion; they may have some suggestions.'

Henry bowed and left immediately.

Teague turned and sought sight of the woman trying to blend in with the castle yard.

'She is trying to escape,' he remarked. 'It's what she's been trying to do for days now.'

'I swear she grows more interesting by the minute,' Rhain said. 'If she was sent here to harm you, you'd think that either she, or whoever set her up, would have prepared her. Do you think I should tell her no one can enter or leave without your permission?'

Teague thought of Rhain talking and smiling with Anwen. 'If you like,' he said, keeping his voice as level as possible.

Rhain ignored his brother's permission. 'If that is what she is planning, you have to admire her bravery. The activity in the courtyard cannot be lost on her; every soldier is alert. What would she think to accomplish?'

'To blend in with the crowd and find the best possible exit to escape.'

'With her hair? Impossible. Even plaited, she has enchanting curls framing her head like a halo. And the colour? It is like a ray of sunlight after a dark night.'

Teague barely stopped himself from growling.

Why should he care that his brother noticed Anwen's hair?

Rhain continued, seemingly unperturbed by Teague's non-committal grunt. 'Maybe she is not so honest. She agreed to fulfil her debt to you and now she's trying to escape. I should be disappointed in such behaviour.' Rhain crossed his arms and smiled. 'But damn if I'm not proud of her.'

Teague's mood darkened. 'You laud her attributes too much.'

'You do not like that I've noticed her beauty or cleverness.'

'I said no such thing.'

'Oh, I know you well enough. Funny, you've never been territorial before.'

'I am not territorial. If I seem displeased it is simply because she is an unknown. There could be no good in bedding her. In fact, it may serve some purpose of hers.'

'Yes, like lessening your foul mood of late.' Rhain snorted. 'You understand, she might not feel the need to escape if you showed her the missives that were sent.'

Teague watched as Anwen disappeared behind the far tower's corner. 'We reply for her.'

'Don't you think she should have an opportunity to reply on her own? She doesn't know Brynmor writes to her. It's curious how you also keep her locked in her room like a prisoner.'

'She's my astringer, not a prisoner.'

'An astringer?' Rhain asked. 'Have you even shown her the mews?'

'No.' Teague had, in fact, been trying to avoid just that, yet he would have to approach her again before too long. He hoped by then his desire for her would cool, or something that she hid would be revealed. 'It matters not. She has a debt to pay.'

'And just how is she to repay her debt?'

'The only way I know.' Teague walked away from his brother and towards the very person he knew he shouldn't approach.

Anwen sagged with defeat against the inner wall. It was no use finding a weakness. The great stone of Gwalchdu was designed too differently than her own home of Brynmor and she loathed every centimetre of it.

Brynmor had flowers and vegetable gardens interspersed everywhere with comfortable benches under the shade of fruit trees. People worked at open trestle tables, while children toddled and ran with the livestock. It was chaotic.

Gwalchdu had a garden, but it was as if it wouldn't dare seed itself wrongly. The rest of the grounds housed no grass, no trees, only hard-packed dirt and rock for working.

The only hope Anwen had of escaping Gwalchdu was in finding a human error, which was why she stood near the small East Gatehouse to observe the comings and goings. If there was any chance of escape, this gatehouse was her best opportunity. But as minutes went by, no opportunity presented itself. Gwalchdu's human defences appeared as insurmountable as its stone.

'There is no escape from here.'

Anwen jumped and turned around.

Trying to calm her racing heart, she said, 'I wasn't looking for escape.'

'Then you disappoint me,' Teague said.

If she only had a sword, or a dagger she could throw. 'Perhaps we are even.'

'You speak of disappointment in me?' Teague peered at the wine barrels she had been standing behind. 'Ah…you speak of the wars.'

'I'll not speak of that time with you.'

'Because I am a traitor and a coward?'

It shouldn't startle her that he admitted it, but it did. He was a warrior, a ruler, and arrogant right down to the tilt of his head. She wondered if he knew the other rumours surrounding him. That his blood was tainted. That he'd made a pact with the Devil. 'Among other traits.'

'So many judgements and yet we've only just met.'

'Yet the first time we meet you kidnap and keep me prisoner. What else am I to think?'

'So though you admit to being a prisoner, you are not trying to escape.'

Teague's head tilted in that way of his before he clasped his hands behind his back. It was a casual pose, but something of his expression darkened before he looked away.

She shrugged. She owed him no answers and, as long as she was here, she would continue her surveillance. Perhaps if she ignored him, he would leave.

'Did you know James of St George from Savoy, the architect, sent his designs for this castle?' Teague said. 'The concentric towers were his idea. No single area or tower is more important than the last. If an enemy struck, he would be spread too thin and easily held back.'

He wasn't leaving, and neither would she, but this conversation needed to end. She didn't need a lecture of the superiority of Gwalchdu.

'Gwalchdu is too big, too dark and juts out like a wound among the castles here.'

Teague nodded. 'Yet it is the future for castles. Were you able to appreciate how it is not solely protected by the outside wall, but also from the river on the west side and the wide water moat on the other sides?'

She took her eyes off the gate to give Teague a scathing look. 'There has been no opportunity to walk *outside* Gwalchdu's walls.'

He shrugged. 'There is more to Gwalchdu's defences than its rock. Most of the men you see were born within these very walls.'

Unwilling to talk of his soldiers either, she turned her gaze to the parapet where six soldiers overlapped on their duties as they walked the barbican. The doors were as thick as the flanking of two horses. They were swung wide to reveal two portcullises firmly staked into the ground. Who needed two at a small gate?

'My men are all well paid, but they fight for more than gold. They fight for their pride and their place in England's history.'

'Pride shouldn't be an issue when it comes to a mere slip of a woman who doesn't belong here.'

A small smile lit his eyes. 'Ah, so you do plan to escape. But you see, pride does enter into it when I've ordered that you cannot leave.'

She'd had enough. 'How can you be so cruel?'

'Cruelty, cowardliness, treason. You judge so readily on my motivations.'

'I care not for motivations when the result is the same.' If she didn't get back to Melun and let him know what had happened to her and to Gully, he might do something foolish, like taking the blame for her actions. 'It has been a fortnight since you spoke of the debt, and of me becoming your astringer. Yet you have not collected. You toy with me and I have the right to know why.'

She was tired of the subterfuge and the secrets. She was tired of noticing the broadness of his back and the strength of his arms. And she was certainly tired of how he made her feel when she stood this close to him: restless and alive in a way she had never felt before.

'I saved your life,' he said. 'Don't I have a say in how and when you pay such a steep debt?'

'If you are wanting an eye for an eye, I fear the only way to repay you would be to save your life. That is not a likely scenario given your legendary ability to avoid death.'

'That is one outcome I cannot avoid for ever.'

If only she could be the one to wield the killing blow. 'Why don't you tell me what my payment is, so I can be set free?'

'The truth. Why were you in the forest?'

Anwen raised her hands in exasperation. So they were back to the forest again. 'I already told you, I was in the forest to capture my bird, then continue on my way to Brynmor. Nothing more.'

'Continue on your way?'

'I visited Bleddyn, the tanner, to purchase new jesses. On my return—'

'Ah! Bleddyn was from Brynmor.' He nodded. 'But what were you doing with the bird?'

'Training it.'

'No one trains a bird this late in the season. I am a reasonable man and you'd know this if you didn't lie to me. You give me snippets, when I need your full cooperation.'

Lord Gwalchdu never asked, he ordered. 'Co-operation I've already given you. I know it matters not because your reputation precedes you. I have no guarantee if I cooperate now that you won't ask for more.'

He didn't move and yet she felt him step away. 'Ah, now you talk of my greed.' He peered over her shoulder and if possible his frown darkened. When she turned and saw Rhain approaching, he continued, 'Since you find my company so objectionable, I will take my leave.'

Anwen watched the silent exchange between brothers as Teague strode away. She could no more understand it than the strange and provoking conversation with Gwalchdu's lord.

'You talk to my brother,' Rhain said, his voice light, almost chuckling.

'A conversation is not what we share.' She didn't want to reflect on what they shared, but knew friendly banter was not it.

'Come, it is not so bad,' Rhain said. 'It isn't only you he frowns at. It would be better for all if you would but tell us more.'

Now he was demanding, just like his brother. 'Better for you, but what of me? You and Gwalchdu's lord expect me to tell you all, but you tell me nothing in return.'

'Ah, trust.' Rhain nodded. 'We seem to lack that commodity here, but there is a way to remedy it.'

'Oh?'

He gave her a look that turned his impossibly amber eyes to a bright gold that matched his hair. He was using his looks to his advantage, but it didn't make her skin flush with heat the way Teague did just by biting an apple.

'We will have to spend more time together so our friendship can blossom,' Rhain said.

A friendship with the Traitor's brother? Impossible. She had no friendships, and even if she did, she knew Teague didn't like Rhain talking to her. It was why he ordered his brother away, why his frown deepened when Rhain approached. Teague didn't like her talking to his brother, so for a moment she was tempted to let a friendship blossom between them. And then she remembered. To have a friendship, there would have to be trust. And she would neither trust the Traitor nor his brother.

'I can see you doubt it,' Rhain said. 'Let me prove it to you. Ask me a question.'

She'd be a fool to let this opportunity pass. She needed to return to Brynmor and the Traitor's brother would give her answers that would allow her to do so. She'd never get such an offer from Teague. 'Any question?'

'Within reason, of course.'

Of course. 'Is it true that prayers are six times a day? I don't see anyone attending that often.'

'Oh! I see you've been talking to my dear aunt.' He offered her his arm. 'Are you cold? Do you want to return?'

She was cold, but she didn't want to be inside. She spent too much time inside, but she pointedly refused his arm when she grabbed her skirts. 'I have to admit I am a little surprised at your choice of question given your present circumstances.'

Rhain began their walk around the bailey.

'I am not a fool to ask you the flaws of Gwalchdu, or of Lord Teague's reasons for keeping me prisoner here. I do not expect you to trust me, as I cannot trust you.'

Rhain's lips curved, but his amber eyes dimmed and he nodded his head. 'I see I will have to make some effort to win your trust.'

'You will tell me about your aunt?'

Rhain continued their walk through the courtyard, but he didn't offer her his arm again. 'No one goes to prayer that often. Teague's men pray at different times of the day so that there is always someone present. The arrangement keeps Ffion content.'

A contented Ffion was not possible to conjure up in Anwen's mind. The Sister battled everything with anger, from the crushing of the herbs to her prodding of Anwen. 'Has she always been so fervent?'

Rhain lifted his brow. 'As in repeating God's Commandments every day?' He stopped for a moment. 'No, she hasn't always been like this. I was about ten when I left for Edward's court. But since I've returned, I sense a bitterness in Ffion that wasn't there before.'

Anwen knew about the bitterness, she also saw the times when Ffion tried to stop it. As if she tried to hide it. Especially when it came to her nephew.

'She talks quite fondly of you,' Anwen admitted reluctantly. 'To her, you are the paragon of all that is good, while Lord Teague is not thought of quite so highly.'

Even she didn't think she could hate Teague as much as Ffion did.

Rhain walked again. 'I know. I think it is because Teague looks too much like our mother, Ffion's sister. She loved Lady Elin. Her death must have brought her great pain.'

'Is that why she became a Sister?'

'I don't know. She went to the Dominican Abbey close to London, which could not have sat well with her, although she was near me. She returned to Gwalchdu about the time I was earning my spurs. I suppose when she took the veil, she took on the black mood of it, as well.' Rhain gave a slight shrug. 'Teague tells me that before Mother died, Ffion was much admired, none more so than by the captain of my mother's guard. There were many men like him. I suppose the attraction was her contrast to my mother. She liked to dance, laugh and plant in the garden. Our mother was more sombre, like Teague.'

Anwen couldn't imagine the Sister dancing or laughing. She'd thought her questions to Rhain as something to distract her from Teague's conversation, but, in fact, she found the subject fascinating.

'I always got the impression something disturbing happened to her when I went warring with Teague.' Rhain held his arm out to protect her from the stable boys walking nearby with three warhorses. 'Since then, she seems agitated and it is getting worse. Greta's been good to her. But then Greta's been taking care of Ffion since before I was born.'

'I can't believe that. To look at Edith and Greta, you would think Edith is older.'

'No, it is Greta. I think she's always been old and as steadfast as an English oak. I often thought her simply part of Gwalchdu, made of the stone itself.' Rhain chuckled. 'I suppose it would take a stone's strength to withstand my aunt, but there does seem to be some understanding between them.' Rhain stopped walking. 'Well, here we are.'

They had travelled the entire outer bailey and returned to the exact spot where they began. It would have been the perfect opportunity to find Gwalchdu's weaknesses without being suspected, but she had been so immersed in Rhain's story that she forgot to look at her surroundings.

'Still looking for a way to escape?' Rhain murmured.

It should have disturbed her that he could read her so clearly, but it didn't. She didn't trust Rhain, just as she didn't trust the Traitor.

No matter how hard, she'd continue to look for an escape. There were lives at Brynmor she needed to protect. They had to be wondering where she was, maybe looking for her. She had to do whatever it took to return to them.

Chapter Nine

Teague heard the laughter before he saw its source, yet he knew it was Anwen. The sun was setting and torches were being lit. Despite the crisp and frosty air, it was the time of day that Rhain and Anwen had taken to walking around the courtyard.

For three days he'd been watching them. Whenever he'd privately question Rhain on their time together, his brother would give him a curious smile. If Rhain hadn't been his kin, he might have put a sword through his gullet.

Anwen's laughter carried on the afternoon breeze until it smacked somewhere in the region of his chest. He turned the corner and could see them. They stood close, almost arm in arm. Her waving blonde hair bound, but still curling like tips of flames around her delicate jaw and her blue eyes were the heat. He wanted to see her throat arch, her eyes beckon, her red lips swollen with his kisses. He wanted to know if she'd laugh in bed and what other sounds she'd make.

Rhain said something again and Anwen threw her head back and laughed, the sound full and rich. It reverberated through him until he wanted it for himself. Wanted *her* for himself. Before he knew it, his legs had taken him closer and their laughter stopped.

'Weren't you to meet with Peter?'

Rhain arched his eyebrows. 'Ah yes, Peter must think our friendship means little to me since I keep forgetting our meetings.' He bowed to Anwen and took his leave.

Anwen's face lost all traces of laughter and even now her eyes cooled. Good, that was how it should be. He needed to keep her at a distance.

'What do you do with my brother?'

His gaze was dark, forbidding and something like menace emanated from him. Anwen's stomach fluttered, but not with fear, as she took in how Teague's red tunic and grey breeches fit against his body. The colour of his tunic complemented his black hair and eyes, and his clothing enhanced him somehow in a way that disquieted her nerves. Irritated at herself for noticing his agreeable appearance, she focused on his crossed arms and his grim expression. But his annoyance didn't hide his appeal. She was tied to him somehow and she resented it.

'We talk, nothing more,' she answered.

It was the truth, but she liked that Teague resented Rhain keeping her company. She had even less power here than at Brynmor. So she kept Rhain's company, laughed and shared words if not trust. And she was aware, so very aware, of how Teague didn't like it. Because all the time she spent with Rhain, she still looked for Teague. And there was something in that which she didn't like.

'See that it is nothing more or you will lose the privilege of the outer bailey.'

'To be more a prisoner than I already am?'

'You know what to do to end your stay,' he said.

He talked of paying a debt, but hadn't given her the courtesy of allowing her to pay it. He watched, but ignored her.

It was intolerable. She could not leave the walls she hated and now he threatened her with even more restrictions. She wouldn't stand for it.

'To pay your debt as your astringer? When you haven't even allowed me near your mews?'

'Only when I'm satisfied with your intent will you get near my birds.'

His manners to her were formal, yet predatory. No, more than that…possessive. She was too aware how he watched her. How his dark eyes would darken more as they lingered on her. Worse still she continually heard the words he'd said that day as she stood in the tub. She began to fear she watched him, looked for him, for the same reasons. As if there was creance tethering them together.

Never.

'You don't want me as your astringer,' she said, proud the venom in her voice was clear. 'You want me to lie with you. That's it, isn't it?'

He looked taken aback for a moment before he hid it. Her words were blunt, crude, but she didn't care. He wasn't listening to any logic, so the reason he kept her here must be unreasonable. It must be lust. By his expression, she knew she was right. For her shocking words did not stop his gaze feeling like a caress across her skin.

She sensed the heat from his eyes, heat from his skin, even from his scent as he stood close. She felt desire from the Lord of Gwalchdu and worse, she feared she returned it.

As if she could lower herself any further. As if Brynmor and all her people hadn't already lost so much...

'That's your intention. To force me to stay, to wear me down until in desperation, or perhaps fear, I spread my legs for you,' she bit out. Men, and their vile treatment of women. She'd seen it often enough. Lord Urien's battering use of women who were vulnerable and afraid of his rages. Alinore, who suffered his hateful words and fists.

Anwen felt no connection to this man. How could she? When Teague forced, just like Urien, when he held her prisoner so she couldn't help those more vulnerable than her? She hated the Traitor. *Hated* him.

'It's why you came to my room while I laid helpless,' she said. 'Why you held my hand as if you had some right to do so and entered the chamber while I bathed. Why you don't want me talking to your brother!'

'You think this is simply lust?' His eyes, cold, black, fathomless even as his mouth curved to a cynical slash. 'You're angry now. You were angry when you climbed that tree. But you forget it was you who demanded that I catch you. This is more than lust. You think I don't notice your own actions towards me? You, who—' Teague scanned the busy courtyard. Greta, her face marred with anxiousness, emerged from behind the chapel and walked within their path. 'Perhaps this is not the time to converse.'

'But you are the one who began this conversation! You're the one playing these…games with no rules!' She could sense him pause, measuring her, but she didn't care. She was finished with waiting for him to come to some decision. 'At least send word to Brynmor I'm here. They may have thought me dead! They may be outside the gates even now ready to take me home!'

'No, there are no people. I cannot have more people here.'

Wrath lashed her insides. She didn't understand this man, his possessive watching, his dominance, his belief he would be blindly obeyed. As if others hadn't duties and fears for loved ones.

Would Melun still have his hands after losing Gully? When she returned, how many more bruises would Alinore have received?

Or would it be like that time on the stairs? When Urien struck Alinore and she toppled to the bottom. While Urien's hands, like manacles, gripped Anwen's arms. Helpless, all she could do was scream for her sister, who she thought dead.

She felt like that now. By imprisoning her, Teague manacled her entire body. When she needed to know if Melun or Alinore were harmed or dead. And this traitor who towered over her would not let her go!

'Why are you doing this?' she said, her voice rising, tightening. 'You don't need me here; just let me go. There are lives at stake!'

Whatever she was expecting from her plea, Teague's reaction was not it. His features went white, then his sharp cheekbones mottled red. So, too, he seemed to grow before her, his shoulders widening, the cords in his neck and arms hardening. In an instant he had become as formidable as Gwalchdu's stone itself, but alive and so very angry.

'What did you just say?'

It appeared as if he would strike her. She raised her arms, but she'd be damned if she'd run. She'd been hit before and had survived. Alinore and Melun needed her and she wouldn't run.

But the blow didn't come. And she didn't get to answer as both Rhain and Ffion intercepted them.

Teague tore his eyes from hers before turning his attention to his brother and aunt. His colouring was still heightened, but his eyes were now unreadable. Without looking at her, he ordered, 'Return to my chambers and do not leave.'

She was being dismissed, but didn't argue. She would get no leniency from Gwalchdu's lord.

Rhain waited until Anwen was out of earshot. 'There was another message.'

Teague motioned his head, and they walked away from the activity in the courtyard. 'Say it again.'

'A message. It was recent and, fortunately, not easily observed.'

'Not easily observed. What do you mean?' Teague felt raw from his conversation with Anwen. Incredulity flooded him so he couldn't immediately understand what his brother was saying. When Anwen told him that lives were at stake, he'd been so sure in that moment she was the enemy. That the lives she spoke of were a threat.

But she couldn't be his enemy, not if what Rhain was saying was true. Anwen had been with Rhain, with him.

He stilled and directed words to Ffion. 'Tell me what happened.'

'I found it, my lord,' Ffion said, her voice strained. 'It was most disturbing. I found Rhain immediately outside the chapel doors. If it wasn't for his bravery, I wouldn't have known what to do.'

Rhain gave her a sympathetic look. 'The message was tied on the hind leg of a young rabbit slit at the neck. It was freshly killed.'

'Where did all this take place?'

'In the nave, my lord,' Ffion said. 'I believe I'm the only one who came across it.'

'Except for the person who did the deed,' Teague answered.

Rhain pulled a rolled message from his cloak. 'The hand is the same. Nothing's different. Except—'

Teague immediately read the contents. 'Except for what it says.' Ffion, who visibly shook, had obviously read the message. He addressed her. 'You saw no one?'

'I was in my personal chambers in the back of

the chapel. I didn't even hear anything. When I...
saw it, I searched for Rhain immediately.'

'You talked to no one else?'

'No, I swear not.' Ffion twisted her hands before her. 'If I may, my lord, it seems that ill fate
has fallen on Gwalchdu.'

'Indeed.'

'Then it seems that Anwen should be returned
home.'

Anwen couldn't now be the enemy, but that
didn't mean she didn't know something. She'd
shown him so much anger, so much hatred. *Lives
at stake.* It was still possible she knew something.
'Anwen is none of your concern, Sister. She stays
under my care and you will speak to no one about
this message.'

'It seems you have grown overly fond of the
wench, my lord,' she said, as if she tasted something distasteful.

Rhain grabbed Ffion's arm. 'My dearest aunt,
perhaps this is not the time to preach on morality.
I am sure you are upset because of the disturbing
sight. Why don't you go and rest?'

Ffion pursed her lips before her eyes focused
solely on Rhain. For a fraction of a second, she
hesitated, then she patted his arm. 'Of course.' She
glanced at Teague again. 'Forgive me, my lord.'

Teague's impatience increased, but he nodded his head. Ffion's preaching was nothing new.

'God's Word is with us always, Sister. We do not need to be oft reminded of it.'

'I have never doubted God is watching you, my lord. I will go now and take rest before evening matins.'

Ffion's black robes dusted the ground and sent soft whirls of dirt as she walked away.

'Will she stay quiet?' Teague asked.

'I honestly don't know. But most of the castle knows to look for those delivering messages.'

'But they do not know the content.' Teague studied the message in his hand.

Right the wrong or you make animals of us all.

'What wrong has been committed?'

'What wrong hasn't?' Rhain said. 'Not to mention the sins of the past. Currently, you defy Edward by staying here instead of protecting his campaign in Scotland and you continue to build on Gwalchdu despite Edward needing the funds.'

'I am a Marcher Lord and I'm well within my rights. It is all political posturing and hardly a reason to slaughter animals.'

'I think the point is your neck is to be slit if you don't correct a wrong that has been made.' Rhain laughed drily. 'I bet this is the only time in your life you've been compared to a leveret. Soft, warm, furry Teague of Gwalchdu. Doesn't have the same ring as the Devil of Gwalchdu, does it?'

Teague slid him a scornful look at the ill humour. 'The wrong could be my going to Edward.'

Rhain leaned a shoulder upon the inner bailey wall.

'That was many years ago and anyone who knows of the situation wouldn't question why you did it.'

'But there are many who don't know the reason.'

'Anwen?'

'Yes, her.' Teague inhaled sharply. She could still know something and he needed caution when it came to her. Even if she had no association with these attacks, his feelings for her were out of his realm of understanding. 'But there are others at Brynmor...'

'Urien?'

Teague shook his head. 'Maybe, but not him alone.' Urien certainly had the most reason to hate him, after Teague went to King Edward. But Urien was nothing but an angry drunken fool and yet... It didn't mean he couldn't orchestrate something like this.

Rhain fingered the dagger at his waist. 'We've been taking in stray Welshmen for years. They would be in a good position to leave threatening messages.'

'But why threaten the very prosperity they enjoy?' Teague was tired of pondering the reasons.

'A vow at stake? It could be anything. A reason we cannot even perceive as yet.'

'Is it of significance that it was found in the nave?'

'I doubt it. The messages are in unsuspected places.'

Teague rubbed his chin. 'I keep feeling we are missing some connection to all of this. It is time for us to pay a visit to Brynmor.'

'Teague, Anwen is not guilty. This kill just occurred and we were both just sharing her company. I think this is proof that she could not have done it.'

It was true. She wasn't the enemy.

Relief and something more was overtaking him. Desire… Satisfaction… Anticipation. But it wasn't enough for him to fully trust her. He knew better than to rely on feelings. He'd been taught that lesson quite young. He could not rule out her involvement completely, but perhaps he could trust her enough to pursue why she intrigued him. Why he wanted her in his bed more than any woman he'd ever known.

But he needed answers first. 'It does not preclude that she had no involvement. I will speak with her.'

Chapter Ten

Anwen paced the large room and stumbled as her foot caught on the deerskin rug. She hitched up her skirts. She was too restless and angry to sit.

She had no idea why she obeyed Teague's order or why she returned to his room. She'd seen him curt and brusque before, but it was as if he could barely leash in his anger, as if he was on a field pulsing with the battle cry to strike.

But he'd pulled all his emotion in when Ffion and Rhain approached. He'd become cold, precise, which alarmed her more than his anger. Something was happening here which she had no knowledge of. Ffion's and Rhain's expressions did not bode well and—

The door swung open. Anwen turned too suddenly, her long skirts catching on a side table, her foot ramming on a chair leg. She tripped.

Teague grabbed her arms to stop her falling.

She caught her breath for a moment before she shoved him away and he let her go.

'Why do you keep me here?' she demanded.

'Your presence complicates matters,' Teague said.

'That does not answer my question. If it complicates things, then take me home and make it simple.'

His anger was not as it was before, but in his eyes were other emotions that swirled too fast for her to understand. 'This is not about my desires or what you want.'

'Then what is it? I am tired of being kept. What is this debt you demand of me?'

'There are matters…' Teague stopped. The look in his eyes changed again. He was looking at her as if for the first time. Assessing her for something she wasn't aware of. She swallowed and his eyes dropped to her throat, bare above the gown she wore. Then lower until he studied her feet she'd exposed with her hiked skirts. She dropped the fabric. Teague's mouth twitched.

'Put on your shoes and follow me.' Teague turned.

'Why?' she asked.

He looked over his shoulder, and raised one brow. 'I give you a boon, Anwen, and maybe some answers. Are you not curious?'

As they walked through the courtyard, it was

late afternoon and the winter sun was already weak. It would be dark soon and the faint rays did not reach inside the mews. She was not sure why they entered the large building, but she understood they were alone.

'Why here, why now? I know you do not need an astringer.'

Teague chuckled and stepped deeper into the shadows.

His laugh sent shivers up her arms and she rubbed them briskly until her eyes adjusted to the dimness of the vast space. As expected, the mews were orderly and precise, but there was more here. The tall ceilings and small windows at the top allowed for fresh air, but still protected the birds from any harsh winds. The fresh hay under feet crunched and smelled sweet and musty.

'What do you think?' Teague asked.

'I've never seen anything like it.' Anwen's attention was riveted on the perches, her mind and heart in awe at the design.

'I took some ideas from Edward's mews, but mostly it was my observation of the birds nesting and the way they perched on a hunter's gauntlet.'

She didn't know what surprised her most. That such housing existed for birds or that Teague took the time and the care to build them. Walking further into the mews, she gaped at the system of cross-beams surrounding her. They were built on overlapping diagonals. The design allowed one piece of wood to be utilised as a perch for several birds, but at the same time gave the birds the illusion that they had their own perch.

Anwen tried to ignore Teague, but it was impossible. With each step she took, he also stepped. Each beam she admired simply reminded her of the man behind the design.

Finally, she turned to him. 'It's beautiful.'

He tilted his head. 'It was born more out of necessity than for beauty, but even I admire the efficiency. I had acquired too many birds and did not want to cause them harm.'

Because the design allowed so many more birds in tighter quarters, she didn't realise how many he had until she truly took note of her surroundings. It was breathtaking. Only the King could have surpassed such wealth.

Pointing to the far wall, she asked, 'Is that a peregrine?'

He gave a wolfish smile. 'Yes, and a female, too.'

'How is that possible?'

'Edward asks the same question, but he is the one who gave her to me.'

Fascinated, she walked among the birds. She was grateful that they were secured to their perches. The sheer force of just one of the predator's talons could shred a man's arm to ribbons.

The peregrine was poised like a statute against the sun's beams breaking through the ceiling's rafters. Up close she could see why its size and hunting abilities were unsurpassed. It was the reason owning a female peregrine was an honour only bestowed to kings and she was so close she could almost touch it.

Teague stood beside her. 'I have something to show you.'

She knew what it was even before he said it. If she admitted it to herself, she had known since they opened the doors. 'You have Gully.'

He did not look apologetic as he gave a brief nod. 'Since the first day we brought you here. It did not take long to bring him to the gauntlet. You had trained him well. He was following on quite well.'

Anwen frowned. When a bird 'followed on', it usually meant that a hawk followed a falconer by flying from tree to tree. It was a technique to help flush out quarry.

Even with this large room full of birds it was relatively easy to spot him. There on the end by the far left wall was Gully, rapidly cleaning his beak on the perch. She never realised how tiny he was, but after seeing the peregrine, she could not help the comparison. The difference was Gully was hers and she still felt pride in that.

She approached his perch that was no taller than

she and gently blew across his face. Her relief at seeing the bird equalled her growing anger and frustration that he was safe.

'Why did you not see fit to tell me?'

'I could neither trust nor believe you.'

'I told you I needed to search for a bird. I am sure you suspected that this was the one.'

'I more than suspected, but it was not verified until now.'

Teague watched her walk to her bird. Her body moved with a rhythm he wanted to match. He didn't think she could be any more beautiful than when he saw her in the forest. But now, here in the dark of the mews, she was transformed. He desired to run his hands through her hair, to see if the curls would wrap around his fingers, like silk caresses. His body burned with need and he averted his head to see what she was seeing.

She was stroking her bird. He noticed that the bird rubbed his head against her fingers as if in welcoming. Her touch was gentle yet firm and all too experienced.

Teague walked towards Anwen and he saw what the darkness could not completely obscure: tears flowing down her face. He reached to capture a droplet, but caught himself and stepped back. 'Do you cry because of this bird?'

'Yes.' Anwen shook her head. 'No.' She rubbed

both her cheeks in an impatient manner. 'The bird is important to Brynmor, and what he catches will continue to provide for the people there, but the bird is not the only reason I cry.'

Anwen took steadying breaths and he could feel her reluctance to speak to him. So he waited.

'There are people at Brynmor who need me,' she continued. 'The falconer, Melun, is old and his sight is not what it used to be. I have been helping Melun with the birds, but now I am not there and I fear Lord Urien will cast him out or worse.'

'But Robert is there. Surely he would be reasonable.'

'Sir Robert is usually reasonable,' she began, then stopped. 'What did I say?'

'You gave a compliment to an Englishman.'

Anwen did not return Teague's smile. 'I am no fool to think that all men are the same. Yet, I cannot depend on Robert to save Melun…it has always been my task. I must return Gully to Urien.'

'Did you think Melun would pay the penalty for a lost bird? Was it his life you feared at stake?' he asked.

'Yes, and…'

'And?' he enquired. There was someone else at Brynmor she wanted to save. Someone important to her.

'There is a woman there and I fear for her, as well.'

Teague watched her for the veracity of her confession. It was vague and he still had questions, but he believed her. It was the way she spoke...it revealed her loyalty for these people.

She was not the danger. In the time she had spent at Gwalchdu, he had found her too direct for any duplicity. Still, he could sense she withheld some facet of herself. He did not believe her to be solely a falconer's assistant and he didn't know her relationship to this woman she spoke of.

But whoever Anwen was, she was not, nor did she assist, his enemy.

She was innocent.

He had kept her here against her will, deceived her and perhaps even endangered her. She deserved to know, but still...how much?

Simply because Anwen was not the enemy he sought didn't mean there was no longer an enemy. Caution was still required, but maybe not so much when it came to her. As the idea took root, his blood grew heavy, hot, pooling lower.

Maybe there was time to explore what they shared—

'Will you let me go now?'

Her eyes and attention had returned to the bird she handled. That was just as well, or she might have seen his response to her. She inspired too many feelings and they came too fast to be trusted. The hope she gave him must be controlled. But he need not have so much caution when it came to the other feeling coursing freely through him now.

'I would have been disappointed had you not asked again.'

She turned to him, her eyes meeting his.

'Will you?'

'No.'

She turned back to Gully, beginning to hum an intricate five-note call to him.

'No arguments?'

'When I told you the truth, you wouldn't believe me. I know now I cannot change your mind with words.' She paused. 'Will you at least tell me the reasons you keep me here?'

'Were you this direct before you were hit on the head?'

She glowered. 'I have no patience for people who hide or mince their words. I only want to know why you keep me here.'

He lifted his mouth. Of course. She was so open, loyal, so very *here*.

Anwen could feel Teague's manner change. It was a subtle shift, like a hawk whose weight had changed on her gauntlet. Yet, she did not feel like the astringer with him. She felt like the prey.

'Why do I keep you here?' he asked. 'I believe you know why, Anwen.'

Teague stepped into the light streaming through the windows. It illuminated the right side of his face and body, leaving the other side in darkness. So like the man. Half-revealed, half-hidden from her. His feet hit the clean hay underneath, soft and heavy. The smell in the air was sharp, pungent. It was dark now; the moonlight from outside barely seeped through the cracks in the wood walls. He filled the room and she lifted her chin to meet his eyes.

'No,' she whispered.

'You deny it now? You know it's there because you feel it like I do.'

'Desire? Lust? Your needs are no different than any man's,' she scoffed.

He slowly shook his head. 'It's more. It's the way I saw you in the tree; it's the way I see you now. The way your breasts curve against your frame as if they do not fit, as if they need a man's hands to support them, caress them.'

He took another step towards her so that they stood a mere breath away from each other. 'And your hips, curved to fit my hands as I lift you to me. Your fleece is so fair and soft looking that I want to rest my cheek upon it.'

Anwen wanted to step back, to distance herself, but she couldn't. He was right. She did desire him. Had felt the insidious snare of connection since she watched him in the lists. Now, so easily his words wove around her, conjuring images which she knew nothing about, but still her body was responding to them.

He stood before her, so large his body blocked out the dim light outside. But she did not need any light. Although they did not touch, she could feel him: his heat, his smell, his strength and power. She knew what he wanted, could feel the force of it, but he did not take. He waited.

Anwen stared at his large scarred and calloused hands held at his sides. The hands of a hardened warrior. She had watched those hands while he trained in the lists and she had felt those hands when they had held hers. She knew those hands well. Perhaps that was why she could almost feel his hands on her breasts cupping and lifting them to his mouth. Her breasts became full, the peaks tightening for a touch he only spoke of.

'I already told you I do not want this.' She meant her words to have force, but they sounded whispery, soft.

His eyes narrowed. 'I don't believe you. Our connection is too strong.'

Anwen's eyes snapped back to his. 'I feel only animosity.'

'Why do you deny it? Even now I can see your eyes darken, your breath hitch. You may not want to, but you desire me as I do you.'

She turned from him, hating that her movement

revealed more than it concealed. He was right. She did want him. Her body, unlike her mind, refused to separate the Traitor from the man who'd rescued her. It bonded her to him in a way she didn't understand.

'I only want Brynmor,' she answered. 'You have lied to me and I know you want me to become your whore, but I won't do it. Return me to my home.'

He shook his head. 'And you state you cannot tolerate those who hide and mince words, but remember, you did not let go of my hand at night. You held it tighter.'

She owed him no answer.

Cursing, he stepped roughly back from her. 'This is madness. But whatever you may think, I will not force this. There is more between us than lust, yet you are as obstinate as a goshawk.'

'I speak only the truth. I have seen and heard Urien's and his men's crudeness to women before. I've watched the debauchery in the Hall after a great feast. There is never *more* between a man and woman. There is just more of man's greed and power over her.'

There was a stunned stillness from him, an intake of breath before his eyes narrowed.

'I will take you to your precious Brynmor.'

Surprise. Happiness.

The torrent of emotion was so sudden it almost made her dizzy. 'Truly?'

A savage curl crossed his lips. 'Do not test me. I owe you nothing and do nothing against my own self-preservation. You have been shown a poor example of men and clearly I have to remedy it. I'll let you return, but only on my terms.' He pivoted and walked towards the door. 'You had best remember that.'

Anwen's sudden lightness of heart was broken by his words. She had forgotten the man, half-light, half-darkness. She would be better remembering that darkness and staying away from him.

Teague stopped before the door. Without turning, he asked her, 'Do these people at Brynmor mean so much to you?'

Anwen contemplated the broadness of his back, the curve of his shoulders, the flexing of his hand against the latch. She came close to feeling his hands on her. Too close to feeling the heat and strength of all his body. Too close, and yet, she wanted more. She had to get away from him.

'If I do not return, I will have betrayed trusts I hold too dear to hurt. They are all I have.'

'We leave on the morrow.'

When the mews door closed, Anwen immediately felt alone. While Teague was with her she was as wound as a tightened creance around a swivel. Now he was gone, she felt as the birds must do, at rest, but knowing their master would be back.

It would take her a lifetime to understand the changes in the man who had given her this boon. She was thankful she would not have to stay around to find out why.

Less than an hour later, Teague ordered another flagon of wine. He had watched Anwen return from the mews, watched as she ascended the stairs, but he had not followed her.

The fire in front of him was banked too low for any heat, but he didn't need any. He wondered whether she was even sleeping. He was a fool for keeping her here as long as he had. And for what? So that he could be as uncomfortable as hell.

Teague lifted the goblet to his lips and grimaced when he realised it was empty. A full flagon of wine later, another on the way and he was still as restless as when he left her. Like some young pup, he had watched her pet her bird. Her hands so small and delicate, yet strong and capable. He wanted those hands stroking him. Fresh blood rushed low in his body and he wanted to howl. There wasn't enough wine in the kingdom for what he needed.

'I thought I'd find you drinking away your troubles.'

'I have no troubles,' Teague said, not glancing at his brother.

Chuckling, Rhain repositioned the matching

chair so that it faced Teague. 'Oh, I think you do, brother.'

'What are you doing up? It is late.'

Rhain slumped into a chair. 'Keeping an eye on you. The whole castle knows you met with Anwen in the mews this evening.'

'Remind me to get rid of everyone.'

'Even Ffion.'

Teague's lips twisted. 'Especially her.'

Rhain crossed his legs and his ankles. 'Blood is blood and according to her we have need of spiritual guidance during these times.'

'Not for too much longer. We ride to Brynmor tomorrow.'

'With Anwen? I am surprised you are letting her go.'

'She is not the enemy.'

'Yes, but that is not a surprise. Why go with her now?'

Teague lifted his goblet, only to find it still empty. 'Because I find I cannot rule out Brynmor's role in this. She still withholds something from me.'

'You've hurt her and she snaps back at you. Is she happy that she's going?'

When he'd told her, Anwen's face had been flushed with joy. It staggered him. 'She won't be happy once she knows I travel with her.'

'You're letting her go, but not completely. Have you wondered at your motivation?'

Teague did not answer.

'Never mind, all in good time, I'm sure. A trip to Brynmor will prove interesting. Ffion will also want to go. She has a bee up her habit about keeping an eye on you.'

'She may come, but you'd better control her until then,' Teague said.

'I shall, as ever, continue in my care of our aunt, but I do not understand it. She seems to be more troubled every day.'

'Troubled or not, she's family and she stays here,' Teague commanded. 'But there are times when I have little use for her type of spirituality.'

'Especially when you're trying to bed a woman you are not married to.'

Teague shot him a look.

Rhain lifted his eyebrows in challenge. 'How early do we leave on the morrow?'

'Not very. It is not a long trip, but I do expect to stay a couple of days.'

'I thought you did not suspect Urien or Robert of any sabotage.'

'Never Robert. But as useless as Urien is, he could orchestrate something and I am running out of options. I am tired of always being on the defence in this battle.'

Rhain stood. 'Since tomorrow is to be such an

interesting day, I believe I better get my beauty sleep.'

'You'll be staying.'

'Of course, I'll be staying by your side. There are threats on your life, I'll not be returning to Gwalchdu merely to be deprived of your company.'

Teague set the goblet down. 'No, you will stay here. This is not an argument. I'll see Gwalchdu passed to you before Edward gets his hands on it, or worse, Urien. The enemy cannot be at two places at the same time. It is safer for Gwalchdu if you remain here.'

Rhain looked as if he might argue, then grinned, and walked away. 'Ah, your precious Gwalchdu. We wouldn't want anything to happen to her now, would we?'

Chapter Eleven

It was late afternoon by the time they cleared the trees and Anwen had a view of Brynmor. She had only been gone for one full moon, but it was as if she'd been gone a lifetime. There was still the walled gate that was the height of two men. The keep, too, was the same: centred in the middle, on a small hill, square and squat. The fields and the hills surrounding them, all covered with a sheen of frost, contrasted sharply to the worn wooden structure that housed people.

When compared with Gwalchdu, Brynmor appeared small and defenceless. It was no wonder the English had defeated the Welsh.

Anwen stroked Gully, who was perched on her arm. What was wrong with her? She was home and it was time to stop comparing Brynmor to Gwalchdu. If it wasn't for Gwalchdu changing sides during the war, Brynmor wouldn't have been defenceless. She was well to leave that cold stone fortress, with all its complications.

Teague's arm tightened around her. 'Anxious to be home?'

Anwen shivered as his warm breath caressed her ear. 'Of course.'

'It appears someone isn't happy to see us.'

The gates to Brynmor were closed. They were never closed in the middle of the day, even in winter, because the fields demanded constant access to the keep. What had happened here?

The soldiers looked to Teague as he sat patiently waiting. Brynmor's soldiers could see Gwalchdu's banner, a black hawk against red, snapping in the wind. Teague was a Marcher Lord. It was Brynmor's duty to welcome him. By having the gates shut, it was at the very least an insult and at the most treason.

Anwen could sense the tension rising, her own included, but then a man appeared above the gate. It was Robert of Dent, the English Governor to Brynmor. Before she could call out and ask for the gates to be opened, Teague interrupted.

'Robert!' Teague's voice boomed over Anwen's head. Startled, Gully let out a low cry.

'Were you expecting someone else?' Robert retorted.

'With this reception, I had my doubts.'

'I had doubts it was you, as you've never graced

us with your presence despite the distance. I needed to see it for myself.' Robert gave a gesture and the gates of Brynmor opened. When they were wide enough, Teague gently urged his horse into her home.

Anwen was grateful for Teague's arms supporting her as she didn't think she could sit straight by herself. The exchange of the two men surprised and confused her. Robert had travelled to Gwalchdu in the past. But the exchange between them was not of vague acquaintances, or of respectful English comrades. The exchange was that of true friendship.

But it could not be. In all the years here, she had never seen Teague and only a few times had Robert left Brynmor for Gwalchdu. Yet, it seemed they were friends, and a friendship between Robert of Dent and Teague of Gwalchdu did not bode well. It made her feel like some pawn in a game she did not know the rules to.

Pushing aside her unease, she glanced at the familiar faces of Brynmor's residents that she had missed so dearly. She was not prepared for the reception she got.

Certainly she had never ridden into Brynmor on horseback nor in the care of Teague of Gwalchdu, but she hadn't expected the hostile stares from people she had once considered her friends. She turned her attention to Robert, knowing he wouldn't bear her any ill will for the temporary company she kept.

She was a child when she had first seen Robert. It was during the years after the first Welsh War and he was one of the soldiers storming the gates of Brynmor in a minor skirmish. Years passed before she saw him again. He rode in with spurs on his heels, marking him for a knight. Anwen's horror at seeing him again only increased since he was made English Governor of Brynmor.

It didn't matter that Brynmor was in shambles or that Robert's position was not that of lord. She still resented him being there. With Urien useless with drink she expected Brynmor to suffer more under the arrogance of an Englishman. Yet from the moment Robert arrived, he worked with Brynmor's people to make it profitable. He treated Lord Urien, a former Welsh minor Prince, with some care, and left Anwen alone to manage the mews. Ultimately, however, even after all his years here, he was English and, thus, an outsider.

Anwen took in the expected changes to her home. After all it had been weeks since she been here. The wintry weather at the least would make the landscape different. But that wasn't the change she noticed most. It was that of the people, *her* people, who gave sidelong glances and avoided her direct stare.

She had no time for their doubt. Once she began her work, they would see she was still the same. The only people she owed her loyalty to were Alinore and Melun, but they weren't here. She tried to concentrate on the bird on her wrist.

Why weren't they in the courtyard?

Teague's slight squeeze of her waist as he dismounted brought her back to the present. Gully made it impossible for her to dismount on her own, but before she could request Teague's assistance, he strode over to Robert.

This was her home and she longed for freedom, but curiosity kept her silent as she watched the two men face each other. Teague's back was to her, but she could see Robert. Despite the fact their earlier exchange had hinted at a friendship, Robert's expression was reserved with a hint of anger. Robert was never angry. All was not as it seemed.

Teague faced the man he had rarely seen over the last five years. His face had aged little. In fact, Robert appeared younger and freer than he had ever seen him before and that was as perplexing as the welcoming they received. Things had changed at Brynmor. Whether the change was at the cost of Gwalchdu or the lives there, he was here to find out.

'Good health to you and to Gwalchdu.' Robert approached.

'I did not expect to see you still here,' Teague said.

'There is more to a man than running away.'

Chuckling, Teague assessed the words that rankled and amused him, but he suspected Robert of Dent knew that. They had trained together at Edward's court and knew each other well, despite what the Welsh wars had brought them.

'Ever the tactician, Robert.' Teague felt lighter, remembering the man of the past.

'I always preferred to use my wits than my arm.'

'It's because your arm wasn't any good.'

Robert's eyes widened in surprise, then he threw back his head and let out a bark of a laugh. 'If there is time, I will see you repaid for that remark.'

'If your arm was as bad as it used to be, we'll need little time.'

Robert chuckled again, but Teague saw something reflective in the other man's eyes.

'It was a long time ago, wasn't it.' It was a remark, not a question.

'Yes, but I am reminded of it often.'

Teague nodded, his lips thinning. 'Urien of Brynmor made that choice when he defied Edward in his true rule of Wales.'

Robert's tone was light, but there was steel underneath his words. 'I am well aware of the choices made.'

'Pardon, my old friend. It still makes no sense to me that you are here when you could have had your own estate.'

'As I said, I do not run,' Robert said. 'Why are you here, Teague? You know your welcome is given solely because of Edward's decree.'

'I have something of yours.'

Robert's eyes went to Anwen. 'Yes, you told me in the last missive you'd be returning her, but what do you do here personally? You know how Urien will respond.'

'I don't give a damn about Urien. It is my right to visit Brynmor and my right to expect hospitality, Robert. I am still a Marcher Lord.'

Robert's gaze narrowed, but after a moment, he nodded and put his hand on Teague's shoulder. 'Come. Let us drink.'

Betrayed. She was betrayed by the Devil of Gwalchdu and her own people. Anwen watched Teague direct his men, but her eyes were not focused on him. Her thoughts were solely on the conversation she heard.

Robert mentioned he received a *last* missive from Teague, which meant there was a first missive. Robert had known she was a prisoner at Gwalchdu. He did nothing to help release her. Nobody at Brynmor came for her.

Then Teague had brought her home. Over the years, Robert had travelled to Gwalchdu to pay tithes and to exchange reports, but Teague had never travelled to Brynmor. Why?

Anwen's mind reeled at the questions and possibilities. There was some reason besides her injury or his lust. Whatever the reason, she wanted nothing to do with it. In fact, she wanted nothing to do with any of them. All she'd ever wanted was to return to Brynmor and return to her work.

Teague gently squeezed her waist. 'Are you well?'

'I am unused to riding,' she lied, supporting her weight on his shoulders as he helped her dismount. The bird in her hand made her awkward, or maybe it was his proximity. For an extended moment, there was nothing but her hands resting upon his shoulders, his hands spanning the breadth of her waist, an almost imperceptible tightening of his fingers. Then he released her and she stepped back.

'Settle Gully and we will talk,' he said.

Anwen quickly strode towards the mews. At her rapid movement, Gully bated, flapping his wings and trying to fly from her wrist, but she didn't slow. She needed sanctuary.

When she entered into the familiar building, Anwen's heart returned to its normal pace. She breathed in deeply, letting the musty smells engulf her as she walked to Gully's empty perch.

What was Teague doing here? If he meant to

simply return her, he could have sent her with a chaperon, but he had brought her himself, along with Ffion and some of his best men. So he must mean to extend his stay. Why hadn't she questioned Teague's bringing her here?

Untying one jess from the gauntlet, Anwen realised she knew the answer. Because she trusted Teague, fool that she was. So excited to be returning home, she'd believed the Traitor of Gwalchdu and fell into whatever game he planned for her. He was not on a mere errand of returning her and the bird to Brynmor, but had an agenda of his own. It appeared Robert thought the same.

So on one hand she had Teague's secret agenda and on the other…betrayal. The people she believed to be her friends and family had not come to see to her health or take her home. Why hadn't Robert come or sent someone to retrieve her? What of Alinore and Melun? They weren't even in the courtyard to greet her. A lifetime of caring and she received nary a message from either. It was as if…as if she was of no value to them.

Willing her tears not to spill, she struggled to release Gully's ties.

'If you had been mine, I would have come for you.'

Anwen jumped at Teague's voice. She had not heard him open the mews door, had not heard his feet crunch across the hay.

'I would have come,' Teague repeated, his voice soft and directly behind her. She did not turn at his words, or his close proximity.

How could he have known her thoughts? She had let him get too close to her at Gwalchdu. That would explain why his words in the mews last night affected her. He had not physically touched her, but it didn't matter. Her body responded to him anyway.

She didn't know how to control or rid herself of her thoughts of Teague. She feared that, with him, she would lose something of herself, like a hawk does its freedom. It was that bond between them again, unbidden, unwanted, but there, and just as translucent and strong, like a newly made creance.

Anwen stroked Gully, still on her wrist. Without Teague's presence, the mews had calmed her, but now she realised her mistake. In this place that provided comfort, she lowered her defences completely. She was vulnerable to him.

If you had been mine.

She could not stop the image of herself belonging to such a man. The feeling alarmed and intrigued her, then she shook herself from her reverie. If she belonged to him, she had no doubt there would be little left of her. She couldn't *breathe* with him.

'You had correspondence with Robert,' she said as lightly as she could. 'You did not tell me of this.'

He tilted his head. 'Was there a need?'

Was there a need? There wasn't any more, but it bothered her.

'Yes, there was a need! They were *my* messages. You had no right to hide them from me.'

'My reasons were well founded.'

'Because you own me now that you saved my life?' she scorned. 'Own me enough to make me your whore? Your well-founded reasons are a little vague to me.'

'I never said I wanted you solely for my lust.'

She waved her free hand. 'You've never spoken of any other reason. Since the start you have spoken of physical desire.'

She watched him open his mouth to speak, but he closed it and just stared at her.

'You talk of lust, of being a whore, yet… Do you know of physical desire, Anwen?' he asked.

She looked at him out of the corner of her eye. 'There are the dogs and horses. I have seen what they do.'

He sharply shook his head as if dislodging images. 'Do you know about the desire between a man and a woman?'

'Why are you asking me this? This will get us nowhere.'

'I'm curious and you are prevaricating. And I think this conversation will get us somewhere.' He tilted his head in that way that maddened and fascinated her. 'You are usually blunt and never avoid subjects, which means you are trying to hide your innocence. I wonder why you do not wish to discuss this with me.'

'If you would listen, you would know I don't wish to discuss anything with you.'

'Now you surprise me. You are lying, too.'

She stole another glance at him, and then wished she hadn't. His black eyes held hers, drew her in, and she closed her own to release the sudden tension in her head.

'I am not a patient man, Anwen, and I cannot deny that I want you. My desire for you has been strong since the first moment I saw you. But if my words lack manners, haven't my actions proved my other desires with you?'

She opened her eyes, not hiding her incredulity. 'Actions?' she scoffed. 'You kept me prisoner! And as for these desires, all I hear from *you* are lies.'

Teague did not move, but she could sense his sudden alertness. 'Again, I have my reasons for withholding some truths from you, but I have been honest in all other matters. I spoke the truth when I said I have never wanted a woman more. Even now I am heavy with it and my palms ache to caress you, but I have shown you nothing but restraint.'

'Restraint? Is that what you call lust and deception?'

'Are you so familiar with both to know it is all

I show you?' he pushed. 'Your manner is bold, but I find you intriguingly lacking in other ways.'

She shouldn't be surprised he twisted her words, but if he thought she lacked charms, why didn't he leave her alone? Releasing the last jess, she turned her back to secure Gully to his perch.

It was a mistake. At least with the bird on her wrist, she had a shield against Teague, who now stepped closer yet. If she leaned back, she could rest against him. As it was, although he wasn't touching her, he was enclosing her.

'I have hurt you. How?' Teague's breath caressed her hair.

'How could you have hurt me?' Gully shuffled restlessly on his perch. She knew she'd been handling him roughly, but it couldn't be helped. Her sole wish now was to secure Gully, unlace the gear and leave. But Teague was too close and her hand trembled as she untied and tugged the leather gauntlet from her arm.

'Allow me.' Teague reached around her until his arms all but held her. Her body responded, her skin prickled. She felt instantly separated from her body as she watched his large calloused hands release the glove from her arm and lay it on a nearby table.

She waited for him to step away. When he didn't, she turned. He still did not move.

'Anwen?' he asked.

She stared at his chest. 'Let me aside.'

'Anwen,' Teague said again, his voice commanding her to look at him. She did.

His black eyes absorbed and searched. 'By my comment, I simply meant you lacked a certain knowledge of carnal ways that is curious given your direct manner.' Brushing her cheek, Teague clasped one of her locks between his calloused fingers.

She felt that touch deep inside her.

'Did you know,' Teague continued, 'that when your hair catches the sunlight, it shames gold?'

Something was happening to Anwen's breath. It was coming in faster and, with every breath, she took in more of the man before her. He continued to caress her hair, letting it slip between his fingers. She could almost feel that touch on her skin. She *wanted* to feel that touch on her skin.

'Does my withholding those missives bother you, or is it that you thought no one wanted you?'

His question dissipated some of the web he wove around her. 'Does it matter?' she said.

Teague dropped the curl and trailed his fingers gently along the side of her cheek and curve of her jaw.

'I think it matters to you. I'll have you know, I reported in my correspondence that they didn't need to come; that you were well cared for and would be returned.'

Anwen tilted her head, trying to remove her cheek from his caresses, but the movement gave him access to the lines of her throat.

She forced the words out. 'So you purposely kept them away from me for all those weeks.'

'Perhaps. But I think them all fools. If I thought you hurt, I would not have been satisfied until I saw you for myself. *I* would have come, Anwen.'

She closed her eyes to shut out his words. It didn't work. They hit her in her heart and some of her barrier cracked.

'I knew your skin would feel like this.'

Teague's tone jarred her from the sensual assault and she roughly moved her head away. 'You touched me enough when I was ill.'

Teague shook his head slowly. 'No, then I worried for your health.'

The Devil wouldn't worry. 'And when I was awake? Or at night?' she interrupted. 'My skin cannot be so different from then, or for that matter, when you have touched other women.' Anwen felt his hand hesitate. 'You are a powerful Marcher Lord. I have little doubt you would know the touch of a woman's skin, as it would be all the same to you.'

Teague's eyes left Anwen's as he skimmed his fingers along her arm until he grasped her hand. Then he pressed his thumb sensuously against her palm, sliding it up to her inner wrist to circle there and back again. Until tiny shivers flew from her wrists to her toes.

'Not all skin is the same, Anwen. And it is a world of difference between what was then and what is now. Now you stand before me, very much alive, and I can feel your vibrancy, feel your warmth. Your skin is not like any others, but more like the down of a newborn peregrine and I can feel how it rises up to meet my hand.'

His gentle hand compelled her, but ire warred within her at his words. 'I am not some foundling.'

'No, you are a woman grown, or else what would Sister Ffion think if she caught us like this?'

Humour. From the Traitor. Anwen's lips twitched despite herself. Ffion would indeed fly into a fit if she knew they were alone. 'I am sure she would think no less than she already does.'

'Indeed, it is difficult to imagine Ffion's preaching worsening.' Teague's hand went to her nape, effectively raising Anwen's lips to meet his own. The movement caught her by surprise.

His humour caught her off guard. She thought him gentled, but the primal feel of his large hand cradling her nape belied otherwise. She was the prey to his hawk and his talons were now gently grasping. He'd been waiting, waiting, and only now she realised she'd been caught.

She *wanted* to be caught.

Teague inhaled sharply as he judged her response. 'But I'd take the risk if I could be here like this.'

He covered her mouth with his own.

Heat seared down her body. Her skin flushed, expanded, stretched. She opened her mouth to breathe, but instead of air, it was his breath, his mouth that she took in. She could smell his scent, taste his skin, feel his heat and she twined her hands behind his neck not for support, but out of need. Her fingers slid along the warmth of his skin, traced the collar of his tunic and then spread upward to thread through the coarse coolness of his hair.

Her throat vibrated with sound and then she felt nothing but hot male body pressing into hers. The kiss was nothing and everything that Anwen needed. It was like the moment a falcon takes flight and is tugged back to the gauntlet by the master.

She felt tied by Teague's arms keeping her at a distance she no longer wanted. She thrust herself upward, trying to break the tension that bound her. But the tension increased as her breasts pressed against his chest and her hips cradled against his.

Abruptly, Teague ended the kiss. Their breaths clashed as their eyes met and Anwen quickly looked away. She feared she was too open for him to read.

'Anwen,' he whispered.

She refused to answer him.

'My men will look for me here.' Teague caressed her cheek. 'I must go.'

Angry with herself, she pulled back from him. 'Then go.'

He lowered his hand. 'We will share a trencher tonight.'

'No! Why? It will not be expected.'

'I wish it and I am an honoured guest.'

Orders again. She was a fool. 'You are more than that here, but what exactly, I don't know. Besides, Urien will never allow me at the table.'

'Urien does as I wish.' Teague's voice held all the arrogance of a Marcher Lord.

'How could I forget?' Anwen said. 'You are Lord Teague of Gwalchdu, King Edward's Welsh weapon. But you are more than that and I do not like being kept in the dark.'

'No, you are not like your falcons, who find comfort when their hoods are on.'

'I have no time for this talk.' She crossed her arms. 'I must find Melun.'

'You will sit with me tonight, even if I tie you to me.'

Images of creances and jesses and gauntlets came to her. Still she tried to distance herself. 'I have been gone too long. There is much to do here.'

'What you have to do is choose your battles.'

'So this is a battle between you and I? And if I lose, will Gwalchdu's lord have me imprisoned?'

Teague sighed. 'It is…burdensome that circumstances allow me only to show you my less-than-better traits.'

'You have other traits besides dominance and betrayal against your fellow countrymen?'

Teague smiled bitterly. 'My betrayal. How could I forget?' He turned to leave the mews, his long strides quickly bringing him to the doors, but not before he uttered, 'Soon Anwen, you will know the truth.'

She would never understand the man. Now that she was home, she should be free from him. And yet he wanted to share a trencher with her.

It did not make sense. She was back in Brynmor, but he wouldn't leave her alone. It was as if he were testing her and her reaction to him. Setting her free to fly, then keeping her by creance or lure.

And that kiss. Her lips felt swollen and her entire body still trembled. If he was setting a lure, he could not have made a more tempting one. But temptation was not the only feeling left behind by their kiss.

Shaking, she focused on the birds and the afternoon light filtering through the cracks. Gully sat peacefully at his perch, at rest in his home, unlike her, who would never feel the same way about this place. Nothing would be peaceful to her and she would give a peregrine to not know the Traitor of Gwalchdu's kiss.

There was more to him than lust and deception. It wasn't the passion in the kiss or the temptation that made her crave him. It was the giving in his kiss that undid her. For the Traitor not only gave her passion, but shared his own. And his was a dark swirling need born of a desolate loneliness.

All her life she thought that Gwalchdu stood out of arrogant dominance and that Gwalchdu's lord must be the same, but she was wrong. It stood alone, because no one stood with it. It was not cold stone out of choice, but because there was nothing that brought it warmth.

If you had been mine.

Chapter Twelve

In the room adjacent to the mews, Melun sat in his favourite chair. His raw-boned frame was thinner, his skin hung in sallow emptiness as if he hadn't eaten in weeks. When he turned his face to hers, Anwen could see he'd been crying and she flew immediately to his feet.

'You have returned, child.'

He appeared to have doubled in age since she was gone; his grey eyes were even cloudier. Yet, he was alive and she could ask for no more blessing than that.

He patted her against the shoulders. 'I am sorry I was not in the courtyard to greet you. I heard riders approach and the shriek of a goshawk. I hoped it was you. I could not have borne it if it was not. So I sat and waited, knowing you would come.'

Anwen let out a small cry. She had wasted time listening to Robert's greetings and Teague's demands; Melun must have thought she hadn't returned.

'I feared you would be hurt,' she said. 'I lost Gully, but even when I found him I could not get here until now.'

'It is like you to always put people before yourself.' Melun smiled. 'I could have managed any punishment meted out by Lord Urien, but I reported to Sir Robert, whom I believe understood my true grief. I did not worry over a mere bird, Anwen, but you.' He brushed her hair aside, his thin hands touching her wound. 'You were hurt.'

'I hit my head. Lord Teague cared for me until I regained my strength.'

'So what I heard is true.' Melun's bushy eyebrows rose. 'Did you ride with him?'

Anwen blushed. 'Since I am unskilled, he insisted that I accompany a rider.'

Melun gave a little smile. 'He thought it a task only equal for himself?'

'I have stopped trying to understand his ways. How is Alinore?'

'Better. That is all that I can tell.'

'What do you mean?' 'Better' was never a word that described Alinore's fragility.

'I don't know, just better.' Melun shrugged. 'There is a certain glow to her cheeks.'

'She is not sick or feverish?'

'No, not at all. Occasionally, she even eats at the table instead of her room.'

'Oh,' Anwen exclaimed. 'These are glad tidings.' She was happy to hear Alinore fared well, but she also experienced a certain sense of loss and more confusion. If Alinore was well, why was she not in the courtyard to greet her?

She squeezed Melun's hand. 'I have missed you.'

Melun squeezed back. 'Am I to assume that goshawk was Gully?'

Flashing him a smile, Anwen stood and brushed the dust from her skirts. She recounted to Melun all that had transpired since she awoke at Gwalchdu. While she did so, she cleaned the room just as she did in the past. Melun's age and diminished sight allowed him meagre skill to keeping a home.

Cleaning for and talking to Melun soothed her soul as nothing else could. When she was done, she knelt again in front of him. 'The Traitor wishes to sup with me this evening.'

'Worse things could happen.'

She raised her hands in front of her as if she could stop his words. 'Ach, are you planning to be a matchmaker now?'

'As I said, worse things could happen.'

'Are there any worse things than being an English lord's mistress?'

Melun frowned and shook his head. 'I do not

understand. The reports told me you were well cared for and no harm befell you.'

'Reports?' she asked, confused. 'You possessed missives from Gwalchdu?'

Melun's frown deepened. 'Of course, but you know that. Sir Robert said he would send our greetings. I believe Lady Alinore also wrote you.'

At Anwen's darkening face, Melun nodded his head. 'Ah, so he continues to be the Traitor after all.'

'I received no reports, no missives. I heard naught from Brynmor and I did not know Gwalchdu sent you replies.'

Melun laid his hand against hers and continued, 'When you stayed, I thought you'd become something more to him.'

Anwen remembered the kiss and the way Teague had shared something of his desire and loneliness with her. Did it mean she meant more to him? No. There could never be trust.

'I am but a simple woman. I am sure for a man of Teague's status, the King would demand a more lucrative joining.'

Melun gave a secretive smile. She was immediately suspicious. 'Why do you smile?'

He poked her in the arm. 'You gave no reasons of your heart that you do not wish to be bound to that man. He has been good to you, hasn't he?'

It was Anwen's turn to frown. What had she

revealed to Melun in her retelling of her tale? Apparently much. He might be almost blind, but no one understood her better.

'Yes, he has been good to me.' It was his goodness that was the worst of it. How could she ever reconcile this man within herself? The sooner he returned to Gwalchdu, the better. She stood to go and Melun rose with her.

The hall was full when they entered. Men argued as they slurped beer, women were moving from bench to bench, servants were spilling food that was quickly lapped up by dogs. This was not ordered Gwalchdu, but home, and she was glad to see some things had not changed.

She walked with Melun to the lower table where he sat. Teague was talking with Robert at the high table, but she could feel his eyes upon her.

'Go to him,' Melun requested. 'He thinks you're about to sit with me.'

'You cannot see.' Anwen made others move to give him room.

'I can see with more than my eyes and he is making his displeasure known.'

Anwen glanced at the high table. It was true. Even Ffion was frowning at her now. Annoyed, Anwen placed Melun's hand on his cup. 'I'll go, but only not to cause a scene.'

The high table was above the seating of others

and that meant she had a perfect view of its occupants and one in particular.

Teague continued talking to Robert, but he kept watching her. He wore a tunic of deepest burgundy and was dressed as civilly as any man she had ever seen: clean shaven, his black hair tied back. And yet, there was something uncivil about him. Brynmor's gently carved table was insubstantial compared to the man who dined at it. Only in Gwalchdu's Great Hall did he belong.

Gwalchdu. Black Hawk.

If she didn't know he was a man, she would have thought him hewn from that very stone edifice.

Teague caught her eye and she quickly glanced at the other table's occupants. Urien sat at the high seat, his great hulking form slumped, his meaty hand grasping his goblet. No one was acknowledging him.

And neither would she, though Anwen wished to never see him at all. The fact he grew fat from food she helped to hunt and drank ale from fields she gleamed revolted her. The fact he sat with honour at this table, when Alinore never sat at it at all because of her fear of him, enraged her.

But she knew keeping these thoughts wouldn't be conducive to sharing Teague's trencher and she forced her gaze to the other table's occupants.

Robert was dressed in forest green, the colour

highlighting his dark brown hair. She had always thought Robert a handsome man, but she could not help comparing him to Teague. Robert was strong, thickly muscled, his features evenly placed and pleasing. Teague's features were more chiselled and harsh, and yet she found he appealed to her more.

Teague. Robert. Brynmor. Gwalchdu.

She made more comparisons. Annoyed at herself, she adjusted her chair.

'Welcome, Anwen, we have been waiting for you.' Urien pronounced each word slowly.

Turning her head pointedly away, she sat and the servants immediately brought great platters of food. Anwen's mouth watered as she spied soup made of honey, spices and breadcrumbs, white peas, fish with ale sauce and boiled rabbit in spicy almond-milk sauce. No expense was spared to feed Gwalchdu's lord.

She tried to concentrate on her trencher, but Teague leaned over. 'I thought you would ignore my request.'

'I want no battle with you.'

Teague arched one eyebrow. 'No? Then what do you want with me?'

Before she could answer, Robert interrupted. 'Let her eat, Teague, it has been a long day. She'll not keep anything down with you towering over her. Anwen, how do you fare?'

'I am well, Sir Robert. Lord Gwalchdu has been most kind in taking care of me these many weeks.'

'I am sure you expected no kindness from one who sides with the English.'

Teague turned to Robert. 'So she gives you no rest in that, too?'

Robert shook his head. 'Not for a moment, despite all these years.'

So like men to talk around her. 'It is difficult to forget, when your very presence is a reminder of why you are here.'

Robert glanced at the stairs leading to the resident rooms above. 'I haven't forgotten why I am here.'

Teague began another conversation with Robert, but Anwen did not join in. She was too famished to be much company and she intended to use the food to ignore the man sitting next to her.

But it was impossible. The shared trencher gave him too close a proximity to her and he was always touching her. Their hands would reach for the goblet at the same time and his palm would cover her hand, or his fingers linked with hers. So, too, he would lean and his leg or arm brushed against her. Each time the ephemeral contact would go through her. It made her warm, then hot. Made her breath catch, her heart pound. Each touch added to another and she was again reminded of his lips touching hers, his fingers thrusting through her hair, his body pressed against hers. Her eating slowed, then stopped as she tried to regain some balance.

'Is something wrong?'

Teague's words skimmed over her ear.

'I believe I am no longer hungry,' she said.

'Are you not?'

Anwen shook her head briefly. The almost-full trencher mocked her growling stomach, but she didn't know if she could get anything past the restriction in her throat.

Teague kept his gaze on her. Slowly, she took in the fine weave of his tunic and how soft it appeared against the cords of his bare throat. Further up to the indentations and shadows of his jaw, and the small curved scar across his cheek. When she reached his eyes, they were midnight intent.

'I find I grow hungrier the longer I sit at this table with you.' Teague spoke in a low voice, the deepness of which hummed under her skin. He tilted his head, his eyes skimmed over her features. 'Ah, you're lying to me again, Anwen. Your face is flushed, the lids of your eyes almost slumberous; these are manifestations of hunger, but I think we'll not be able to find our repast here at this table.' Teague leaned closer. 'I cannot eat for thoughts of your lips touching me instead of this food.'

Anwen forced ale down her throat. What was

happening to her? Before she could answer him, a high keening sound exploded across the hall.

It was Ffion. Sprawled on the floor, her black gown askew, she twitched and kicked the air. Vomit and food smeared her face.

Teague and Robert reacted immediately. Urien blustered and stuttered at the sudden commotion. Shocked, Anwen watched Teague force a wooden spoon between Ffion's teeth. Robert restrained her arms and legs. The entire hall hushed; people stilled, wide eyed and afraid.

'What must be done?' Anwen knelt next to Robert and grabbed one of Ffion's arms to hold it to her side.

Teague held Ffion's head between his two hands. 'We wait until it stops.'

When Ffion's shaking slowly decreased, Teague lifted her. 'We need to get her to her rooms. She will not want to waken here.'

Robert stood. 'I will show you the way.'

Anwen caught Melun's worried eye and followed the two men.

An hour later, Anwen still sat at Ffion's bedside. The Sister's sleep was less fitful, but her greyish complexion remained. Standing, she addressed Robert and Teague, who stood as if guarding the door. 'I will go and get some hot water, linens and food. She may also want some repast when she wakes.'

Teague's eyes were tired. 'Thank you.'

Anwen nodded before closing the door behind her.

Robert pointed to Ffion lying on the bed. 'Is she possessed?'

Teague closed his eyes briefly. 'No, it has been her condition since childhood.'

'It is like that boy at Cilmeri.'

'Without the bloodshed or the trauma,' Teague added. 'I wish Greta from my household was here. She and Edith have some understanding with Ffion's afflictions and is a great help.'

'She is resting, perhaps that will be enough.' Robert crossed his arms. 'The Church knows?'

Teague nodded. 'It has never been spoken of aloud.'

'It is a wonder she has not been burned.'

Teague's expression darkened. 'She is family and I am rich. A fact the Church appreciates.'

'It is good you are much favoured,' Robert said. 'I will do what I must to keep this quiet.'

Teague placed his hand on Robert's shoulder. 'I appreciate it, but do not tax yourself.'

'Yes, but if Edward discovered your aunt is afflicted, the consequences—'

'Edward knows,' Teague interrupted.

Astonished, Robert was silent a moment, before

he replied, 'Your Devil's blood. That's why you're called the Devil of Gwalchdu.'

'At first the rumours were pointed to her, when I could—'

'You took it for your own advantage,' Robert interrupted.

'Not without some penalty.' Teague nodded at Ffion. 'She has paid much because of that rumour that started before I was born. I regret that I could not dissipate it sooner for her sake.'

'Hence you pay the Church and use her affliction so that men fear you on the battlefield?'

'My skill with a sword should have been enough; what I wished was to slash every tongue that spread such whispers.'

'I think they knew that.' Robert released his arms. 'What are your intentions with Anwen?'

Teague had expected this conversation with Robert since the moment he requested to share a trencher. Even so, he did not know how to answer. His request was impulsive. In the mews he had been reluctant to let her go and sitting next to her at the table was an opportunity to keep her close. But his intentions? Of those, he was not certain. His emotions when it came to her were foreign to him.

Keeping his voice neutral, he answered, 'Why do you ask?'

'She is much loved here. The people need her, respect her, follow her. She has worked hard for that respect and shares their burden and their pleasure. If she were hurt, it would damage what peace there is between Gwalchdu and Brynmor.'

'Is it only the people who would be displeased?'

Robert's jaw locked. 'No, I would be, as well.'

Teague pounced at the confession. 'What is she to you?'

Robert glanced at Ffion's sleeping form. 'I have known Anwen a long time and have come to respect and care for her as a sister. That is all, but it is enough. I will not see her hurt.'

Teague assessed Robert's words. 'I do not wish her harm.'

Robert nodded once.

Teague's lips twisted wryly. 'You believe me?'

'Your word has always been enough for me.'

'But we have not fought together for a long time and there has been much conflict between us. Matters and politics have changed greatly in the last ten years.'

'My trust in you has not,' Robert said.

Teague have a low laugh. 'You have softened, my friend.'

'In many ways. My needs have changed from the times of the wars and conquests. I now value hearth and home.'

'But Brynmor is not yours as long as Urien is here. Why is he still here, Robert? If you value

Brynmor so, Edward would have easily given it to you as a prize.'

'There is something here I value more than land.'

'Is it Anwen?' Teague felt a flash of possessive anger.

Robert smiled secretively. 'No, but I find it interesting that you ask if it is she.'

Teague did not like secrets. 'I will be staying a few days.'

'Why?'

'I need to ascertain a matter concerning me at this time.'

'What you do with Brynmor concerns me, Teague. I have a right to know what it is.'

'Not in this, you don't.'

'If it involves Anwen or anyone else—' Robert said.

Teague interrupted. 'You mention Anwen again, Robert. What is she here? You have told me nothing about her position, yet it is clear she is no mere astringer or servant.'

Robert turned towards the door. 'It seems we all have our secrets, don't we?'

'I will find the answers I need. I merely wished for your cooperation.'

Robert stopped at the door. 'As long as it is in Brynmor's best interests I'll cooperate, but it is best you remember I am not under Gwalchdu's rule.'

* * *

Sitting at her bedroom window, Anwen stretched the sleep from her shoulders. The morning sky was a cloudless light blue, making the day colder than usual. She was surprised she'd slept at all since her chambers were next to the guest rooms and, consequently, near Teague. More than once she glanced at the door, expecting it to open, but he never came.

Running her hands down her skirts, she gave an exasperated snort. Whether she felt relief or regret, she wouldn't think about it any longer. She had returned to Brynmor and she wouldn't waste her time on the Traitor of Gwalchdu.

She was leaving the garderobe when Ffion approached. Teague said that his aunt would not suffer long and might have no memory of the episode. To ease her transition, they all agreed no one would mention what happened in the Hall. Although the Sister had made her stay at Gwalchdu unpleasant, Anwen didn't want to cause her additional discomfort.

Perhaps it was Rhain's description that softened her towards Ffion, but Anwen also saw how hardships shaped people. Sometimes making them stronger or leaving them bitter. The Sister had, at least at one time, been kind. The least she could do now was give Ffion some courtesy.

'Good morning, Sister.' Anwen waved her hand

in the direction of the garderobe. 'It appears we are of the same ilk this morning.'

'Perhaps.' Ffion's eyes barely flickered to the closed door. 'Did you sleep last night?'

'Very well, thank you.'

'Alone?'

Ffion was clearly recovered, if she was back to lecturing on her favourite sin. 'Of course, Sister.'

'It appears not for long, my child. Your manner is too bold by far and you are not escaping the lord's notice. If you are pure, you'll not stay that way.'

'I do not understand what you mean.'

Ffion's pursed her lips. 'I wonder if you are truly that naïve. I watched you during dinner last night. You have not escaped his notice and now he seems even more taken with you. Take a care, or you will lose more than your freedom, you will break God's commandment.'

Even a trip to Brynmor did not end Ffion's seeming obsession with adultery. Only the visibility of Ffion's black circles under her eyes kept Anwen's patience. 'Thank you, Sister, I appreciate the concern.'

Ffion stepped closer. 'Be careful. You know not what goes on. It may cost you dearly.'

Anwen didn't knock as she entered Alinore's rooms. As expected this early in the morning, her sister was on her knees in prayer, and the morning's light cast her golden hair as if in a soft halo.

'How long will I have to wait until you're done?' Anwen asked, as she held her arms out wide.

Alinore's entire body jerked before she swept over to Anwen. 'Oh, it is time you visited me!'

Anwen closed her eyes to savour the light gossamer feeling of Alinore's arms around her. 'Please let us sit and talk again.'

Anwen pulled open the coverlet on the bed and sat at the head, while her sister snuggled beside her. This was just what they always did and Anwen's heart filled with fond memories, but also other…darker memories.

'You will not find any bruises.' Alinore's lips curved.

Anwen stopped scanning her sister's arms. 'Was I that obvious?'

'Yes.' Alinore giggled. 'You know Robert protects me and has since he returned.'

But there were times Urien risked a swipe or foolishly forgot Robert's wrath. 'You are Urien's daughter and he hurts you! I've never understood why you still care, let alone tolerate him, when all he ever does is shout and hit you.'

'Patience. He is my father and I do not simply tolerate him. I love him as God wants me to do. He's your father, too.'

Urien would never claim her as a daughter.

Not her, bastard-born. He hadn't been her father since the day he struck her aside and went after Alinore.

Alinore's hands fluttered as if to stop Anwen's thoughts. 'Pray, no anger or tears. I share not your grief.' Her sister's gentle eyes reflected the truth of her words.

'I'm sorry I wasn't here to help you.'

'You cannot protect me from everything.' Alinore gave a teasing smile. 'Although you always did try.'

'I couldn't help it. You are too dear to me.'

Alinore squeezed Anwen's hand. 'I know. I love you too, though I see you are still too stubborn to say it.' Putting her hand back into her lap, Alinore added, 'But in truth, it has been weeks since he tried anything.'

'It's good to see that Urien was so in his cups that he couldn't hurt you.'

'No, it wasn't that, and it wasn't just Robert delaying his hand either.'

'What has happened?'

'Things have changed since you have been gone. Robert has taught me how not to get hit.'

'You were always good at avoiding Urien before,' Anwen answered, more defensively than she intended.

Alinore shook her head. 'It is not the same. I avoid, not by hiding like a child, but with words and deeds. In fact, Father is much easier to control than I ever thought possible!'

Anwen was taken aback at these words. Anwen had learned long ago how to control and avoid Urien, but she always thought Alinore too fragile. Now, with Robert's help, it appeared she found confidence.

Alinore gave a light laugh. 'Anwen, do not be sad, be happy for me.'

She tried to smile. 'Of course I am happy. It's only—' She stopped and waved a hand. She realised what her sister said was true. Looking at Alinore, glowing with happiness, she could have hoped for nothing else, even if Robert of Dent played a part in it. Was Alinore in love?

'What is Robert to you?' she asked.

Alinore blushed, her hand covering her mouth. 'Oh! I can see that getting hit on the head has not changed you.'

Anwen remembered how Teague had asked whether she'd always been direct. She also remembered how the moon's light hid his face and body in its darkness, but his words, though softly spoken, still vibrated through her.

I watched you.

She believed him. He saw her, not only physically, but also something of her heart. Perhaps in the forest or in the nights he held her through her pain, but she gave him something she could not take back even if she wanted to. There was a connection between them.

Alinore raised one brow. 'Or maybe it *has* changed you.'

'Nonsense.' Anwen shook her head. 'It was merely a minor injury.'

'That is not what I understood.'

'So, you were given correspondence, as well.'

'Very much so. When you did not return, I worried the rains made the river too full for crossing and somehow you were swept away. But we received a missive from Gwalchdu that very night telling of your accident and we have waited ever since.'

They waited, but didn't come. Anwen suppressed the thought, but not soon enough. She should be happy to be here again.

Melun said Alinore was better. It was true. There was a certain glow to her and a strength that hadn't been there before. Alinore still moved with the grace and serenity of those of the convent, but she had gained some strength and happiness.

Anwen smiled. 'I'm starving! Shall we break our fast?'

Chapter Thirteen

Anwen clapped her hands briskly against the morning frost as she knelt in the rich dirt of the south field.

It had been three days since she returned to Brynmor and she had spent that time planting winter wheat. The planting was behind and some of the fields hadn't even been tilled.

Brynmor hadn't lain fallow while she was recovering from her injury, but there was no denying the fields needed more hands. Anwen welcomed the work and the exhaustion for she needed the distraction to her thoughts that strayed to a certain traitor and the declaration he made.

Would Teague have come for her? She watched his determination in the lists, heard of his legendary exploits in the field. All that she knew and saw of him suggested he spoke the truth. He would have come for her.

But now the man who declared such words was

as distant from her as the sea was from Brynmor. She sighed and rolled her shoulders.

They still shared a trencher at evening meals, but he no longer touched her. Yet, it didn't matter. Each night, she was too aware of how his hands lifted his goblet and how his throat moved when he swallowed his ale. She would watch in helpless fascination as he caressed his spoon handle, his fingers sliding along the round smoothness of the pewter. Occasionally she'd risk looking at him and feel guilt and relief if his gaze was elsewhere.

If you had been mine.

She was too aware of him, too tied to him.

Anwen sunk her fingers deep into the pouch of seeds around her waist. All these seeds needed to be planted to feed the people of Brynmor.

Brynmor was her home, her life.

She didn't belong to the Traitor of Gwalchdu, even if he said he wanted her. She had no place at Gwalchdu and didn't want one. Brynmor needed her, not Gwalchdu.

It was late morning by the time she rested. The day had warmed, but not by much. She interlocked her fingers over her head and stretched.

Villagers were returning the few sheep from the outer fields and stable boys were resting plough horses, but she could also see Teague's soldiers patrolling. They didn't lounge about like guests, nor did they lazily pursue the serving wenches. Instead they systematically walked the perimeters of Brynmor's fields, tower and gates.

They searched and guarded just as they did at Gwalchdu, but why? She wasn't wrong to think Teague had his own agenda in coming to Brynmor. The proof surrounded her. He had brought her from Gwalchdu, but stayed. His many soldiers scanned the landscape and interfered with Brynmor's people. She knew Robert wasn't pleased despite the friendship between the two men.

Anwen worried over Teague's extended stay, because if Teague was annoying Robert, then Urien was probably furious. And when Urien got angry, he usually abused Alinore.

But for three days Urien stayed his hand. Alinore even joined them for evening meals, a circumstance that had always before provoked Urien. Now, he remained belligerently sullen. For Anwen, his worsening table manners were a welcome change as long as he left Alinore alone.

Yet, her sister was never entirely alone because Robert was often by her side. He never stepped over the bounds of propriety; his manner was gentle, almost tender, and Alinore's responding smiles tentative and sweet. They shared something together that wasn't there before Anwen left.

Robert must know an Englishman's courtship with Alinore would never be sanctioned by Urien. She couldn't bear it if Robert broke Alinore's heart.

'Why are you frowning?'

Anwen jumped at the voice behind her. God's breath, she must have been too deep in her thoughts to not have heard a full-grown man come up behind her. But she was not surprised that Teague noticed her frowning. For three days, he might have exchanged a handful of words with her, but over those days, he had watched her. When she was doing the laundry or checking winter supplies, she felt a tingling at the back of her neck, a light caressing of awareness. When she looked up, he would be near and his black eyes would pull her into him. Could she never break the creance tying them together?

'You startled me.'

'A hundred foot soldiers could have been through this field and you wouldn't have noticed.'

'I'm thinking on unpleasant subjects. I am sorry if my frown displeases you, but I thought myself alone and my frowns are for myself only.' Anwen grabbed her apron and wiped her hands. 'What do you do here?'

'You do nothing for yourself.' Teague pressed

his lips together. 'I want you to show me Brynmor's land.'

'You have already seen Brynmor,' she pointed out.

'Have you been watching me?'

'It is a logical conclusion. You have been here three days. What have you been doing other than observing Brynmor?'

Teague stretched his hand out to her. 'I want you to show me your home.'

Anwen could see the calluses and scars of his warrior's hands. This was a man of power, of dominance. Even in the light of day, how could she forget he carried darkness within him? How could she show the rolling fields of Brynmor to a man with these hands?

Ignoring his hand, she answered him. 'I have much work to do. We are not at Gwalchdu. You do not command here.'

Teague dropped his hand to his side. 'I am not commanding you; I am asking.'

Anwen searched his features, but as usual, she could not tell what he was thinking. There was no reason for his request other than for them to share company. But he had ignored her for days.

'It is going to rain.'

'So it rains,' Teague said. 'Robert has managed this place and well knows the profits from him. I'll get my tithes, but I wished to see this place from your point of view. It is apparent there is much to be done here.'

Anwen opened her mouth to decline, then stopped as a thought occurred to her. His words were persuasive, but maybe not for the reason he believed. It was true there was much work to be done at Brynmor. Maybe it would do him good to see the English Wars' damage to her precious home. 'I will show you, but I have much work to do still and cannot be expected to spend the rest of the day showing you about. Some of us do not have a multitude of servants to do their work for them.'

'I hope not to hinder you.'

She refused his suggestion of a horse ride. He would see more if they walked.

She wasn't about to tell him the real reason why she wouldn't ride. If they did, she would be cocooned within his arms. She would feel again the hard planes of his body and his thighs would touch hers as they straddled the horse. After the kiss, she didn't want to be that close to him again. Simply thinking of touching him disturbed her in ways she didn't understand.

Anwen walked through the field and away from the man she agreed to spend time with. She was pleased to be in one of her own woollen gowns again. The hem was greatly shortened and her ankles, which showed, were cold when she moved, but she was able to move more easily through the deep rutted fields and her cloak was adequate for the cold.

Teague walked alongside her. She showed him the soil that had rested too long because there was no one to till it. She explained that if there were people to care for it, the supply of food would almost double.

Then they walked along the road that led to the village. Mixed with the occupied cottages were empty cottages and buildings. Most of the good wood had already been used and the empty buildings were no more than frames of planks barely holding together. When the snows came, even the decaying wood would be used.

When they reached the end of the village, they were the furthest from Brynmor's keep and close to the river. By then the sun was fading, and the sky darkening with mist and rain; it was time to return.

She turned to him. 'As you saw, Brynmor pales in comparison to Gwalchdu. There are too many needs and too little resources to fulfil them.'

'Yes, Robert told me much the same, but it was informative to see it from your standpoint. I appreciated your introducing me to the villagers. They respect you.'

Respect was not what she needed. She cared for these people and intended to look after them as long as she drew breath. 'Respect won't feed them or provide a roof over their heads.'

'No, but the potential is here. The untilled fields are rested; the soil is rich. The abundance of resources here is remarkable.'

Bitter pain sliced through her heart.

She'd shown him Brynmor's weaknesses and poverty. Shown the Traitor the hardship and destitution since the English War. He'd interrupted occasionally with questions. He wasn't rude, argumentative or even arrogant. He didn't act at all the way she expected him to and it left her confused and troubled. Now it seemed he saw beyond what Brynmor was, to the hope of what it could be. Nobody else had ever expressed how she felt about Brynmor. Not even Robert, who worked hard to make this place viable.

But Brynmor would never be prosperous again. It needed money that Urien didn't have and that Gwalchdu surely wouldn't loan. All Brynmor's potential was wasted because there weren't enough people to harvest the food and no market days to sell it. Many made the trip to Gwalchdu to sell the food, but it was never enough. It was as if all their efforts were in vain. Familiar anger coursed through her sorrow. It hadn't always been this way. Not until they were betrayed by the man who stood before her.

She must have been silent too long, because

Teague spoke again, his voice low. 'It is too far for Gwalchdu's protection, Anwen, or I'd offer the help.'

Anwen wiped her cheeks in haste. When had she started crying?

'Ever the English greed,' she scoffed.

'In a way.'

Teague kept his distance from her. He wore a heavy woollen cream-coloured tunic with brown breeches and a heavy leather vest trimmed with fur. His sword belt hung at a slight angle and his hair was loosely tied back. It was a simple outfit that covered a complicated man and she was too tired for complications.

Waving her hand as if to dismiss him, Anwen walked to the river's bank. It would be mostly empty this time of day. The darkening clouds turned the blue water almost black, but there was still beauty here.

She heard his footsteps behind her. Intending to ignore him, she increased her pace. He continued to follow her and was just as silent as she was. Her frustration mounted. Why wouldn't he leave her?

For every step she took, he matched it and she found that even the crunching of his boots on the gravel was grating. She whirled on him. 'Why won't you leave me be?'

Teague stopped, his eyes scanning the riverside. 'There could be danger.'

'I've been out here many times without your benevolent supervision.'

'But I am here now.'

'We're not at your precious Gwalchdu any more. I can take care of myself.' She wanted to be alone, not followed by this man who disturbed her thoughts. 'Just leave me be!'

His lips curved at the corner. 'No, not now.'

Anwen ignored the tightening in her stomach. Why did she have to find hidden meaning in his words? She hugged her arms around herself, suddenly feeling the cold.

'This place has upset you,' he observed. 'Why don't you walk away, let it all go? So many people from Brynmor have left and have sought Gwalchdu's protection.'

'As long as I am welcome here, I'll stay.'

'But what is Brynmor to you? I understand that you do not care for the English, but this is all English soil now. Robert may have the title of Governor, but even you know he is more than that here and could be legally so if he requested it. King Edward has been most unusual in his treatment of Brynmor. Even you must be aware of that.'

Leave her home? She might not have much at Brynmor, but she had some control over her life. She was needed here. Anywhere else, she would be vulnerable to the whims of those who had more power. She would never put herself in that position. Worse, she wouldn't put herself in the position of the very man who made Brynmor weak and vulnerable during the war. 'Why would I seek protection from the Traitor of Gwalchdu?'

'Yes, why would you? But everything is not as it would seem.'

'I see and know nothing else to the contrary.'

Teague tilted his head. 'What did you see that day in the forest with me under the tree? Why did you fall to me?'

So he knew about her betrayal. For weeks she reasoned with herself about the choices she made. She'd had no choice that day, but that hadn't stopped her feeling of trust. When she fell to him, she trusted him.

'This is a useless conversation.' She took a step away. 'What else was I to do? Die? You act as if I had a choice.'

Teague pressed his lips together and stepped towards her. 'Then later? When you were recovering? Why did you seek me through your pain?'

'I didn't seek you.' She took a larger step backward. 'You were already there. Again, what choice did I have? I should be asking you why you were there!'

He ignored her question and took another silent, predatory step towards her. 'But you responded to me in the mews and again when we dined. And how about now? Your heightened colour, the intake of breath?'

'I am simply frustrated at this ridiculous talk.' She couldn't take another step back. The river was soaking the back of her leather shoes. The mist was turning heavy, colder, soaking them both.

'You are more than that. There is something more here. It is confusing, yes, but I, unlike you, am not avoiding it.' He took the final step towards her. 'I don't think I can avoid it any more.'

He stood so close she could see the thickness of his eyelashes framing dark eyes, the arch of his eyebrows, the curve of his cheekbones and fullness of his lips. All these features somehow softened him. Or was it her softening to him?

She trusted him in the forest and again when she sought his care when her pain was bad. She had the excuse of exhaustion and pain, but they were only excuses. She had wanted him by her bedside.

That day when he'd shown her his birds, they shared their common interest. Was she bonding to this man? Was her trust of him not some temporary madness brought about because of the circumstances, but because he earned her trust?

No. He betrayed his own country and kin. He was still a powerful lord, and she knew all too well how powerful men treated those weaker than themselves. There could be no trust with him. 'You speak of things that do not exist. There is rain coming and we need to return.'

Teague did not move and she watched as he slowly perused her face and his gaze rested on her lips. The look was so tangible, she could almost feel his black eyes tracing the curved outline of her bottom lip and her body started an odd humming vibration of anticipation. She waited, knowing he intended to kiss her.

'Soon.' He turned and walked, without waiting to see if she followed. She did.

Peter, his captain, intercepted them at Brynmor's gate and Teague took his leave. When his back was turned to her, she finally let go of her held breath.

He was a relentless man; even when he wasn't talking to her, she could feel his will. While he was close it was difficult to determine her own feelings.

He wanted her. She had felt that in the mews. No, before that, when he comforted her in the night. So, too, at Brynmor as he watched her. It was in the turn of his lips, the way his gaze turned from watchful to calculated, then became closed again before she could dismiss him. But did she want him? How could she when he betrayed his own people? She could never trust him. She wouldn't bend to his will.

Seeking a distraction to her thoughts, she

scanned the courtyard until she saw Alinore and Robert standing near the stables. Alinore was laughing at Robert, who was talking quite animatedly.

'Anwen!' Alinore's light blue eyes twinkled with merriment. 'Robert was telling me about his difficulty the first time he went on a warhorse.'

Robert's expertise with horses was legendary. His knowledge of their care was relied upon here even with Brynmor's meagre stables.

'Difficulty?' she said. 'I could hardly imagine.'

Robert addressed Anwen, but quickly glanced at Alinore, their eyes sharing their secret. 'Oh, horses haven't always liked me.'

Alinore laughed. 'I suspect he is telling me this simply to get me on one of these beastly creatures.'

'On a horse?' Anwen blurted. 'You've never wanted to ride before!'

Alinore nodded. 'Oh, I know you've been trying to get me to ride, but they are big and have these hooves and teeth. Yet Robert promises me that he will be there and I think I might do it… since he's making me.'

'I'm not making you.' Robert chuckled. 'And think how grand you'll look at the Martinmas parade!'

'Ah, you would bring up Christmas,' Alinore said.

'Only because I know it's your weakness.'

Anwen watched in astonishment as Alinore pretended umbrage at Robert's words. In all the years she had lived at Brynmor, she never saw such a change in Alinore.

In the mere weeks she'd been away, her sister had become a stranger who didn't need her; who had distractions of her own. She doubted Alinore or Robert even noticed her departure.

Feeling at odds, Anwen took time to prepare for the evening meal. A thin silver circlet bound back her hair and although the veil she wore was transparent, she hoped it covered most of her scar.

Her gown was a fine light blue wool, with a bright yellow surcoat. The sleeves required lacing from the purple ribbon that went from wrist to elbow. The gown was not as short as her day gowns, but swirled about her ankles when she walked. She might be late for the meal, but she felt better by the time she descended the stairs.

Taking care not to trip, she fisted her hands into her skirt. As she approached the dais, she noticed that everyone, except Alinore, was sitting at the high table. 'Where is Alinore?'

Robert's face darkened with anger. Teague leaned over and whispered into the man's ear.

Nodding at whatever it was that Teague whispered, Robert addressed Anwen. 'Resting in her room.'

Having seen Alinore an hour before, Anwen

was alarmed. 'Resting? Nothing happened to her with the horses?'

'No, her time with the horses fared well.'

Anwen uncurled her hands from her skirts. 'But something happened. I can see from your face.'

But Robert did not answer her; instead he peered over her shoulder. Alinore was descending the stairs. Anwen breathed a sigh of relief, but before she could walk towards her, someone grasped her wrist.

Teague. His grip did not hurt, but it was firm. Although she arched her brow at him, he merely nodded his head at the seat beside him, indicating for her to sit.

'It's about time that you joined us,' Urien slurred from behind his goblet. Ever the lord of the manor, he sat in resplendent sprawl, his tunic stained with spilled ale. But it was not Urien's slur or his dishevelled appearance that sent a shiver of warning through Anwen, it was his smug tone. Urien was pleased with himself. 'Thought I'd have to have another talk with you.'

Anwen inhaled. She knew all about Urien's 'talks'. But before she could move, Robert was by Alinore's side and giving a deep bow. 'My lady, you look as fair as ever this evening.'

Alinore's bowed head did not hide her blush at

Robert's remarks, nor did her long sleeves hide her tentative hand reaching for Robert's.

Alinore rarely came to dinner and she never let anyone touch her. Melun said Alinore was changed. Anwen wondered in what other ways her sister was different.

Urien waved his goblet. 'Come, girl, and take your place. I'm hungry.'

Alinore flinched at Urien's crude behaviour and it was then that her headdress moved, revealing a dark red bruise across the side of her face.

Standing, Anwen gasped, but Teague's hand on her arm stopped her. 'Easy, Anwen. See how Robert attends her.'

'If he attended her, she wouldn't be hurt.'

'Watch, Anwen.'

She didn't want to listen to anything Teague said. How could he know what happened here? But causing a scene would embarrass Alinore, so she looked.

Alinore wasn't sitting next to Urien, but between Robert and Ffion—Robert must have done that.

So, too, Robert shared his food with Alinore, helping her cut pieces small enough to pass through her swollen lips.

An odd twisting happened in her stomach as she watched Robert gently handle Alinore's fragile pride. Her sister's gentle smile behind such bruised and swollen features should have emoted only pity from Anwen, but it didn't. Alinore had never smiled before, not like that, not with courage.

Anwen grabbed her ale and took a long draught. She should be happy that Alinore fared well while she was gone, not crying at the loss that she was no longer needed to protect her sister. She merely had to find other ways to be useful to Brynmor... to her home, so that she wouldn't be thrown away like her mother. But what?

'Peace, Anwen. It is for the better.' Teague handed her a bite of chicken.

Anwen took the morsel he offered. 'What do you know of better?'

Teague watched her close her mouth around the succulent meat. 'I don't know as yet, but I hope to find out,' he answered.

Chapter Fourteen

Anwen awoke with a start at the creak of her door. It was black in her room, and silent, but she was not alone. She turned her head to see a broad figure standing in the doorframe.

She did not need light to see who it was. She would have recognised him even in the blackest of nights. She suspected it was an awareness born of those many nights when he sat by her bedside.

'Teague, what do you do here?'

'Come out with me.'

Although she'd never admit it, he possessed the Devil's own voice, low, seductive, like a caress, and in the darkness of night when there were no other distractions, his voice took on a heightened power. It took a moment for Anwen to understand what he was saying.

'It is night.' She pointed out the obvious.

'A time of the day that I find most pleasant.'

'It rained and it's cold.'

'Walk with me, Anwen.'

His coaxing words held a hint of urgency and were waking her despite her exhaustion.

'Turn around while I dress.' She wasn't taking any chances. He was, after all, known to have the Devil's blood and she could believe it. Anybody that got her out of bed in the middle of the night must possess some ungodly powers. She certainly couldn't be doing this of her own volition.

'I don't think this is wise,' Anwen said, as they walked up through the fields. Peering over her shoulder, she could just make out a diminished Brynmor lit with only a few lamps. It appeared lacking against the night sky filled with stars.

'It was necessary. Do you not trust me?' Teague asked.

'No,' Anwen answered, although in truth, she must or else she wouldn't have travelled this far with him. 'We could fall into a hole and nobody would see us until morning.'

'You are with me.'

'I do not feel safe simply because you say so.' Still, she continued to walk with him. 'I hardly see what is practical about risking our necks in the middle of the night. If you needed to show me something, it might be easier in the daytime.'

'I didn't say it was practical, I said it was necessary.'

They cleared the trees and Anwen gasped. It was a fairyland. The full moon illuminated the darkness with soft, gentle light, shone like a giant pearl on the water. The river rippled and flowed against the wet rocks, boulders and dark fertile earth. The brisk night air was like a cloak blanketing them and carried the sounds of the river and tiny creatures to them.

Anwen always found this spot of the land tranquil, but she never came at night. It was a place transformed.

'It's beautiful,' she murmured.

'It is better than I imagined.'

Anwen turned to him. 'Why did you bring me here?'

Ignoring her question, Teague walked along the river's edge. She followed him as they walked further away from the village and the keep. Their silence wasn't uncomfortable since his presence and the river's beauty were enough company. It was surprising what a difference a few hours could make. Whereas earlier, she had been irritated at his company, now in the dark of night it was almost comforting. So, too, though she was freezing in the night's air, she was soothed by the sounds of the meandering river.

Peace. She found peace here and he had given it to her.

'Thank you for bringing me here tonight.'

He glanced at her. 'All these days, I couldn't understand why you so often came here, as it was out of the way of all your usual activities.'

She was not surprised that he noticed. 'You have been watching me.'

'Yes.' He took a couple more steps and then stopped. 'After dinner you disappeared. Did you come here?'

She wouldn't hide the truth from him. He had brought her back here. The least she could do was repay him with honesty. 'Yes, I did, but...'

'You didn't find your peace before. And now?'

'Maybe,' she said. Was she confessing that somehow, miraculously, she found some peace with him? Perhaps it had simply been having the time to ease her thoughts or maybe it was that there was something different about him. He was giving, not demanding.

'Returning to Brynmor has not been easy,' she continued. 'There have been changes since I was gone.'

'You speak of Alinore?' Teague watched her too closely.

'Yes, she has changed. As you said, it is for the better, but...I miss the old Alinore, as well.'

'She is happy now.'

'Oh, she is, she is.' She waved her hand in front of her.

'Is it that she has grown while you were gone?'

'Yes… No, more than that.'

'It is her relationship with Robert that makes you uncomfortable.'

She glanced at him. 'How did you know?'

'I've known Robert a long time.' Teague peered over her shoulder before he continued, 'Robert and I fostered together at Edward's court. He is younger than me, but despite that and the difference in our backgrounds, we became friends. Even at such a young age, he appeared older, more able to keep his head while training, and he trained hard, as if to prove something. We fought together for Edward during—' Teague stopped, and his eyes caught hers.

'The Welsh fight for independence,' Anwen finished for him.

'Yes, for that. During that time and before the signing of any treaties, we came across Brynmor in our fights. For reasons I could not fathom until recently, Robert asked to be appointed Governor of Brynmor. I think it is your Alinore that prompted Robert to stay.'

'She was a child at the time of the fights.'

'Did Urien already treat her wrongly?'

When they were younger, their father's abuse had been public. 'Yes. I never understood it because despite Urien's abuse, she continually cared for him. Still does.'

Teague swiped some rocks at his feet. 'Knowing Robert, he would not tolerate injustice done to Urien's daughter. Growing up, he fought the rumours of his peasant blood and he was always there for the disadvantaged. With his sword skill, only fools challenged him.'

Anwen reflected on Teague's assessment. It all fit. When Robert returned, Urien's beatings had mostly ceased. She had always thought it was her own protection of Alinore stilling Urien's anger, but perhaps Robert protected Alinore, too.

Teague threw a rock and it skipped across the river. 'I think he stays because he cares for the woman she has become.'

Anwen remembered Alinore's small secret smiles, how her eyes lit up when Robert was in the room. Alinore was in love. How simple and how complicated.

'Urien would never allow their marriage.'

'No doubt. However, if she still cares for Urien, it explains why Robert has allowed him to remain Lord of Brynmor even though Edward would have granted Robert the keep as a spoil of war.' Teague rolled a rock between his fingers. 'With Urien's health, it is merely a matter of time until he dies.'

'That would be a tidy ending.' Anwen hugged herself against the cold. 'But that doesn't explain why he closed the gate against you.'

'Doesn't it? My presence here is sure to anger Urien and given Alinore's fresh bruise tonight,

I'd say Robert was justified in his displeasure at my coming.'

'Why did you come here?'

Teague's lips curved wryly. 'It's no secret that Urien and I have little liking for each other.'

Anwen waited. Her eyes adjusted to the dark and the moon's reflection on the river cast enough light for her to see most of Teague's features. He did not look at her as he skimmed another rock across the water with a thrust of his arm that caused his cloak to stretch against his back.

His loose hair looked soft, thick and warm as it rested on his shoulders and she wanted to feel the thick texture of it. She could almost touch him now and her breathing hitched at the thought. Instead, she shook herself against the cold and paced to warm up.

Teague threw his last rock. 'What is a secret is that Urien's hatred of me goes beyond the Welsh Wars. At one point, his ambition went beyond the walls of Brynmor.'

Anwen pivoted. Urien wanted to rule Gwalchdu? 'How?' she whispered.

Teague held out his hand to her. 'Come, it is cold and we have been longer here than I intended.'

She shook her head. 'I don't want to go back.'

'Your teeth are chattering; take my hand, we're not going back to the keep.'

Curious, she took his hand. She was colder than

she thought. Quiet, watching their breaths rush in front of them, she held Teague's familiar grasp. She could not seem to let him go. It was as if she needed his support for just a while longer.

Up the hill he took her, just skimming the houses outside of Brynmor's gates, far enough away not to disturb the animals inside the buildings with the sleeping villagers.

'Where are you taking me?' she said, just as they crested a hill.

There, close to the top, was a small hut, thickly insulated with a fire vent. A hunting hut for winter time that hadn't been used in years. Anwen thought it derelict, but with the warmth of the indoor fire making its lone window glow and smoke rise above the frosty night, it looked inviting.

'What have you done?'

He squeezed her hand and opened the door. 'Come, just a bit more.'

She had to, her teeth were chattering, and her hand in his was warm, but her other one was like ice.

He stripped her of her damp cloak and his own cloak and vest, then wrapped her in a warmed woollen blanket and took another for himself.

She shivered inside the blanket. It was dark with shadows in the room, but the fire lit it enough.

'You've repaired it.'

'I made it better. It was necessary.'

'And that…' She pointed to a pallet with fresh linens and heavy furs, waved her hand to the cauldron near the fire. She could smell warmed ale. 'Are those necessary as well?'

He poured the ale into goblets and handed one to her. 'On a night like this, very much so.'

She took the goblet and soaked up the heat as she took a sip. There was nowhere to sit save a stool and the pallet. She chose the stool. 'Tell me of Urien.'

Teague's lips quirked as he saw where she chose to sit. 'I have said enough and too much thought is being wasted on the past when it is the present that occupies my thoughts.'

'I followed you because of what you said by the river.'

He sat on the pallet and stretched his legs. The hut was not meant for more than four men with hunting gear and the pallet took up most of the room. She scrunched herself up on the stool, but Teague's legs touched her nonetheless.

'I know.'

Deceptive Devil of Gwalchdu. She looked around at the comfortable room, the quiet of the night, the seclusion and intimacy. She should have expected a trap, had been prepared for it all the time she was at Gwalchdu, but she'd let her guard down at Brynmor. As if home was safe from the Traitor. Nowhere was safe when he was around.

'We need to return,' she said.

'Soon.'

He'd used that word before, when she thought he was going to kiss her. Now his gaze arrested her as it had then. It was as if her sole purpose for coming out this evening had been to look at him.

Teague tried to gather his thoughts, and couldn't. Anwen's blue eyes were wide, direct and just a little unsure. She was never unsure. 'I did not tell you how beautiful you were tonight. All through the meal, I could not wait to be here with you.' He bent and pushed his hand through her damp curls, his thumb gently touching the scar at the side of her temple. 'Does it hurt?'

She pulled her head away and he felt the loss of the warmth of her skin.

'No, the headaches are gone,' she said.

He watched as her eyes changed from curiosity to challenge. He couldn't believe he once thought her capable of subterfuge. She was not capable of hiding anything, and that went for more than just her thoughts. For three days, he watched her ceaselessly work beside her fellow Welshmen.

'There is barely a scar, Anwen, and the swelling and redness are completely gone,' he noted.

'I know what it looks like.'

'Do you?' he asked.

'The day I had my first bath.' She turned her

face away from him and took a sip of ale. 'I saw my image in the water.'

'That was weeks ago.' Teague took a long draught, and set his cup on the floor. 'You are still wounded.'

'I said that I am well.'

'It surprises me that you display such womanly vanity.' Teague bent forward and lifted the goblet out of her hands and set it by his. Though her chin was raised, and her gaze held steady, hurt flickered for a moment in her eyes.

'Anwen, I have seen you wash floors until your hands were cracked and bleeding. When the cold wind increased, you gleaned the fields with the servants until your face reddened. All your dresses have holes because you're constantly tearing them with hawk's talons or forest shrubbery chasing after your birds.'

He leaned further forward, cupped her hands in his. She did not wrap her fingers with his, but neither did she pull her hand away. She also turned to make their position easier. She would listen.

'You have the least vanity of any woman I have ever known, not because you have no need to, but because of your merit, your strength, your purpose.'

'You compare me like you would a horse.'

Kneeling in front of her of her, Teague let his breath out softly; he would need patience to woo her. 'You have a noble heart, a strong spirit and a fire inside you, Anwen of Brynmor. That is a rare beauty. One little scar that is covered by a lock of your golden hair is not a blemish, but a testament to your beauty. You risked your life to capture a mere bird. By doing so, you saved that bird's life and the livelihood of an old falconer.'

Teague's thick callused fingers wrapped with hers, and she almost leaned into the warmth of his body and the black heat from his eyes. He knelt in front of her. The Devil, the Traitor of Gwalchdu knelt, comforted her with words, with his hands. She tried to shut out the warmth, the heat, but his words…his words somehow slipped inside her. 'What is the point of this conversation?'

'It is necessary.'

'For what?'

'For letting you know my desire.'

'Your desire?' She choked over the two words.

'For you. Haven't I shown you how I am different than other men you have known?'

'Other men…like Urien? Like his men?'

'You insult me, insult us. I'm not like them and what you described to me.' He pressed her hands. 'That is why we are here. It was necessary to have this time together so that we can come to a more civilised arrangement.'

She remembered his words from her bath, in the

mews, and the way he watched her at Gwalchdu and again at Brynmor. There had been lust there, but desire? No. This kind of desire was softer, deeper. He could not desire her.

'For three days I have barely seen you,' she pointed out.

'A testament to my veracity,' he said. 'There are grave matters that I cannot tell you of, but that concern all. As much as I wish otherwise, now is not the best time for us to meet.'

'Our meeting could hardly have been avoided because you were the one standing under the tree.'

'True.' He continued caressing her hands, but his body shifted so his front almost touched her knees. 'Despite that this is hardly the time or the place, we have met now. This is not something I wanted, but it is also something I will not avoid. We are one, Anwen, and have been since the moment I caught you. I won't deny this bond does not exist or that even now as I sit next to you, I...yearn for one word from you to end my need.'

Anwen extricated her hands from his and stood to the side. 'I am tired from today's work. We should return.'

He stood beside her. 'You are changing the subject.'

'There is no subject.'

'There is. You are hardly unaware of it.'

Tightening the blanket around her, Anwen forced her eyes to look anywhere but him. Even so, she knew he spoke the truth. She could feel her skin flush at the thought of him, of need, of want, of desire. She hoped the shadows of the room hid her reaction. She wished she could pace, but the room was so small, standing had only made their proximity closer to each other. 'What did you mean by an arrangement between us?'

Teague stood, measuring and calculating her response. She kept her face still to not reveal anything.

'I want you, Anwen. No, need you. Need to know what it feels like to hold you close. To know the taste of your skin, feel how your breasts fill my hands, to skim the softness of your stomach with my fingers, my mouth—'

'*Rutting* is your arrangement?'

He shook his head. 'I wish to give you pleasure.'

'You are no different than those men. You want to lay open my body so that you can slake your lust. All you desire is coupling!'

Dropping his blanket, he placed his palms against her shoulders. His light grasp was enough to stop her. Stop her, so she felt the warmth of his palms spread waves of heat through her body.

'There are many reasons not to be here. I, of all men, know this should be avoided.'

'Avoided? You planned all of this.'

'Never. If you knew my past, if you knew what—' He shook his head. 'This isn't planned. This is hope. I keep hoping; it's why we're here. So I talk of coupling,' he whispered, his thumbs caressing and rubbing against her shoulders. She realised she could move, but her legs, her body, were strangely not like her own. Nothing of her was her own. She stood inside the tiny hut but her skin felt like a thousand warm winds brushed against it, her heart beating as if she'd run to the top of a cliff.

'I think of coupling,' he said, with more sweeping caresses across her shoulders. Caresses that changed her breath as if gusts swept them away as she stood poised on that cliff, waiting to vault.

Shifting, moving closer, against her, his movements restrained, her body responding as if he tightened the creance holding them together. Holding them on that cliff, about to soar. Her own feet and legs lifting her up…up to Teague's lips, his head bowing. Then his words against her lips: 'I want nothing but coupling—*with* you.'

Desire slammed into her as Teague's lips and body crushed hers. She spun, once, twice, trying to think, and then no more as she flew. As she felt the firm softness of his lips, his hot hands tracing from her shoulders to the small of her back and lower, until he pressed her more fully to him. Her feet were no longer on the ground. She released the blanket and grasped his arms; her fingers curled around his biceps, the tendons taut from holding her.

His entire body was rigid. Her breasts moulded against the hard mounds of his chest, her hips cradled his, her legs, lifted by his arms, wrapped around his thighs. Her body softened, became moist, and she soared higher.

'Anwen, please, please tell me this is what you want.' Teague's kisses trailed behind her jaw, where they became firmer, more insistent, before he lightly bit along her neck. It was fierce but gentle and very, very possessive. 'Please tell me you know this is different.'

'Yes,' she murmured. Her relief, coupled with her need, was too much. She gripped his shoulders as if she was flying too high. 'Yes, again.'

He made an answering groan against her skin as he laid her gently on the pallet.

There was a momentary adjusting as he knelt beside her, his hands gliding along her collar bones over her heart before circling the undersides of her breasts.

Needing more, she arched and pressed herself fully into his hands. It wasn't enough.

'Here.' He gestured with his hands, he asked with his dark, dark eyes.

She raised herself up. Deft fingers unlaced her gown, released her chemise and pushed the tangled clothing over her shoulders. Her skirts bunched at her waist and bared her breasts to his touch.

'Anwen.' His voice low, gruff. 'You're beautiful. More than I imagined. More than I could ever imagine.'

His words brought her back from the cliff, to her actions, to the man that knelt before her. And she only wanted to fly again.

His eyes softened. 'I am a warrior, Anwen. I know more of battlefields than I do the tenderness of maids, but I swear I will be gentle.'

He pulled his tunic off. She'd never seen him this close. His skin was smooth, but hard, the muscles built upon each other, giving bulk and length to his form.

The small room and flickering firelight enhanced his sun-darkened skin. She could see the scars of his training, of the warrior he claimed to be. She wanted to touch him, to test the heat of his skin, but before she could lift her arms, he stood to unbuckle his belt. He suddenly glanced through the window, and stopped, his hands frozen at his waist.

His face turned from passion, to doubt, to fury. 'No!'

Teague's vehemence broke Anwen's thoughts. She pushed herself to her elbows, but Teague was already grabbing his tunic, pulling it hurriedly over his head.

'Get dressed.' He gazed down at her, his brow furrowing. She was not prepared for the urgency she saw in his face.

'What's wrong?' She stood, pulling her chemise and gown over her head. Her fingers shook from confusion and passion as she tied the surcoat under her arm. The world was crashing around her.

She hadn't been thinking. One moment she was accusing him of making her his whore and the next she was lying beneath him. Beneath the Traitor! Now, all signs of passion gone, he was leaving her in cold embarrassment. Then she turned and looked through the window.

Brynmor was in flames.

They ran, pulling each other through the mass of people fleeing through the castle gates. Eyes watering from searing smoke, Anwen searched every blackened face in the courtyard.

'You have to get out of here!'

'No!' Anwen gasped. Brynmor's wooden towers blazed like giant torches in the night. Half the manor was nothing more than black fractured beams and swirling ash. The upper apartments were gone, the foundation disintegrating in the heat.

Peter, his clothes half-burnt, rushed forward.

'Where's Robert?' Teague demanded.

'I don't know; I've been trying to gather the men since the fire first started in the apartments.'

Alinore! Anwen surged forward.

Teague grabbed her arm. 'I can't worry for you and others!'

There was nothing left of the apartments now, Alinore had to be somewhere else; but the fire was leaping from the manor to the mews and she couldn't take the chance. Tugging her arm free, Anwen ran for the mews.

Anwen shuffled closer to the supply building almost fully engulfed in flaming spires. She no longer paid heed to her exhausted body's stabbing aches or to her limbs shaking. Hours before she'd wrapped her hands in cloth to protect them from hot debris, but now they blistered and bled through the blackened cloth.

Shouting servants and running villagers swarmed the courtyard. There were still more household items to find, more people to save. Earlier, she'd found one child under a burning table, but more children could be missing.

Through the crackling of the building, she heard a shout before a thunderous crash of a wall falling. Intense heat and black smoke swirled. Anwen clenched her eyes against the sting of flying ash and gasped as the air became saturated in red fire.

She couldn't see who shouted. She lowered herself to her hands and knees.

Something gripped her leg.

It was a demon, with hair and eyes as black as night and a body singed and covered in soot. His body was beneath a structure leaning at a deadly angle.

'Teague.' The increasing smoke made her voice raspy, her lungs weak.

'Get out!'

She was on her knees, and couldn't see his legs beyond the structure. He was trapped.

Her heart leapt. 'What happened?'

'It's my leg. I can't free it. The rest of the building is going to collapse.'

Wildly she looked around, but there was nothing to pry him free. She couldn't move the timbers with her bare hands. 'Give me your hand.' She took his before he offered and grasped just under his elbow before tugging hard. The structure above wobbled and she stopped.

'Leave before it collapses on you, too.'

The Traitor, stuck in a burning building. The Devil of Gwalchdu, who betrayed the Welsh, made Brynmor vulnerable to the English King, who increased Urien's rages, who kept her prisoner, was trapped under Byrnmor's flaming collapse.

It was almost horrifyingly perfect. Her own home, which would soon be nothing but molten ash billowing in the wind, would kill him. Teague, who was still pleading for her to leave, who was even now trying to save her. Teague, who needed her.

'I have to find help!'

He grabbed her hand and clenched hard, so hard she finally felt it through her bandages and the pain. 'It's too dangerous!'

Gripped by his obsidian eyes, by his roughened hand that she clenched in return, it took all her strength to release him before she fled out of the building.

She ran blind until she could see Peter and veered in his direction.

Images flashed before her. Teague. Alone. Flames reaching for him, his eyes, so black, so black.

Waving her arms, crying out, she caught Peter's attention, who ran towards her.

She would return Peter to Teague and with his sword, he'd pry away the timber to drag him free. Teague would be safe. She closed her fist, still feeling the strength of his hand in hers.

His hand. She stumbled, started to topple, only frightening realisation kept her moving forward.

Teague hadn't grabbed her hand to gain her attention. He clenched it as if he'd never hold it again. At that last moment, his black eyes gripped hers, not in anger, but in bleak desolation as he yelled for her to leave him.

He expected her to leave him…and never return.

'Help!' she cried past the hoarse dryness in her throat. 'Help!'

Chapter Fifteen

Anwen heard the crunching of the gravel beneath her ear before she opened her eyes to the river flowing in front of her. She wondered how she found herself at the river again, but it was the sounds of villagers coughing and animals bleating that broke through her confusion. She pushed up and gave a low cry. Her hands, freshly bandaged, felt like splinters of wood had been shoved in them. Before her eyes, bright red blotches appeared.

'How do you feel?'

Rhain stood over her. Behind him were people with armfuls of kindling. Some were carrying blankets or rope. Some were sitting, leaning against the sparse birch trees or lying down. All of them were still blackened from the smoke and many of them slumped as they walked. It was as if the burden they now carried was slowly crushing them.

'Where's Teague?' Clasping the blanket around her, she stood.

'Woke up before you.'

How had she fallen asleep? She'd been worried for Teague, trying to make him comfortable, to tend him as he directed his men. She remembered him laying down, his warm hand rubbing low on her back...

Anwen glanced behind her. There was Teague, his hair wet, his clothes fresh; the only indication of their hellish night were the bandages around his leg. He was talking to Peter and pointing in the direction where some soldiers were building makeshift tents.

'How is his leg?'

'He hasn't mentioned it.' Rhain's gaze followed hers.

Of course Teague didn't mention it. Peter had said it wasn't broken, but still Teague had to be in pain. Toiling, pushing himself. Already he wasn't caring for his leg. He hadn't even told Rhain about the injury, as if it was insignificant, as if he hadn't almost lost his life.

'Timber fell on it. It's badly burnt and should be taken care of.'

Aware of Rhain's assessing gaze and that she spoke of Teague's care, she said, 'You arrived quickly.'

'I saw the fire from Gwalchdu's towers and was

already on my way here when Teague's messenger arrived. I sent him on to Gwalchdu to bring soldiers back.'

'You were coming to Brynmor's aid by yourself?'

'It was faster and the least I could do for my brother.'

Melun, with a blanket covering his shoulders, was sitting quietly with other older villagers. Ffion was tending the injured, her pouch of healing herbs swinging along with her black robes. Anwen didn't see Urien or Alinore, but the bend in the river didn't allow her to see everything.

Rhain offered her his arm and she rested a hand there. 'As long as the weather holds, we'll set camp here until we clear Brynmor of anything useful. Teague is already making decisions to move people to Gwalchdu.'

'There's nothing left?'

'The keep is gone. There are a few buildings, but the fire extended to the outer wall.' Rhain's eyes softened. 'With the loss, it would be unrealistic to repair.'

Especially since it was hardly adequate before. Her home was gone. 'What needs to be done?'

'We have brought provisions from Gwalchdu and are slowly taking some of the more wounded villagers to Gwalchdu first. It is slow as Teague wants no one unprotected and there are many working on the small fires still burning at Brynmor.'

'Unprotected? What do you mean, unprotected?'

'You should be resting,' Teague ordered, as he walked towards them. Clean clothes and a fresh face didn't hide the circles under his eyes, or the strain around his mouth. He limped, though he tried to hide it. Still, he appeared as indomitable as Gwalchdu's stone.

She was still shaking with what had happened last night. 'So should you. I merely need to know what I can do to help.'

'You don't know when to stop, do you?' he said.

'Goshawks are my favourite bird.' The bird was known for tenacity in the face of adversity.

'Yes, and they are foolhardy stubborn birds.'

Rhain glanced from Teague to Anwen. 'I think I will take my leave and pull charred splinters from the horses' hides.'

Anwen watched Rhain walk away. Her arguing wouldn't return her home, nor was it the gracious response in light of the sacrifices made.

'Thank you,' she said. 'For helping.'

Teague's eyes searched hers with a light so bright in their dark depths and yet some equally dark hesitancy. 'I should be thanking you.'

She was shaking from her fear, shaking from what he revealed to her in the fire. Shaking from something she didn't trust and didn't want to think about just yet.

'The houses,' she said. 'Rhain told me what you are beginning. It is not an easy or profitable task.'

Teague's eyes lost their light. 'But the most fair.'

'I thought the English didn't know that word.'

He peered over her shoulder. 'It was taught to me at an early age.'

Another revelation. She feared knowing more about him brought her too close to him. This man of power, of control. A man, who ruled. Worse, not only did she now owe him the debt of her life, but the debt of her people.

All through the night, as she desperately tried to save what she could of her Brynmor, she saw Teague fighting to rescue her people. Now, he was giving a kindness she could never hope to repay. Her life was becoming so entwined with the Traitor's, she didn't know how she would ever be free of him.

Teague grabbed one of her hands, tenderly cupping it between his thick palms. His brow furrowed as he contemplated their hands before his dark gaze returned to hers.

'Urien was not found.'

She nodded. Unfit, unwell, it would have been too much to find him alive. After hating him for so long, she wouldn't grieve over his loss, but that wasn't how everyone would feel. Alinore would be devastated.

'I should leave. Alinore will need me now,' she said.

Teague's hand jumped over hers. The movement gave him away, more so than his eyes shifting. 'Teague?'

His eyes darkened, softened.

'No,' she whispered, shaking her head, willing Teague to mimic her movements, but he simply let go of her hand.

'No,' Anwen repeated, her soul in agony as she realised the awful truth.

Robert walked by, his clothing charred and torn. His short hair was covered in soot, dirt and sweat. He looked like a man who came from the fires of hell. She knew what those fires felt like because she survived Brynmor's fires. But not Alinore.

'Where were you?' she accused.

Robert blankly looked from her to Teague. She wouldn't let him go easily.

Swiping pebbles from her feet, she flung them. 'Weren't you supposed to be her great protector?'

Robert didn't block the rocks hitting his chest. She heard each tiny rock hit the ground as if they were her own tears falling cold and unforgiving.

Teague pulled her to him before she could throw another handful. When his strength broke through her madness, she curled around his arm, and he carried her further up the bank and away from the villagers.

There weren't enough tears, not enough to ease her pain. Her tears eventually dried up, leaving her sorrow hollow and dry. Teague was still there rubbing her back and murmuring soothing words she couldn't hear.

When she could, Anwen wiped at her soot-and-tear-smeared cheeks. 'Where is she?'

'Robert is tending her body.'

Anwen inhaled sharply, trying to swallow the lump in her throat. She'd hurt Robert in the most heartless of ways. 'Where?' she repeated.

'You mustn't—'

'Where, damn you!' She slammed her fist into his chest.

Teague nodded towards a grove of trees just uphill from the river.

As guilt quickly overcame her grief, Anwen ran up the hill. She hadn't been there, hadn't saved her. Though Alinore would never know, Anwen raced hard to reach her. When she crested the hill, she came to a precarious halt.

The rising sun was already fading the moon and the stars. The grey light was enough to see two figures surrounded by a circle of young sparsely leafed birch trees.

One was laid out, as still as the earth and the fallen leaves she lay on. Her face and hands had been washed so her skin glowed white against the morning's light and her hair, so carefully brushed, spread like gold against the green darkness of the grass. But for her dress, which was as black as Hell's fires, she appeared as radiant as a fallen angel.

The other figure was deeply bent on his hands and knees. His body jerked and rocked as his hands alternately gripped, then caressed the woman laid on the grass. Anwen recognised him though his back was to her. There was no mistaking the sounds coming from the man before her. Robert of Dent wept over the dead body of Alinore of Brynmor.

Anwen took two quick breaths, enough to sustain her suddenly starved lungs; then silently she turned and walked down the hill and back to the river. As she did, she knew she left someone whose grief was even deeper than her own.

When she returned to camp, Anwen swayed on her feet. She didn't know where to turn to first, but she hoped Melun would need her. She needed work to distract her from her thoughts, from what she should not have seen under the birch trees.

She felt rather than heard her name behind her. Teague was there, his impenetrable eyes assessing her, his lips moving. He was saying something she could not hear over the stark hollowness roaring inside her.

When he gestured and walked, she followed him. Away from the river, away from the din of the camp, up the long hill until they reached the hunter's hut.

Again, Teague prepared it. The fire was burning, warming the hut, warming her body, which was cold. But it reached nothing of her insides, nothing of her heart which had seized up inside her.

'She was more than someone you grew up with.' Teague sat her on the stool by the fire.

Anwen nodded, knowing whom he meant. The emptiness inside her was too revealing to hide anything. 'She was my sister.'

Teague set her blanket away.

'My half-sister,' Anwen continued. 'I was Urien's child too, but bastard-born. In the great import of a legitimate heir, I was quickly forgotten.'

Teague took a rag and dipped it in a cauldron of water resting by the fire. 'Will you let me?'

He had cleaned, but she was still black. Yet in this tiny hut, when she felt so raw, did she want his touch, his attention?

He took her hand and held out her arm. 'Come, this water is warm, unlike the torture of the cold river I had this morning, and I brought you clothes.'

It wasn't his thoughtfulness that had her agreeing to his ministrations. In fact, those made her more reserved. No, it was that…dark hesitancy he'd shown her this morning. There could be no harm in this, so she nodded.

'Your leg?'

'Ffion's salve is doing its work. I have some here for you, too.' She inspected her hands as Teague untied the loose bandages, and dropped them.

'What happened to your mother?' Teague gently used the water and linen against her skin. Gentle, but her cuts and burns stung.

'I was told she was a young servant girl, who just started her menstruating. I was given to a wet nurse immediately. Despite my bastardy, I was Urien's, a Welsh prince's child, and couldn't be left to a servant girl. I don't know what happened to her. Melun eventually came to take me and claim me in his care.'

She breathed in raggedly, shivers now rattling her body. 'I'm cold.'

'It's the shock; it will go after a while.'

She didn't want to argue with him, but she was too scared her coldness would be permanent, that she'd never feel warm again.

Teeth chattering, she inspected her now clean hands. There would be more permanent scars. More changes that were for ever.

She wanted to cry again, but couldn't. She was too tired for tears and she was too tired to protest when Teague pushed her hair away from her face and took another linen to wipe the dirt there.

'She lives on in you,' he said. 'When Alinore walked down the stairs that first night, the candlelight hitting the gold in her hair, I thought then how alike in appearance you were.'

'Don't.' There were several cauldrons, several linens. It would be more expedient for her to bathe in the river than Teague's slow gentle cleaning and soft words.

'Just a bit more.' Teague took her other hand, careful not to touch the burns as he squeezed more water down her arm. 'Her hair and eyes were lighter than yours, but she had your dimpled chin and particular way of walking. I knew then you came from the same sire.'

Anwen inspected her blistered, scarred and callused hands that were so unlike her sister's. 'When we were small we'd play a flower-picking game. It was a game she'd always win since I was too impatient and lost most of my petals. My sister was good and she was the one taken.'

'Yes, she was good, and gentle, and softer than you. She lacked your fire and blunt tongue, but a part of her was in you and you in her. That part is still there, as well as all her memories. She is alive in you.'

She didn't stop the tears flowing then and she didn't stop Teague when he cradled her head just under his chin and wrapped her within his arms.

It was a long time later when Anwen could breathe again. The setting sun darkened the little hut despite the fire. But the fading sun was not the reason she was cold. She knew why she was cold. The desolate changes inside her were becoming permanent. At least while Teague held her, the coldness was kept away. But her tears were done and now there was no reason for him to hold her. Unless…

She shifted away from his body and stood. With uncoordinated fingers, she untied the laces of her gown and let the outer garment fall. She quickly untied her ankle boots and fisted the material of the chemise.

'What are you doing?'

'Bathing. My arms and face are not enough. I thought you could do the rest.' She pulled her chemise off.

She should have been colder than ever, but she wasn't, not with Teague standing almost against her. But he did not touch her. So she lifted the small cauldron of water and held it out to him. 'My hair needs washing,' she whispered.

The cauldron's weight and handle stung her hands before he took it. Before he set it down

again. 'This isn't what I came here for; you don't
want this.'

She had never known a man, but she knew no
other way to keep his arms around her. All she
could think was that she must stop the pain. 'Lie
with me.'

Why did he hesitate? This wasn't easy for her.
'Make love to me. Now, here,' she said, firmer
now, not backing away from her decision.

'Why are you asking this?'

That stopped her. Only the night before, he
had wanted this. Perhaps the fire changed him,
as well. She didn't care. Merely the suggestion of
this heat between them was taking the coldness
from her. She *needed* this.

'I don't want to be alone,' she said.

His eyes narrowed. 'You ask this solely because
of your grief, your emptiness.'

'Then fill me.'

He let out a harsh breath as desire and need
darkened his eyes. She felt absorbed in his eyes,
as if she could sink into their fathomless heat. 'I
should refuse you.'

'Why? This is what you wanted.' She didn't
know what else to do. Her body shook. She would
break if he did not touch her.

'No, not any more, I want something more now.
In the fire, you came back for me. Do you not
know what that—?'

'You refuse me?' She was going to be denied? *He wouldn't*. Before he could step away, she feathered her fingertips along his neck, tracing the cords that arrowed and dipped. So unique and so male. The movement whispered her breasts across his torso. His sharp inhalation matched hers.

Moments passed as he held still, as his eyes roamed over hers, before he dipped his head until she felt as if he kissed her. Until she licked her suddenly dry lips and parted them to let in air and his gaze snapped back to hers and held there. His brow furrowed as if what she showed him pained him. Then he cupped her face, and his eyes softened.

'No. I cannot refuse you.' He stepped back and tossed each piece of his clothing across the upper pallet rail until he stood before her naked, except for his short braies, and the wrapping around his leg.

So many bandages. The injury was extensive and it must pain him, but he stood strong before her as he lifted the first bucket. 'We'll make a mess.'

'I didn't say it was practical.' She echoed his words from the night before. She closed her eyes and lifted her face up to the cauldron. She was aware of his eyes on her, aware that this was beyond anything she experienced, but she wasn't cold. Not when the warm water sluiced over her body and she heard Teague's almost predatory growl.

She opened her eyes.

The water splashed on him, as well. She watched it flow in currents over his chest and arms to a waist rippled with tight muscle. His skin was darkened by the sun, shadowed by the flickering light, yet she could see how it was lighter at the base of his waist and hips, where the fabric of his braies bunched, wet, thinned, outlining what he could not hide.

He gripped the rim of another bucket. 'No, not practical...' When she closed her eyes this time, she braced her hand against his chest, felt his heart speed up as he cradled the nape of her neck, lifted her hair, and waved the water through her locks and down her back.

She felt a quick movement from him, his hand impatiently at her neck, lifting her hair. His roughened fingertips sliding across her sensitive skin as he dumped the last bucket of water over her.

When that bucket clattered to the floor, when he pulled her into his arms, she wasn't prepared at all. It wasn't the feeling of his almost bare body against hers. It was the way he held her as if she was fragile, as if she was precious.

She opened her eyes. Oh, his obsidian eyes, absorbing, so much darker than she had ever seen them before.

'Necessary,' he whispered against her lips.

She couldn't have known what it would feel like for his lips to skim over hers, for his tongue to beckoningly trace the seam for her to open. To feel the light slick slide of his lips as he pressed more of his body, until she shivered for more.

'Needed.' He sucked her lower lip slowly, sweetly, into his mouth. She heard rumbles through her body, mews of impatience. Her own.

He took a step away.

'No,' she whispered. 'Now.'

'Yes, now.' His eyes were heavy lidded, his cheekbones flushed, pronounced, his lips full and sensual. Battle-scarred chest, muscular thighs. A line of black hair starting on his abdomen, that arrowed lower.

He grabbed a linen. 'Turn around.'

She did, heard the inhalation of his breath and looked over her shoulder. Teague's eyes roamed from hers, then slowly to the bottom of her feet. His hand gripped the linen tight and tighter yet as his eyes travelled upward.

'I don't want to dry you,' he rumbled. 'The way the light flickers across the water droplets, just here.' She felt a slow finger along a shoulder blade and then trailing down her spine to her lower back before it was quickly removed.

'Lift your hair.' His voice was a low growl she hardly recognised, but with both hands she lifted the strands off her back and he wrapped her hair in the linen.

With each gentle squeeze, she felt the tension in him coil tighter, and in her tighter yet. Until he dropped the linen to the floor, took her hand and laid her down on the pallet.

'You're still wet.' He knelt one knee on the pallet's edge.

He skimmed his hand down her throat, gently caressing the cords that gave her breath, feeling the pulse of her blood through the veins.

Her body clenched, shook, trusted as she felt his hand tremble and she understood he was as affected as she was by his light touch.

More droplets of water allowed his hand to slide gently over her as he went lower, flattening his palm. He paused over her heart. 'You were like this in the bath that morning, standing there defying me. The water beading on your skin in the sunlight…in my chamber.'

He lifted her hand against his chest, and she felt his heartbeat. Strong. Sure. 'My heart felt then as it does now. Even then, you affected me.' His heart pulsed harder the longer she held her hand to it, the longer she held his eyes. He caressed her hands, a slight frown rippling across his brow.

'Do they hurt?'

Her hands stung with every movement she

made, but she wouldn't stop. She shook her head. 'Your leg?'

He shook his head, telling her he knew she lied about the pain. 'You saved me.'

'I owed you my life, remember?' she said.

His eyes lost their heated glimmer. She felt the pain in him then and her own increasing. It wasn't what she wanted. 'I want something more now, though.'

'Yes,' he said, his lips curving at the corners. He cupped one breast, letting the soft weight fill his palm, and rubbed his thumb across the peak. He bent his head and she felt a soft brush of his breath, a lock of his hair against her stomach, and then he kissed her breast, licking her nipple in one slow swipe, and an arrow of pleasure arced through her.

She clung then to his shoulders as he settled more fully on the pallet to set slow, purposeful kisses on her other breast, to blow cool air across it. He shifted again and went lower still.

His calloused palm and thick fingers lazily skimmed her abdomen. The water eased his thumb rubbing across her navel in firm circles. His kisses followed his hands, his fingers, the path of droplets she swore could not exist, even as she felt every one of them skimming crazily across her skin.

He went lower yet. His fingers weaved through

her soft curls, his own loose locks caressing her hips, his tongue dipping into her navel, circling it. 'Almost dry here now,' he whispered. Then he went lower.

One finger traced just at the place where she ached. Provoking a growl from him; a gasp from her. 'But not here.'

She was wet. She thought the water skidding on her body eased his finger's heated path, but this…this was much more. Now her wetness allowed Teague to rhythmically slide his fingers as he touched her.

She couldn't stand it and grabbed his wrist. 'Wait.'

He eased his hand away. 'Am I hurting you?'

'No, it's—' Her eyes flickered across him sitting next to her. At some point, he had shucked his braies. She'd never seen a naked man before. Never seen anyone look like him. He was Gwalchdu's lord. Fortified with more strength than any man should have. She watched his body as he trained in the lists. He fascinated her then; now he was mesmerising, and within her touch.

So she touched him, and he eased into her touch. She felt the textures of his skin, the roughness of his hair along his abdomen, his thighs. With skimming hands she wondered at the curves of his wrists and arms, his shoulders. Caressed with her fingertips along his collar bone. Rested her hand against his chest and felt his erratic heart thumping like her own.

'How could I resist you?' He captured her hand, placing it to her side as he covered her body with his. As he kissed the curve of her abdomen down to the fold of her hip and inner thigh.

'I cannot wait,' he said, his voice hoarse. 'To see you. Touch you like this.' He gave more kisses, a slick taste of his tongue. He raised his head. His cheeks were flushed, his eyes hardened with need. 'I could only hope—'

Rising to his knees, he nudged her thighs apart and cupped her fully in his hand. His hand was hotter than before as he rocked his fingers, gently, more urgently, against her slickness.

'What…?' she gasped. 'What… are you doing?' With each rocking of his fingers, the bond between them grew taut, tense, strained.

'I have to ease you.'

She didn't feel ease. 'It's not working.' She felt as if what was between them would snap, and she would fly away. As if sensing her sudden need, he anchored her with a firm hand on her hip, while his other…

'So stubborn. Don't…fight it,' he said. 'I only want to give you pleasure.' Her body listened, won whatever battle it waged against her thoughts. Her body began to move in rhythm with his fingers and to accept the pleasure he gave her.

She sensed a change in him then. His great chest taking in rapid breaths, his skin no longer dry, but glistened with sweat. Whatever he was doing to her was costing him. Her emptiness was now an ache in intensity, the wanting undeniable.

'No more.' She gripped his wrist.

His breath coming harshly across her skin, he rested his forehead against her shoulders, pressing his lips there. 'I do not wish to give you pain. It would be better if—'

'I need you.' She clasped his shoulders, and pulled him closer. 'Please, Teague. Now.' She didn't care if it hurt.

His breath came in one long sigh as his grip on her hip tightened. Her words had hit him. Covering her body with his own, his hands raised her to him.

'Yes, now.' He moved his hips; a long gentle firm slide against her as her body shivered. And another, as her hips arched to keep the slide that much longer. His eyes pinned hers, as he held himself just over her.

'Now, it's…necessary.' He surged in one swift motion.

She cried out as her body tensed in pain.

Through the haze, she heard his haggard breath against her ear. But already her pain eased, already the emptiness began inside her. She didn't want the emptiness. She glided her hands up his back to cup his broad shoulders.

'Please,' she whispered again.

'Soon. We must wait.'

'Now,' she demanded and pressed her hips more firmly to his.

He moaned, kissing her cheek as he lifted himself up, as he pulled his hips away, before he surged into her again. Deep within, her body fluttered and tensed.

'Anwen.' He froze and shuddered. She froze with him.

When he moved his hips in a rhythmic circle, it compelled her to follow him. She asked him to fill her, but she was overflowing, the force of his movements pressing. Her body arching. Wanting. 'More,' she gasped.

'Yes!' he cried, his movements giving her more, demanding more until she cried out too as her body tensed. As his did against hers and he enfolded her in his arms tightly, so tightly, before he collapsed beside her.

It was over. Anwen gathered the covers when the heat ebbed from her. Already the cold began to intrude, and she kept her eyes on the formidable man beside her to keep it away.

Teague lay on his stomach beside her, his head rested on his arm. When he raised his head to look at her, a dark lock of his hair caressed her cheek. She did nothing to remove it.

'Are you well?' he said.

The pain, every loss that brought her here weighed her thoughts, but lying next to Teague pushed them far enough away for her to rest. It was the most she could hope for now. 'Yes.'

He closed his eyes as if in relief, as if he savoured the one word.

'Now do you know?' He trailed a finger along her cheek, catching it just under her chin to turn her head to his. 'Now will you admit to what is between us?'

His words sent a fissure through her and she tilted her head away from his touch, but she didn't lower her eyes from him.

She had sought him to avoid thinking of her sister, of her home. Teague thought otherwise. Was it the truth? Had she sought him because of that connection between them? She had felt loss before... heartache, more than most, so what made this time different? Why had she sought comfort with him? To seek such answers, she feared her pain wouldn't stay distant much longer.

'I admit nothing,' she answered. 'Nothing.'

Two fingers under her chin lifted her face, forcing her to feel his touch. 'Don't do this. In the fire, you came back for me, gave me your body. Admit, Anwen of Brynmor, what you feel.'

She expected his arrogance, but there was too much light to his eyes, too much...emotion. She turned on her side away from him. It was probably a telling move, but she didn't care. Something was stronger between them. Something that had strengthened in the fire…when he needed her.

'I admit,' she answered. 'I admit to grieving and needing a closeness with someone. It's over now.'

'You lie,' he growled.

Ah, this is why she fought the creance between them. His sudden arrogance reminded her of who he was. He was a lord. He wanted control and power, just like Urien. Abruptly, she scrambled off the pallet. In the fire's light, she pulled on the clean clothes he had brought, struggled to extricate her wet clothes from his.

The task kept her busy. Anything to forget the warmth in the Traitor's eyes. That warmth, when she sought only forgetfulness. Lying with him was a grave error. Of course, the Lord of Gwalchdu's greed would encompass her in his bed, as well.

Teague stood, grasped her wrist and spun her to face him. 'This is not over.'

She could feel his will to move her. Realisation of his dominance swept through her. She hadn't been thinking. Only feeling. Her sister was dead. But nothing could change between them.

She wrenched her hand away. 'Don't touch me! *Everything* is over.'

She didn't care if he watched her flee the hut. She only hoped to forget how he stood framed in the doorway by the firelight. Clutching his clothes in one hand as if he meant to follow her, Teague, Lord of Gwalchdu, stood still as cold stone. Stood half in light, half in darkness…and alone.

Chapter Sixteen

Teague stretched his arms above his head and searched for Anwen in the crowd of people walking through the camp. When he didn't see her, he had to dispel the now familiar unease he felt whenever she was not in his immediate sight.

It had been almost a sennight since he talked to her, touched her. She did her best to ignore him and he would give her time for now.

Everything's over, she said. He knew otherwise. His need for her was a thousand times more powerful since he held her.

Had he ever known a woman like her before? No. His unexpected reaction to her in the forest when he had caught her didn't trouble him so much now. *She's mine*, he had thought. And she was. Despite his ill treatment of her, she'd come back for him in the fire. She risked her own life trying to save his.

Hadn't he realised her loyalty before? Climbing

the tree, she made her devotion to Melun clear. In the mews, she told him of Alinore and how she had to get back to her. He just never thought...never hoped, she would be loyal to him.

She'd come back for him and yet she fought him. And why not? He didn't deserve her loyalty. Not when he knew what she did not.

Someone was trying to kill him and that person had miscalculated, terribly, when they chose a fire to do it.

In all the damage to Brynmor, one certainty was terrifying and relieving. If he had not taken Anwen out to the hut that night, she would have died, just as Alinore had.

The majority of damage was done in his chambers and the two connecting ones. The location of the fire was too calculated. He was sure it was linked to the death threats, thereby he was responsible for the consequences. By coming here, he had put Brynmor in jeopardy, killed Alinore and Urien, and risked Anwen's life.

And what had she done? She came back for him. Gave him a gift he'd never received before. Loyalty.

He argued she owed him a debt for her life. He knew he now owed her and he knew how to pay her.

By staying away from her. By keeping her safe within his protection, within Gwalchdu, just never in his arms again. His enemy couldn't know of her importance to him.

He knew that last night, though it had been born of lust—no, it was more than lust. Her body glistening with water wasn't what compelled him to touch her. It was the need in her eyes. After she came back for him, how could he refuse her need? He knew what it was like to be alone.

But that wasn't the worst of his weakness. That moment was when he demanded she acknowledge there was something more between them than mere desire. It was good she refused him. He knew what connections did to those who felt bound to them. He needed no weaknesses now.

Now he needed to sever any remaining feelings between them, which should be easy. After all, she didn't trust the connection, didn't trust him. To ensure that distrust, he would tell her of the threats. She wouldn't forgive him then; he could hardly forgive himself.

'Some families will not cooperate.' Rhain strode over and picked up a saddle to place it on to the cart.

'What is their reason this time?' Teague gathered some bridles and threw them on the cart, where they made a splintered clang.

He'd worked tirelessly to remedy the damage of the fire. There was little left of Brynmor's keep and buildings, and what little there was wasn't enough to rebuild. It was best for the people to move to Gwalchdu for shelter and protection. The weather held thus far and only gentle rains had fallen, but it was turning colder.

'They are not giving any excuses now. They are already occupying the undamaged huts outside Brynmor's fallen gates.'

'They have to move.' Teague's voice left no room for argument. 'They are too vulnerable to an attack.'

'A persuasive argument, but these people are not exactly in favour of the English. They do not want your protection.'

'I am half-Welsh.'

Rhain gave him a pointed look.

Teague stopped in his lifting. 'Give them a monetary reason then. Those outbuildings aren't meant for winter occupation. I'll provide them with better homes, give them extra supplies. We'll provide them with whatever they need.'

Rhain gave a low whistle. 'There are hundreds left here. It may deplete your coffers more than your Spanish armour did. With certainty, there will be those who'll take advantage of the situation.'

Teague gazed over Rhain's shoulder, seeking answers there. There were none. Now that the emergency of the fire was over, he was beginning to feel an anger that not even the slaughter of the Welsh Wars had instilled.

Visions of Anwen going into the burning building blurred with her saving him, with her lying with him. In his dreams he didn't know what to protect her from: himself or the fire.

Returning his attention to Rhain, he said, 'Let them have it. I'll not take this chance again.'

'This is guilt speaking.' His brother crossed his arms. 'What gave you suspicion?'

'Most of the damage occurred in my private rooms, which spread to Urien's, Alinore's and Anwen's. The fire was too widely dispersed. If it was accidental, it would have happened in one spot and spread slowly from there, giving time for people to escape.'

'But two did not escape. We can at least mark Urien off the list of possible enemies.'

'Even so, we are no closer to the truth. Why set fire to my room when I wasn't there?'

Rhain shrugged. 'Everything this enemy has done implies they are not working with reason.'

Teague's anger was too close to the surface. 'It is senseless to destroy an entire manor and endanger others simply to get to me. The fire left such a waste and all for nothing.'

'But it seems they did get to you. You are shaken by this.'

Shaken was too tame a word. He still couldn't see the bright golden halo of hair. He'd have to search for Anwen soon. His unknown enemy had little regard for whatever destruction he wrought or whom he killed. He would not allow any harm to come to Anwen.

'Ah, you look over your shoulder again.' Rhain nodded. 'Perhaps your worry is for another? After all the time you took to save Anwen, you certainly wouldn't want your hard work going to waste.'

Teague's glare would have quelled a king.

Rhain raised one eyebrow. 'I understand that expression, brother, but I'll let it drop for now. You are not yourself.'

'Remind me to teach you to talk plainly one day.' Teague lifted up another saddle and Rhain took the other side to help him set it down gently.

'I think what you feel is plain enough, but if you wish to hide it from yourself, it's not for me to reveal it for you.'

He owed no explanation to his brother. Teague shoved the saddle deeper into the cart. 'It is my responsibility to protect her and everyone else who belongs to Gwalchdu! Just ensure everyone from Brynmor is moved to Gwalchdu. I don't want them making any more excuses.'

Rhain bowed. 'I'm at your command.'

Anwen stared across to the river's opposite bank. Tomorrow, Gwalchdu's side of the river would be her home. Even with nothing for her left at Brynmor, she fought the truth.

Alinore was buried in the circle of trees, where Robert tended her the night she died. It was a beautiful spot and that eased some of Anwen's heartache.

Melun left for Gwalchdu a few days after the burials. Once the services were done, Ffion and the rest of Brynmor's residents left, as well. Anwen was grateful for the Sister's healing medicines and implacable character. In the chaos following the fire, both were needed in abundance.

Anwen had not left for Gwalchdu to help with the unloading, but she heard that carpenters and blacksmiths were already building new cottages. Teague was sparing no cost. He had spoken of fairness, but he was going beyond that. Why? Her people could have been separated, sent to faraway villages and manor houses.

It was another aspect of the man she would have to reconcile within herself. How could one man be a deceiver, a traitor, but also a giver and lover? A warrior, yet one willing to give her gentleness?

Why was she thinking about him when she knew he had betrayed the Welsh by siding with the English King? He was the downfall of Brynmor, of Wales. He was a man of power and dominance.

Yet she sought his comfort when she was in pain, when she grieved for Alinore. From the first moment they met, she had trusted him to catch her. He made her feel safe. Should she—?

'We need to talk.'

Teague stood to her left. He wore a tunic streaked with sweat and dust. His breeches were crusted with mud. His hair was tied back, but whole strands were loose. He had been working as hard as she. Yet she noticed other aspects of him, as well.

She noticed the strength of his arms, but she remembered all too acutely how those arms enveloped her. She knew the texture of his skin, the roughness of his hair. He had not spoken to her since that night in the hut and she was grateful for the reprieve. It allowed her time to build her defences against him. With the way her body responded to his nearness now, she needed all her defences.

Teague did not wait for a response, but took long strides away from the camp. Away from the camp, down the river's bank and not up the hill towards the hut. Was she disappointed? No. That night in the hut felt a lifetime ago.

Feeling her feet sink into the rocky pebbles, she hurriedly caught up with him.

Teague stopped when he believed no one could hear them. He didn't know how Anwen would react, but if it were he, his anger would know no bounds. He counted on her to be angry so he could keep her safe.

He hesitated. He hadn't been this close to her for a week. The wind loosened her plait and her hair waved in angelic golden curls. He wanted to smooth her hair, feel its springy softness between his fingers. But angels could be vengeful and he was about to disclose grave tidings.

She seemed to sense it; her body was motionless as she clasped her hands in front of her. Her even blue gaze gave him time to say what he needed to say, but gave him no comfort as to how his words would be received. No matter, he didn't deserve her comfort. He simply had to pay a debt.

'It was my fault,' he said. 'The fire. It was my fault. I think it was against Gwalchdu, that they wanted to take something from Gwalchdu. It should have never happened here.'

'How?' She stepped closer to him, pressing his arm, pulling his attention more sharply towards her. 'How is the fire your fault?'

'Your hands are cold.' He took both her hands in his, chafing them between his. Touching her, feeling the pull to take the extra step until he could hold her, overwhelmed him. He resisted. 'They've never been this cold before. That's my fault, too.'

She tugged her hands away. 'The coldness of my hands is just because they're cold.'

He could see she did not understand. She wouldn't be standing this close to him if she understood. 'I have an enemy.'

She raised her eyebrows. 'Yes...'

'No, this is recent and, I believe, personal. They have been plaguing me for months now, but I don't know who it is.' Teague exhaled slowly to let some of the anger out of him. 'He leaves messages. There are often gaps in their frequency, but never a doubt in their meaning.'

She stood still, but he could see the slight tremors in her hands. She was beginning to understand.

'The first message was hidden in the saddle on Rhain's horse. Since then, there have been more messages tied to the slaughtered carcasses of small animals. Even if I don't understand the messages, I cannot avoid the implied meaning. He wants my death and the destruction of Gwalchdu. It is one of the reasons I went to Brynmor, to see if this place had any play in the part of the messages.' He paused. 'I suspect this enemy may have started Brynmor's fire.'

A stark hollowness clouded her eyes as his words sunk in. 'Are you telling me,' she said, 'that I, and hundreds of others, lost their home, that Urien and my *sister* were killed because you chose to visit Brynmor when there was a threat of death against you?'

'I am.'

Her face was pale, her body unnaturally motionless, but she understood. He wouldn't have to give her any more information.

'Did you suspect this before or after we lay together?'

He paused.

'You bastard.'

Ignoring the greetings and cries calling out to her, Anwen weaved through the packed carts, cattle and people. She needed to breathe, to think, to get as far away from the Traitor as possible. She didn't see Rhain until he grabbed her arm and forced her to stop.

'I am sorry, Anwen. Teague told me you lost more than your home.'

Was this entire family bent on humiliating her? She didn't want to shed any tears in front of the Traitor's brother and pressed her hands to her cheeks to stop the tears from coming, but it didn't work. It seemed nothing was in her control any more, least of all her hurt and anger. 'Yes, we all seem to have our own demons, don't we?'

Rhain raised his eyebrow. 'So he told you of the threats.'

She wished she could avoid him, but there wasn't any place for her to go. 'I wish I didn't know.'

'If you had not suffered life-threatening injuries, he would never have brought you to Gwalchdu. He knew the risk. Everyone's life at Gwalchdu is threatened.'

She snorted. 'The lives at Gwalchdu are threatened, but Brynmor was innocent.'

'So is Gwalchdu.'

'I do not believe anything Gwalchdu does is innocent. Your brother's past decisions ensured Gwalchdu's stones are covered in blood.'

'Teague made the choices he needed to make.' Rhain's jaw tightened.

Anger flared again in her. The choices the Traitor made were to remain in power and control. To cruelly wield them over those weaker than him. What a fool she'd been. 'Yes, and it's easy for a second-born to sit on the decisions of his older brother.'

'Don't ever say it is easy for me being Teague's brother!' Rhain took two steps towards her, anger etched in every beautiful plane of his face. 'You know nothing of the past and what sacrifices were made.'

Why was she even trying to talk to him? Gwalchdu's men were all the same. 'I know your brother has taken my home away. Taken my very way of life!'

'Is that your worry?' Rhain pulled up short. 'There is enough for you to do at Gwalchdu now.'

She thought of all the work before her: the farming, planting, building of homes and helping of the sick. All her life she helped Brynmor's people. How was she to help Gwalchdu when it had always been an enemy's home?

'Brynmor's people feel as I do. No one would stay at a traitor's fortress.'

'Teague ordered Gwalchdu's gates to be locked. Essentially, there's nothing to do but to work.'

'Of course, he'd imprison everyone.'

Rhain shook his head. 'He cannot allow people to leave Gwalchdu. The enemy is amongst us. Teague does it to protect you. He feels respons—'

'He is responsible!' she interrupted. 'It is his fault my sister is dead because he brought the danger to Brynmor. I wish all of you would leave me alone.'

'You know that will never happen.' Rhain tilted his head in that familiar way that Teague had. The movement brought a bitter poignancy to her chest. 'And there's a part of you that wants that. You battle with yourself. That is why you are angry.'

Anwen brushed past him. 'Don't ever presume to know what makes me angry.'

'I'm going now.' Robert tied the final crate on to the cart.

Teague turned to his friend. Robert had changed dramatically since the fire. It was as if his soul had been consumed in the flames and all that remained was a shell of the man he fostered with.

He expected Robert to leave long before now, but had been grateful he'd stayed to help. They accomplished much in the last sennight, but none of it would have been possible had Robert not persuaded the families to move to Gwalchdu. Teague owed him a great debt.

'Where?' Teague asked.

'I'll return to King Edward's court; he'll have need for my sword.'

'I have need of it as well, Robert, you are welcome—'

'I can't.'

Robert's grief tore through Teague. Just weeks before he'd mocked his King's worry over his wife, Eleanor. Now that he had received the gift of Anwen's loyalty, Teague couldn't mock or dismiss Robert's loss. If he lost Anwen, he would grieve, too.

'You always have a home to return to.'

'Thank you.' Robert placed his hand on Teague's shoulder, but Teague rebuffed it, giving Robert an embrace and pounding him on the back for good measure.

Robert winced. 'I'll feel that for some days to come.'

Teague chuckled. 'That was the point.'

Robert lifted his mouth, a ghost of recognition fluttered across his face, but it was quickly replaced by the lines and furrows that appeared to have grown permanent overnight.

'Goodbye, my friend.'

* * *

It was close to the end of the day when Anwen spotted Robert saddling his bags to leave. If she intended to apologise, she'd have to face him now.

'Robert?'

Robert did not turn to address her, but he stopped in his task. It was the most she could ask for. He had ignored her since Alinore's death, as she had him. What she had accused him of was so terrible that no apology could possibly make amends, but now she had to try.

'She…' Anwen watched his back flinch as if she struck him. She regretted causing him further pain. He did not look at her and that, too, caused her regret. Although he did not mean it, his withdrawal from her and leaving hurt. He was English, but she had known him for most of her life.

'Yes?' he prompted.

'She may not have told you. But I wanted you to know she loved you.'

Robert shuddered, as if his body was suddenly and terribly cold.

'She told me, in confidence.' Anwen brushed her tearing eyes. For a sennight, she deliberately hadn't mentioned Alinore. She swallowed to keep her voice still. It didn't work.

'She told me; then she smiled. You made her very happy.' Anwen clenched the folds of her skirts. She needed pain in her healing hands to stop the pain in her chest. 'That's all I wanted you to know.'

Robert turned. The hollowness in his eyes ripped through her. 'I failed her.'

Anwen swallowed, and answered, 'Me, too.'

Then she walked briskly away so she did not see him leave. She had seen too much leaving.

Chapter Seventeen

It was time to go. Anwen walked to where Teague and his soldiers readied the horses. Her anger from yesterday deepened. She knew he had his own agenda in taking her to Brynmor, now she knew what it was. She could not judge him for seeking the killer, but she would judge him on the risk he took by coming here.

He gently stroked the neck of his destrier and adjusted its bridle. She felt those hands as if upon her own body. His warm palms, with thick calluses had pressed into the flesh of her calves, then her thighs as he slowly moved up her legs. She, too, like his horse had gentled for him. Her body hummed. She didn't understand how she could hate him, yet want him.

That was yet another betrayal she made to herself when it came to the Traitor. She didn't regret lying with him; it was her decision. But she did regret this wanting him still, especially when she knew what he had done. Brynmor had paid for his need for power. She would do well to remember this.

He turned when she came nearer. His stance showed him in profile, the curve of his shoulder, the indentation of his back. Anwen brushed her hands on her skirt to wipe off the sudden moisture there.

'Where do I ride?' she asked him.

His eyes were impenetrable. 'With me.'

She assessed the other riders and their heavy satchels. Only his horse was bare of burdens. He left no room for her to argue, but she wasn't pleased about it.

'Ready?' he asked.

She nodded as he put his hands on her waist. He hadn't touched her so intimately since that time after the fire. Her body was all too aware of the fact. His men watched, so she kept silent, but she challenged him with her eyes.

He was looking at her again in that arrested way of his. She felt locked to his gaze, forgetting the stamping destrier next to them and his men on their horses flanking them. All she could see was his blackness and the heat. Desire, fast and hot, hit her. She lifted her chin, hoping he'd mistake the flush of her skin for anger instead.

His eyes flared and his fingers pressed just a

little deeper before he lifted and settled her on his horse. Then he pulled himself behind her.

She was immediately impacted by his muscled thighs and hard chest. She pulled herself forward in a vain attempt to give more space between her body and his, but he was wrapped around her. Even the way he smelled wove through her senses.

She had no weapons against her wanting him, but she must try...if not for his past betrayals and his need for power, then she must remember he had killed her sister.

Raising his arm in the air, Teague urged his horse forward and his men followed. Anwen sat stiffly in his arms and she was trying not to touch him. He knew it was right; he needed her hatred, he owed her protection and safety by staying away from her.

Still, he wished he had waited until they crossed on to Gwalchdu land before he told her of the threats against him. It would be a full day's journey before they arrived at the fortress's gates. If he had waited to tell her, they could have had a pleasant, if not pleasurable, ride. But her anger meant it would be a full day of hell for him and he only had himself to curse.

He made the primitive decision of having her ride with him because the alternative, of her being this close to another man, was unacceptable. He had not accounted for what it would feel like to put his hands on her again. He'd had only one night with her and it was not enough.

Anwen was sitting against him, forbidden, but she was not immune to him. She tried to cover it up, but he felt her desire when they mounted.

His body tightened as the image assailed him. He needed a distraction from this need for her. If it was hours like this, he would not be able to get off his horse when they reached Gwalchdu.

'Tell me about your precious hawks,' he asked.

'You want to know of my hawks?'

Her voice was low, husky. Ah, yes, she felt what was between them even as she sat stiffly away, trying not to touch him. She was angry about her desire. And he still wanted her despite the fact he knew better.

'It might take our minds off what we truly want to speak of and do.'

'I want to do nothing with you now,' Anwen lied. 'I don't want to talk to you either.'

'We have hours to go and we both need distraction.'

She hated to give in to his demands, but he was right. She couldn't sit with only her anger and the knowledge that, if she turned her head, their lips could touch.

'I don't remember a time I wasn't in the mews,'

she said and felt the exhalation of Teague's breath as if he'd been holding it. 'Melun was the head falconer and he eventually trained me.' It was good to talk of past times…happier times. Birds fascinated her, both with their beauty and deadliness. But mostly, she loved the way they could soar.

'When Melun began to lose his sight, I tried to become his eyes. I didn't want Urien to know. If he did, I feared he would send Melun away, or give him tasks that would damage his pride.'

'What of Robert? Would he have not provided protection?'

She paused, remembering Melun's words to her. 'I didn't think he would, which was why I was worried for Melun when I was…recovering at Gwalchdu. But he told me Robert intervened when Gully went missing.'

'Why an astringer, why not become a falconer?'

'Hawks can be difficult to train because of their unpredictability, but I like the challenge of them.' Some of her tension eased as she talked of her training. 'I like Gully in particular—sometimes he would catch the lure quite willingly and at other times he would act as if I insulted him.'

Teague chuckled before asking another question. Anwen found it was surprisingly easier to talk to Teague, but, then, given the beauty of his mews, it was clear he liked the training of birds. And it did take her mind off other matters, like her body's betrayal in wanting him, or his risk leading to the death of her sister. But more importantly, it helped her avoid thinking about the way his laughter warmed her in a place she thought closed to him. Her heart.

When they passed over the river, Anwen saw the castle looming and the villagers' new homes being built. It was late when they arrived and torches were being lit.

Teague helped her dismount and she took a step away before realising she didn't know where to go.

'I don't know where I'm to stay.' She yawned.

'I took the liberty of securing your room.' Teague gave the horses' reins to a stable boy and walked away. 'Edith will show it to you.'

Watching Teague return to his home, Anwen felt more like a reluctant guest than a resident. The fire had taken away her home, her shelter, her place in the world. Teague might be master and lord here, but she was supposed to make a life here, as well.

A temporary life.

She couldn't stay at Gwalchdu, not knowing Teague's past and his present actions. Not with her sister's death. She had no reason to stay under the roof of another man of power. Her home was gone as was her family. She might have stayed at Brynmor for Melun and Alinore, but she didn't have that here. Melun didn't belong here either. Neither she nor the old falconer were needed. Gwalchdu was efficient, orderly. When winter ended, she and Melun could go and find the life where they were needed, where power and dominance didn't threaten the home she always longed for. A home with chaos…and love. She couldn't make her home within Gwalchdu's controlled walls ruled by an even more controlling lord.

Edith and Greta pounced the moment Anwen entered the residence tower.

'Oh, there you are! Whatever was he thinking, making you take that trip with you barely well and all! Oh, we worried, we did, didn't we, Greta?'

Greta nodded her head emphatically.

'Look at you, more slender than a blade of grass.' Edith pushed Anwen's hair away from her scar and started to pull her towards the stairs. 'That looks well and is healing just fine. What with your hair, you can't even see it.'

It was almost a relief to have someone give her directions, but that feeling disappeared when Edith opened the door adjacent to Teague's room.

Her sudden halt caused Edith to stumble.

'I can't be next to Lord Gwalchdu's rooms. There must be some misunderstanding. That room is for the lady of the castle, not me.'

Edith firmly patted Anwen's arm. 'The room's

ready for you, I say. Come, you're just tired. I know you won't be having me and Greta working on somewhere else this late.'

Anwen scowled, knowing she couldn't argue now. 'I will find more appropriate rooms in the morning.'

'Gwalchdu is full.' Edith followed behind her. 'The stables, too. With all this space, I didn't think we'd ever be full. But don't mind me, dearie. Complaining I'm good at. I'm too used to Greta's silence and must talk for the both of us.'

Anwen smiled. She couldn't help it.

Despite the fact that it had been dormant, the room was freshly cleaned and aired out. Yellow linens covered the walls, a green crisp coverlet and drapes adorned the bed. Ornamental chairs padded with the same pillows and blue tassels were placed beside tiny tables. Every comfort was there for a lady, but it was the bed that beckoned and Anwen crawled under the covers.

The next morning, she found Teague training in the lists. It reminded her that he was a warrior, not a gentle landowner, and he'd been away from Gwalchdu for almost a month.

The weather had turned ever colder and he wore clothing this time. But it was thinned, well-worn, and clung to a body that glistened with sweat. Indomitable man.

'You shouldn't be here.' Teague nodded to Peter, who bowed and left.

She didn't need a greeting. 'That's why I wanted to talk to you.'

He crossed his arms. 'I have a feeling we are not talking about the same matter.'

'You have placed me in the rooms adjacent to yours. They are the Lady of Gwalchdu's rooms.'

'Yes, I did. My servants would not presume those rooms for anyone. They were my mother's and I have left them empty.'

'It isn't appropriate. I have no intention of being the lady of this castle. I need to change with someone else.'

'No. There's no other room. Everyone is settled and it won't matter anyway. You were put where I ordered.'

There the lord was again. Arrogant, autocratic. She clenched her teeth to keep her voice even. 'You are being unreasonable.'

'I never said I was reasonable.'

'Why?' she pressed.

'Because I want you in that room. No one knows what happened between you and me. I have purposely stayed away from you so there will be no gossip-mongering. You'll stay in that room and that's that.'

He was already walking away. She was dismissed. Anwen unclenched her teeth to let him hear her anger. 'I'll not stay! I'll find somewhere else.'

He peered over his shoulder. 'No. You won't.'

Anwen never found another room. She did find Melun, however, in the gardens.

Brynmor might have burned to the ground, but she recognised some flowers had been successfully replanted here at Gwalchdu, where no flower had been planted before.

'My child, you should have warned me about that pestering woman. I would never have left the peace of Brynmor if I'd known that harridan was waiting here for me. Wanting me out in the garden, standing by her with buckets of spades and eggshells like some squire to a knight. All day long…chatter, chatter, chatter!'

Anwen laughed. 'Sister Ffion is not so bad!'

'Sister Ffion? Oh, no. You could not find a gentler soul than her. I am talking of that woman with the fluffy hair, chatters up someone so much you don't even know you're being bullied until you're there, stuck, doing her bidding.'

'Edith?' she guessed.

'Yes! Everywhere I turn, it's, "Oh, dear Melun, could you do…?" and "Master Melun, do you have the time…?" I'm tired, I'm telling you!'

Melun wasn't tired, he was invigorated. All of Anwen's worry since she'd sent Melun ahead of her melted away. He found a new purpose, a new life here at Gwalchdu. It seemed Melun did belong here at Gwalchdu.

Giving the elderly man a hug, she said, 'It's simply her way.'

Melun tried to replace his grin with a cross look. 'Man of my station doesn't need to be hen-pecked. Think I'll go and give her a talking-to right now.'

He departed, leaving her alone again. Anwen had no one to talk to. Alinore was gone, so too was Robert and now Melun was slipping away from her. She had thought to make plans to leave with him. But Melun did not need her any more. It was a loss she wasn't expecting. It seemed she was the only one suffering a loss of home and purpose.

In the inner bailey, she found Ffion sitting on a bench near the rosemary bushes. Her eyes were half-closed and she feverishly rubbed her rosary beads. Ffion had been like this since the fire.

'Sister?' Anwen whispered, not wanting to startle her.

Ffion had worked tirelessly helping the people after the fire, but it appeared to have taken its toll on the older woman. Dark circles hollowed her eyes and the wrinkles on her brow had deepened.

'Child, I have not seen you in prayers all day.'

'There are evening matins, Sister.'

'There is nothing as important as prayer.' Ffion placed the rosary in the folds of her voluminous gown. 'Especially in these times.' Her lips pursed. 'I don't think I'll forget the fire's destruction. It was so fast…'

Anwen sat beside her. 'None of us will.'

Ffion slid her a glance. 'No. I suppose you won't, will you? It is hard to understand God's will, or what He has planned for us. Some things are out of our control.' Nodding, she added, 'I understand you are in the rooms adjacent to Lord Teague's.'

'It appears those will be my rooms as long as I stay here.'

Ffion voice drew flat. 'Those were my sister's rooms. She died tragically, but Lady Elin was a great lady. I thought Teague understood. He never before allowed anyone in those rooms. Never. There have been too many changes lately. Combined with too many dangers. I believe it is evil portent.'

Ffion was in a religious fervour. Not wanting to aggravate the Sister, Anwen stood to leave. 'Gwalchdu and Brynmor have suffered enough danger.'

'There is more to come.' Ffion grabbed her rosary and pushed the beads through her fingers. 'It's not safe here. Lord Teague's arrogance will

cause us harm. If it wasn't for Rhain's commanding presence, I don't know what would happen,'
Ffion whispered. 'What wickedness to put you in
that room! If you knew the past—'

She didn't want to hear any more. Bidding the
sister good day, Anwen walked away.

'You should not be in that room!' Ffion called
out.

No, she shouldn't be in that room; she didn't
want to be in that room. At least Christmas was
coming. There would be work to do for winter at
least; then she could leave.

When she passed into the outer bailey Anwen
jumped sideways as a pack of dogs chasing two
squealing pigs swept by. Then she froze and
thrust her arms in the air when shouting children swarmed around her as they chased the
whole lot.

Lowering her arms and gathering her breath,
she was overwhelmed by the clanging of metal,
the pounding of wood and the flares and sputtering
of controlled fires. People building new structures
called out, laughed and strode to different work sta-
tions. There was a fight at the cordwainer's and two
women were gesturing madly over soiled laundry.

Chaos. At Gwalchdu.

Anwen's heart skipped and skipped again. With
the sudden arrival of people, Gwalchdu couldn't
remain precise, controlled or orderly. Brynmor

was not quite lost after all. Lifting her skirts, she charged forward. Gwalchdu might be a temporary home, but for now, she'd see where she was needed.

Chapter Eighteen

It had been too long since he'd held Anwen. For weeks, Teague had watched her with a type of hunger he didn't know was possible. He worked to erase the craving, but it was still there. It didn't help that she was always nearby. If he was directing how many crofter huts should go up, she was there directing how they were to be built. If he was ordering supplies, she was there with an exact count of how many pots to provide. It wasn't just her presence, it was the glimpses of her bared skin. Her wrist as she reached for a cauldron or the back of her neck as she bent to talk to a child. He suffered from those glimpses and his ache deepened.

Teague stretched, his eyes scanning the winding narrow road between the houses. Anwen was talking with Rhain and the tanner, Bleddyn, both men dwarfing her. She was resilient, but she'd lost weight and there were shadows under her eyes. She had not slowed since they returned from Brynmor. He had purposefully avoided her, but he noticed her anyway and she'd collapse if he didn't do something. It was past time she took a reprieve.

'The roof looks well repaired. I can hardly wait to tell Sarah.' Bleddyn patted her on her shoulder before turning to leave.

'Oh, Teague will hardly notice the additional labour and supplies to build a thicker thatch,' Rhain added.

Rhain's tone wasn't lost on Anwen; she rounded on him. 'If these houses are to last, then they need to be thick. It will keep more people warm, using less firewood and not deplete Dameg Forest. Teague needs the forest for the animals that feed his belly.'

Rhain put his hands up. 'I have no argument with you and I'm sure Teague will not resist, given his motive.'

'Yes! He shouldn't argue. If it wasn't for him—' She stopped. 'What do you mean, "given his motive"?'

A slight flush mottled Rhain's finely sculpted cheekbones. 'It is not my place to say.'

Anwen poked the man's chest. 'It is your place to say. You owe it to me for not telling me of Teague's enemy. All those times we talked you never warned me and look at the consequences. I lost my home and my sister.'

Rhain visibly winced. 'I believe I no longer envy my brother for your attention. Your words are worse than any sword cut. Deserved, no doubt, but painful.'

'Rhain...'

'Very well, but in truth, I'm surprised I have to tell you what drives Teague to work.'

Over the last month, she had tried not to notice Teague working, or the way exhaustion and determination furrowed his brow. She shook her thoughts away.

'It is guilt over Brynmor's loss. He should be guilty,' she answered. 'Although I'm surprised he should feel such an emotion given the sins he's committed in his life.'

'No man lives without some sin on his soul.'

Anwen rarely heard Rhain so reflective. She'd seen him use his charm and wit as weapons and she wondered, not for the first time, what depths he hid behind his golden handsomeness.

'No woman, as well.' Rhain's fingers flitted over the small dagger at his waist. 'But it is true guilt plays some motive with my brother. He repairs to make amends for what he's inadvertently done to your home. But what do you believe drives him to give to Brynmor's families, who have no need of his gifts?'

She didn't know and didn't want to know.

'He does it for you.'

Never. 'You are mistaken. All my life, Teague has preyed upon Brynmor's vulnerabilities and made it weaker. The sole reason I am here is to see Brynmor's people settled this winter.'

'They are settled. I've heard you talk of Christmas. That isn't merely settling.'

'Christmas is a time for joy. You'd deny my people that?'

'I see it makes you happy, as does staying here. I think you stay for another reason.'

'No! That is twice you've wrongly judged my motivations. You are as overbearing as Teague. I cannot wait to leave the lot of you.'

'That is unfortunate since I have need of your company, Anwen,' Teague said from behind her. 'If you'll follow me?'

Anwen turned to round on him as well, but he strode away before she could make a response. He was always doing that; this time she wouldn't let him get away with it. Fisting her skirts, she ran after him.

'I'm not getting on that,' she said a few minutes later when she could see his horse saddled. 'I have too much work to do.'

Teague was familiar with that mutinous expression on her face. 'You have done nothing but work since—'

'Since the fire,' she interrupted. 'But since it

was not but a month ago, there's still much to do. The rains have delayed setting foundations and there are homes to thatch before it snows.'

'It'll soon rain again. The day turns dark from clouds and a few hours' reprieve will not make much difference.' Teague offered her his hand. 'I am not making a command, but a request.'

Anwen inspected her dry, cracked hands. Even as busy as she was at Brynmor, she had used oils and brushed her hair. Now she hadn't bothered to look at her image since the day she fell from the tree.

The day she almost died.

She took his hand and he swung her up on the horse. The dark clouds were rolling in fast, and a cold wind was increasing. He was right. A couple of hours would not make much difference.

Teague took her south alongside Dameg Forest and away from the sea and Gwalchdu. She hadn't been so close to him since they rode from Brynmor. She remembered the intensity of the heat between them. She expected the same again, but it was not so. Instead, the warmth of his body, the smell that was distinctly him was soothing almost and she fought the need to rest against him. She would do best to remember she was not safe with the Traitor.

Despite the dark clouds, the sun caused the rolling meadow to be covered with shadows and shards of brilliant light. It was as if they were steadily leaving one world and entering another. No longer did she hear the pounding of hammers and shouting, but instead the song of birds and the soft creak of the saddle. No longer did she need to weave and run around the many obstacles in Gwalchdu's baileys, but she rested, feeling the gentle sway of the horse's gait. Then, all too soon for her, they dismounted and Anwen walked to the river's edge.

It was colder here and she wrapped her arms around her cloak. But the sun still shone, so she closed her eyes, lifted her face to it and let the river's sounds and smells surround her.

When she opened them, Teague was watching her with a mound of rocks in his hand for skipping over the water. Over the last month she'd seen just that look on his face. It didn't bother her today. Maybe it was the tranquillity of the river, but her heart felt lighter.

'So you take me to the river again and I find some peace. If I was at all superstitious, I would want to leave to make sure Gwalchdu was not burning down.' Anwen raised a brow. 'But I supposed you're not worried about it.'

'No. I am not.' Teague fluidly skipped a rock, then another. His breath curled visibly in front of him with every powerful throw.

'Do you want to try?' he asked, holding out a stone.

Some day she would try, when she was far away from here. 'Did you bring food?'

Teague nodded to the pack on the horse as he tossed another rock. Eagerly she lifted the satchel, spied the insides and grabbed a loaf of bread.

'Do you regret coming?' he asked.

Tearing a bite to eat, she shook her head. 'No.'

She did not regret coming here. What she wondered was why he was able to compel her to come. She was like a falcon to his lure, or more like prey to his talons.

She took the last bite of bread. Her enthusiasm for the food was waning. Since the fire, her eating had been sporadic and she'd been sick more than once. At first, she thought it was the worry making her ill, but now she missed her monthly flow. It was startling evidence that she was pregnant.

'You look tired,' he said.

'I am not sleeping,' she confessed. It wasn't morning sickness she suffered from, but all the time. She took another bite of bread.

'Is it Alinore?' he asked.

'I don't wish to speak of my sister with you.' Anger and grief coursed through her again. Emotions more welcomed than the bewildering peace she felt with him, or the ramifications of carrying the Traitor's child.

'You grieve, and have thrown yourself too far into work.' Teague looked away and seemed to gather himself before he spoke again. 'Would it help to know that Brynmor's loss was not my intention? I thought my enemy only wanted Gwalchdu.'

She looked sharply at him, but he kept his gaze resolutely away from her as he swiped more rocks from the ground to skip across the river.

What was she doing alone with this man? Why did he compel her to his side? He had betrayed her people and left them vulnerable during the Welsh Wars. So, too, he confessed he caused the fire that killed her sister. Yet, he cared for her when she could have died and now made sturdy homes for Brynmor's people. How could he both give and take away?

'Would you have not gone to Brynmor?' she asked.

His mouth thinned. 'I would have taken precautions.'

She remembered his soldiers walking Brynmor; he had taken precautions. 'The results would have been the same. I am still without a home.'

Teague's eyes flashed disappointment before he answered, 'You have a home.'

'I have no home or weren't you there?' Anwen's agitation increased. 'It is nothing but ashes.' This was good; this anger was right and familiar. She did not want any feelings of giving or any acceptance from Teague.

'Gwalchdu is your home now,' he said.

Home. With Teague. A myriad of images flashed before her. Him standing under the tree defying the branches to hurt her, him holding her hand at night taking the pain away, him fighting through the fire to help others. Yet, he was the Traitor with little regard for the consequences of his actions. Could she have a home with the Traitor of Gwalchdu? *Never.*

'A temporary home,' she said. 'I'll stay and help for the winter, then go.'

He stepped away with a sound, a huff of breath, as if what she said hurt him.

She knew it was a lie. She knew who she was and who he would always be: powerful. Controlling. Despite his recent generosity, she couldn't forget. They would die enemies. Him siding with the English had left Brynmor and Wales vulnerable. Urien's hatred had turned towards her sister then.

No, she couldn't forget.

'Is it because of the fire?'

She nodded. 'And your past.'

Frustration flashed in his eyes before he started to pace. His movements were long paces, but somehow short, like a warhorse wanting the reins. It was then she noticed how he was dressed.

Under his cloak, he wore a thick leather jerkin and his breeches were soft leather. His sword hit against his leg as he moved and she could see a dagger in his boots, its silver handle flashing. There would only be one reason a man would dress as he did: for protection. It must be a madman who threatened him.

'It is probably best you leave after winter.' He turned to her. 'But until then…could we not have some accord?'

'For what purpose?' Her eyes narrowed. 'Because you need to spend your lust?'

'Ah, yes. Now you snarl and snap at me.'

Snarl and snap? Anger crawled up her spine and boiled in her heart. 'What else did you expect? You came to Brynmor and it suffered from an enemy who pursued you! It burned to the ground because of you!'

'I accepted the responsibility.'

'And the other time?'

Teague tilted his head. 'You speak of my siding with the English King Edward during the Welsh Wars.'

'It's as if you can't harm Brynmor enough, yet you speak of it so calmly.'

'It is the past. It is done.'

She released all her hurt and frustrations in a sigh. 'It's never been done. After the wars, Brynmor's homes leaked, livestock diminished. People lost families because they moved away. Then the work doubled because there were no people.' She pushed her hair from her face. 'Tools broke, but we couldn't replace them. All of Brynmor's skilled workers left. I have seen good friends get into fights over stale bread, people become sick and children went hungry because of what you did!'

She was releasing the venom, but it wasn't helping. The talking merely built her rage until it was hot, rolling.

'And what of Alinore?' she continued. 'My sister, who played with flower petals, wore the worst of it. Her face bruised, her arms scarred from burns. Urien would not leave her alone; his fist hit like a mace and I could do nothing to stop it!' Anwen hit her chest to free some of the pain constricting her heart. 'I tried. I used my own body like some of your precious Spanish steel, but he swatted me away. Why her? Why not me? I was the bastard-born.'

Teague's silence incensed her more, for she wanted a response from him. Something. Anything! 'And for what?' she questioned. 'What! Just so you can have your stone walls, thick tapestries and your precious beeswax candles.'

He started and she stopped talking, leaving her discordant breathing the only sound. The air surrounding them was swirling, heavy and thick with moisture, the wind was sharper, abrasive. It whipped at Anwen's hair and moulded her gown against her body. The coming rain would bring a storm and when Teague finally spoke, she knew it to be true.

'You think I sided with Edward for my comfort?' Teague said. 'You, who give generously of yourself to others, judge me by my wealth?'

It was too late for caution; too much damage had been done. 'I see what I see and I see what you have and what Brynmor had not!'

'You do not see! You see my mews, my thick walls, but you have no idea what it took for me to hold on to it, or what sacrifices I made to build it.'

'I know what happened; we all know what Gwalchdu's lord did. When the rightful Prince Llewellyn was preparing for war against King Edward, you ran scared to the lap of the English dog! Brynmor, unprotected by the forces of Gwalchdu, didn't stand a chance of defeating Edward. You betrayed us!'

His body was like stone, but something bubbling with life breathed just beneath the surface. 'There was betrayal, Anwen, but not by me.' Teague raised his hand. 'No, wait! It is time you hear what I have to say.'

Anwen wrapped her cloak around her and crossed her arms. She'd listen to him.

But should he tell her? Teague could feel Anwen's eyes on him and it was all he could do to ignore her as he must. It showed his weakness that he took her here, that he noticed she was tired.

The enemy was here and he could not be weak. He could not soften towards her. He wanted to laugh at the irony. At first, he stayed away because he thought her the enemy and now? Now there was true animosity between them.

'Are you cold?' he asked.

She shook her head. 'Get on with what you want to say. I'll return soon enough.'

She was obstinate. Brave. Grieving. But she would believe him.

'You, no doubt, know my mother was Welsh, my father English.' Teague swiped more rocks. 'She sacrificed much when she married an Englishman, but she fancied herself in love. She died giving birth to Rhain on the day we received news of my father's death. I was five and Gwalchdu was left vulnerable. What do you think happens to an estate the size of Gwalchdu when it is defended by a boy who cannot hold a sword?'

Teague tossed a rock, which sunk into the moving river. 'The caretaking of the keep fell to Ffion. Gwalchdu had always been Welsh and it seemed it would remain Welsh. At that time, Llewellyn was the Prince of Wales and in good graces with the English King Henry, King Edward's father. Luckily, too, the captain of my mother's guard stayed and helped to defend the fortress. I think he was smitten with Ffion. Ffion had many suitors and I thought she'd marry, but she never did.'

Teague grabbed a flatter, wider, rock. When he threw it, it shot across the river, hitting the opposite bank. A small victory, when he had to talk about his greatest defeats.

'Prince Llewellyn's power was great and so was Urien's. King Edward ruled England when I was ten, but Urien and Llewellyn refused to respect the new English King. It broke whatever fragile peace there was between Wales and England.'

Teague picked through the rocks at his feet until he found one that satisfied him, but this one he didn't want to let go. 'For most of my life, I heard only Ffion's point of view on Welsh superiority. I was as deeply Welsh as any boy, and I despised the fact my mother married a weak Englishman.'

'Urien knew peace was about to end. I was but ten when he rode to the gates of Gwalchdu with forty of his own men.'

Tossing the rock to catch it, he dared glance at Anwen. Her arms were still crossed, but her face was not quite so mutinous. Did she need to know this now? Did she ever need to know it? He wondered if he told her for his own selfish purposes. So that she might look at him in a different way.

That was a weakness, perhaps, but then, when hadn't he been selfish when it came to her?

Teague continued, 'I know now he did it in case there was a protest to his taking control of Gwalchdu. Forty men behind a leader would have been a considerable force, but Ffion did not protest and neither did I. After all, he had been visiting and giving advice to us in those early years. It was natural for him to take over. That is my regret and has been all my life.'

Teague threw the rock upstream, watching it cut through the flow of water. 'Soon, it became clear Urien's interest wasn't in the betterment of Gwalchdu, but in stripping it of all its money and resources, so he could fortify Brynmor and increase its soldiers. He didn't care about Gwalchdu's people.

'By the time Edward declared war, I did not see how my home could survive it. The servants were gaunt; the soldiers who stayed were more farmers than warriors. Gwalchdu's walls, mostly wood at that time, needed repairing. Urien, through ignorance or ill intent, stripped it of any way to defend itself.' Teague breathed in. 'That man robbed me of any heritage, with no care of what he left behind. Gwalchdu was closest to the English borders and we were like reeds to the scythe.

'After Edward kidnapped Prince Llewellyn's intended bride, the time came to regain control of my family heritage and oust any Welsh sympathies from my home. I paid homage to the English King.'

'Gwalchdu's people starving, vulnerable?' Anwen scoffed. 'I never heard of such a tale.'

'You wouldn't. I ensured it didn't last.' He closed his eyes. Her anger was there, but so was her shock. She was listening. 'It didn't last, but Greta was there, as was Edith. If you doubt me, ask them.'

'What happened next?' she said, waving her hand at him.

'I do not need to say what risks I took travelling the miles to Edward's camp, or what would have happened to me if I'd been caught, by either side, before I was able to talk to the English King,' Teague said. 'But I did it because I knew people easily betrayed each other, but that stone was for ever. I would save Gwalchdu with my life and damn the consequences.'

'Where was Rhain during this time?' she asked.

'When I gained Edward's alliance before he declared war on Wales, I sent Rhain away to train at Edward's hands. He was nine or ten at the time and as you know has recently returned. Ffion couldn't stand what I'd done and soon left for the convent. Never fond of me, her opinion of me turned bitter and it was even more so when she returned.' Teague picked up another rock, tested its weight in his hand.

'But why didn't King Edward hang Urien for his treachery?'

'You want to find flaws in my story. Know this, there are flaws, not of truth, but of my own actions.' Urien might be his greatest regret of all. 'For this part of the tale, I have only myself to blame. King Edward showed mercy at my request.' Teague huffed. 'When I returned from the first war of the Welsh uprising, Urien already showed signs of what he would become. Drink was heavy on his breath, his clothing unkempt. Having to live life with bitter defeat, he was already suffering far worse than any executioner's axe. It could only get worse and it did, didn't it?'

Anwen's stricken look told him everything.

'I regret not having Urien tried for treason.' Teague threw the rock. 'Especially for your and Alinore's suffering.'

'What hatred I felt for the English ended with Urien of Wales. I earned my spurs and my home when Llewellyn signed the Aberconwy Treaty conceding Edward's conquest of Wales. I was about fifteen at the time. Your anger is not with me. I did not turn traitor. Urien did.'

A smattering of raindrops hit her cheeks and nose. The heavy rain was coming, but she kept her eyes on his and he did not drop his own gaze.

'I need to return,' she whispered.

Chapter Nineteen

They barely entered the outer bailey before Anwen slid from the horse. Through the roaring in her ears, she heard Teague call out her name, but she didn't turn to face him. The icy wind shoved her skirts against her legs and she lifted them with both her hands as she ran. She knew where she needed to go.

The wind helped her open the heavy doors of the mews, but she pushed, hard, to get them closed. She was immediately surrounded by the smells of damp wood and hay. Behind the closed doors, she could hear the wind batter against the heavy oak building and rain pound against the rooftop. Breathing the much-needed musty air deeply, Anwen spun around.

The birds were awake and restless. The storm would be a bad one. She suddenly felt like a plump rabbit as heads swivelled and predatory unblinking eyes focused on her. The cold weather increased their appetites and, although she knew Teague fed them well, she was grateful they were all secured as she strode to Gully.

'Greetings, old friend.' She brushed her hand over his head, going against the grain of his thick winter feathers. Gully blinked his eyes in pleasure.

'Melun tells me your training's complete,' she said. 'It must have been hard to learn from another's hand, but I guess we both have had our share of adversities recently.' Softly, she continued, 'I may have to have some retraining of my own. I hope I can be as successful as you.'

She struggled to find the falseness, the treachery in what Teague said, but everything rang true. It was staggering, heart hurting, but she could not deny the truth.

Teague, Gwalchdu's lord, wasn't the Traitor.

She had been eight when Teague earned his spurs. She was young, but old enough to have seen the difference of Brynmor before and after the Welsh Wars. Before the wars they had many soldiers, costly comforts and luxuries. After the wars, there had been few necessities and gardens became barren.

Never had she thought Brynmor's prosperity before the war was because Urien stole from Gwalchdu. Brynmor was a great estate and so she assumed Urien must have been a great Welsh minor prince. Yet, had she ever seen the man who had sired her work a day in his life? No.

It wasn't the wars that changed Urien; he never had the character to build Brynmor into a powerful estate. He stole from Gwalchdu to make Brynmor glorious. In turn, Teague had suffered.

All her life she insulted Gwalchdu's lord and she wasn't the only one. How many insults and slurs had he had to bear? Even one would have been too many and for no good cause. Teague had changed his fate by courage and intelligence. He hadn't given in to Urien or Edward. He took the opportunity to benefit Gwalchdu and its people. In doing so, he sacrificed himself.

She justifiably mourned the way Brynmor had been before the wars because the poorer they became, the more Urien's abuse grew out of control. He caused so much harm, so much pain, and she always blamed Teague.

But Teague wasn't a traitor, and he wasn't responsible for her sister's death. Hadn't he shown, with his past, that there were matters he couldn't control?

But that didn't solve her dilemma.

Teague was still a man of power, still a lord who ruled according to his wishes. He had imprisoned her and risked the lives at Brynmor to seek answers regarding this enemy of his. This enemy who had killed her sister.

Understanding the past did not help the present. Not when she was sure she was carrying his child. She carried a Marcher Lord's child. With his power, he could not marry her, but she'd be damned before this child would be unloved and harmed like her. What would happen when Teague realised? She didn't know.

But there were some truths she did know. She wouldn't be carrying Teague's child if she hadn't felt some connection to him. And it wasn't just desire, because she sought comfort and safety from him. She hadn't rescued him from the fire only because she owed him the debt of her life. It was because of his loneliness, too.

He built homes for her people now, and gave kindness. Brynmor's chaos wasn't gone. Gwalchdu was almost like a home with Melun living here. Perhaps she could…make a home here.

Was it enough for her to tell him of their child? There were so many questions she needed to ask him, but she needed to find him first.

Rain drove down as she ran from the mews to the resident tower. She was cold and soaked as she scanned the Great Hall looking for Teague. Ffion was walking towards the stairs that led to the private apartments. Anwen stopped her.

'Pray, Sister, have you seen Teague?'

Ffion, both her hands wrapped around her rosary, blinked rapidly. 'Teague? He is usually on the ramparts at night.'

'On a night like this?'

Ffion shook her head. 'No, probably not. Some of his soldiers are outside guarding, but I doubt Teague could handle the storm. You know his constitution is not as strong as Rhain's.'

Anwen ignored the taunt; she had no time to change Ffion's views.

'Why do you want to know the whereabouts of Gwalchdu's heir? It is late. You should be alone and seeking prayer.' Ffion's eyes flashed, a mixture of some fervour and anger. 'You have lain with him, haven't you?'

Anwen had enough of this slander against Teague and herself. 'Sister Ffion, I simply asked you his whereabouts.'

Ffion took a step back, horror on her face. One hand now clutched the rosary, the other reached out with fingers spread like claws. 'But you *shouldn't* have lain with him, child. I told you how he craved you like no other; how determined he was to have you. Why did you challenge him?'

Anwen had never seen the Sister this angry before. She just stopped herself from clutching her arms around her middle to protect her baby from Ffion's cutting fervency. Even so, Ffion's eyes glared at Anwen's stomach.

'He has spilled his seed in you and now all is lost! Lost!'

Ffion swayed and Anwen rushed to hold her.

'Heathen! Adulterer!' Ffion spat, spittle spraying out. She said no more words, but staccato animalistic noises came from the back of her throat as she flung out her arms.

The Hall was deserted. If Ffion collapsed as she did at Brynmor, Anwen couldn't hope to keep her steady as Teague and Robert did.

If Ffion reacted like this when she only suspected Anwen carried Teague's baby, how would she react when she learned the truth?

The older woman shook more violently before soon her tremors eased and she slowly sagged against her.

'Sister Ffion?' Anwen shuffled her towards the small hearth.

'I need Greta.'

'I don't want to leave you just now.'

Ffion slumped into a chair. 'Please, child, bring Greta to me. I must speak to her immediately!'

Anwen found Greta in the kitchens, her great arms deep in a copper pot. Anwen clutched her arm. 'Ffion needs you.'

Greta dropped the pot unsteadily on the carving table and shoved her cloth into the drawstring around her waist as she followed Anwen out to the Hall.

When they reached her, Ffion appeared half-alive. Her upper lip held beads of sweat; her skin was white as if it hadn't a drop of blood. Greta lifted Ffion in her arms.

'Will she fare well?'

Greta, her brow furrowed, nodded.

'What can I do? Do you need me?'

Greta shook her head once.

Anwen paused. It didn't feel right to just abandon them, but she needed to find Teague. Maybe when she found him, she could tell him of Ffion's episode.

If Teague wasn't in the Hall, he could be many places, but Ffion was right when she said Teague was usually on the ramparts at night. If his soldiers were there on a night like this, then he would be, too.

'I'm going to find Teague,' she told Greta, before racing along the long corridor to the soldiers' towers.

He couldn't find her!

Rain plastered Teague's hair and clothes to his body; his chest heaved from running. He'd searched the entire grounds for Anwen, but no one had seen her.

She appeared almost stricken when she jumped off his horse that he let her go, but it had been hours since she'd run to the mews. She was no longer there. She was no longer anywhere.

There was only one place she could be: the ramparts. It was the dead of night and a storm raged. The few men guarding never patrolled the ramparts on a night like this. There would be no visibility gained and they were slippery and too dangerous.

Lightning speared the horizon, illuminating the night sky as Teague grabbed a torch and ran up the stairs to the battlements on the north tower. The thick oak door separated him from the storm outside, but he heard a faint cry before the thunder cracked and any sound disappeared.

He pulled the door's handle. It didn't budge and his keys were in the chamber below. Lowering his torch, in the flickering light he could see the crushed keyhole. Even if he had a key, it would be useless.

He slammed the torch into its wall mount. Using his weight, he rammed his shoulder against the door. It shook with the force, but it didn't open.

'Teague!'

Blood rushed to his feet and a cold sweat instantly set on his back. The voice was barely audible, but he heard it. Anwen was on the other side of the door, on the slippery narrow ramparts, in a wind that had already felled trees.

His heart rammed against his chest and he

shoved at the door again. For the first time, he was cursing the defensive construction of his doors. He would have to get a tool, something heavy and sharp to break the door. The sword at his side would be just as useless as his shoulder.

The thought of leaving her sent him almost into a panic. Pounding his fist on the door, he yelled, 'Stay low!'

He had no idea if she heard him. He slipped his way to the armoury where he chose a double-sided battleaxe. He ran back up the steps and hoped he wasn't too late.

'Anwen!' he shouted. 'I need to axe through the door!' Only the wind hurling rain against the battlements answered him. Teague swung the heavy axe against the door and felt the impact shudder through his hands. The door didn't move. He cursed the narrowness of the stairwell, another construction meant for defence, for it limited his strength.

He swung again. His forehead beaded with sweat, but it wasn't from exertion. How long had she been out there? An hour? Two? While he ran on the ground cursing the mud, she could have fallen to her death. He couldn't hear her any more. If she was on the other side of the door, he might axe right through her. But he had no choice.

Again he swung, splitting the thick oak. The door shuddered. His rage built with each swing.

The axe handle was cracking. He would reach her. There was no other choice, no other possibility.

He swung. The double-thick iron-and-steel lock fell with a crash of metal upon stone and he kicked it to the side. Dropping the axe, he rammed the door open.

The full brunt of the storm slammed into him. Blinded, he stumbled on to the battlements. Without the protection of the stairwell, the rain slashed at him like relentless knives and the wind tore at the sleeves of his wool tunic. Leaning into the wind, he raised his arm to shield his eyes.

He couldn't see her anywhere. This part of the castle was not built for the comfort of his soldiers, but for scanning the sea for ships. There were no shelters for the weather, but there were some taller ramparts towards the rear. Anwen might have sought some protection there. He pushed himself forward a few steps until something small hurled itself at him and clutched on to his shoulders like a thrown cat.

His arms immediately encased Anwen, his thankful words whisked out of his mouth before any sound could be made. Carrying her, he ran down the stairwell to his rooms and set her on the floor. Her lips were blue, her hair sodden, the tendrils flattened around her face. Deep shivers racked her body.

'What were you doing; what were you thinking?' With trembling hands, he stoked the fire and scattered kindling. 'What if I couldn't find you?' The fire swelled, sending a blast of heat into the room. 'The wind could have flung you off the ramparts. People die in weather such as this!'

There was a puddle of icy water pooling at her feet. She was frozen, terrified.

Teague cursed the rain, the wind, the night; swore at the weak fire and that he had to set her down to tend it. With an unforgiving rendering, he tore the soaked clothing from her body. He saw a flash of her chafed flesh before he wrapped her in a heavy wool blanket and sat her by the fire.

Whipping his hair back, he threw off his tunic. He was cold, wet, and he had been outside mere minutes; she had been out there for hours. When he tried to unlace the wet leather strappings of his sodden breeches, he cursed loudly in a stream of invectives that would have had lightning striking, if it hadn't been already storming.

Anwen was cold, so cold. Cold such as she had never known her entire life. She could not stop the shivering despite the fire or the blanket she clutched to her chin.

Teague stood naked before her. The fire lit his skin so it shone burnished bronze. 'Open the blanket.'

She clenched it towards her, but did not take her

eyes off the corded muscles in his arms and legs, the ripples of his stomach muscles. She was cold, but her body was warming and responding to the male beauty before her.

'Do you wish to freeze?' His voice was harsh, but his hands were gentle as he pulled at her clenching hands. He made a place for himself, pressing his body against her before closing the blanket around them. He inhaled sharply as the cold of her body touched him.

She didn't say anything at all. It was like being held against hard fire. She hadn't expected this, but she wanted it. She had many questions to ask, but for now she was cold and he was heat. She pressed her lips against his chest.

Teague hissed. 'Your lips are like fire, but your body is like ice.' He rubbed his hands on her back, increasing the warmth as she increased her kisses. When his hands slowed, pressing long caresses along her back, she grew hotter.

'Anwen.' He caressed from the base of her neck, then down, following the curve of her spine. His thumbs pressed deep in the small of her back, before he spread his fingers wide along the curve of her buttocks. 'Again, you've caught me un-awares.'

'You didn't plan this?' She tried to tease, but her voice was low...husky. Her hands felt as greedy as his. Her response to him this time was different, deeper than before. Now she was responding because she knew him. Because again, he kept her safe. His rugged form, his actions. Everything about him made her greedier yet.

He shook his head, a look of desire and longing in his eyes. There was longing, even though his hands greedily stroked her skin. 'By Gwyn, no. This is not my intention.'

She pressed another kiss. 'And if it is mine?'

She felt another sweep of his hands, his fingers curling and just stopping from clutching her closer. 'With you against me like this...' he said. 'I meant only to give you warmth and comfort.'

Frightened, alone, the wind had shoved at her until she gripped the unforgiving stones to keep from being flung off the sides. In all of it, she never doubted he would come. 'You gave me comfort. You're giving me comfort.'

'That's all I should be doing. But you keep kissing, and,' he breathed, 'touching me.'

She kissed and touched him more.

He dipped his head and she lifted herself to meet him. As their lips brushed, her teeth immediately stopped chattering. His heat poured into her and she pressed herself tighter against him.

He pulled his mouth away and hungrily kissed the cords of her neck. 'It is too soon. You are cold, frightened.'

It might be too soon, but she knew one certainty. He was not all darkness. She twined her hands around his nape. 'I need more.'

'You are blunt. Bold. And yet...'

'I was never bold before you, never like this.' She arched her neck to give him more access. 'I need you.'

'You're impossible to resist.' With a groan, he swept his hands to cup her breasts. He skimmed the tips with his thumbs until desire thrummed more tightly through her.

Lifting her, the wool blanket forgotten, he set her on the bed and sat beside her. She explored him freely with her hands, with her mouth.

When Teague stretched beside her, she explored even more. She revelled in the roughness of the hair on his chest and legs, the warmth of his skin, the ridges of muscles twining underneath, the thickness of his bones beneath that.

She caressed and kissed lower along the path of hair on his abdomen, trailed her hand to the rigidness of his hip bone, felt the soft vulnerability of bared skin there until his breathing became deep overlapping shudders.

'Anwen, what do you do?'

'What you did to me in the hut when you kissed me. Is that not right? It's what I want to do.'

His dark eyes, darker yet, were unfathomable, consuming. She saw more of that longing she sensed in him when he held her. But it was sharper now, urgent, as a fist curled at his side and his leg twitched as if he might spring out of the bed…or on to her.

'How could I…' his eyes lost their focus as he gave a harsh breath and looked away '…refuse?'

She continued until he made impatient sounds that only encouraged her. So she kissed him more, her fingers tracing the inside of his thighs until he shivered, until he groaned.

'Enough.' He forked his fingers through her hair and dragged her up to capture her lips with his. The blood through her limbs pulsed and he twisted until she was underneath him.

His hands were on her now, firmer, without rhythm. She widened her legs. He growled in satisfaction, fervently kissed her breasts, the inside of her wrists, her stomach. Clasping her hips, he moved her further up the bed. Then he cupped her underneath and lifted her to his mouth.

It was her turn to flush, to let out a breath, but she didn't look away. Not when his glittering obsidian eyes held hers; not when he had that curve of sensual satisfaction on his lips. Not when he said, 'You are necessary.'

Clutching the blankets beneath her, she couldn't move, but she could see how his dark loose hair swirled against her inner thighs. And she felt his kiss, so much and not enough. As he held her firmly, she tried to press herself more fully against his mouth, wrap her legs more tightly around him. She needed to move; she needed more. But he kept his kisses light, teasing, until she moaned in frustration.

He raised his head and the black heat of his gaze seared her. Then he touched his lips softly to her thighs, to her hips.

'I didn't think you could be any more beautiful to me,' he said. He pressed more kisses to the curve of her stomach and navel, his fingers skimming along her legs. 'I didn't think I could want you any more than I did.'

He unwrapped her trembling legs, lowered her shivering body gently back to the bed, kissed along her flushed skin as he moved upwards. 'But I only want you more than ever.'

Every muscle in her was tight, coiled, aching. She caressed him now, echoed his skimming gripping touch. She could feel the cords of his back, the swells of muscles in his shoulders and she kneaded his hips as he poised above her.

'Please,' she demanded.

And he answered her.

Chapter Twenty

$\mathcal{O}\mathcal{O}\mathcal{O}\mathcal{O}$

Anwen woke to the sound of dry logs popping. Teague crouched by the fireplace and prodded the logs until the flames flared and increased the warmth and light. He'd thrown on a woollen tunic against the chill of the room. The loose tunic and braies seemed to highlight his rugged form she had become all too familiar with, and still seemed to need.

Averting her gaze, she noticed on the table by the fireplace lay a large tray covered with food, a pewter flagon next to it. The shutters were closed and the room held a dim light, but she could hear the sounds outside telling her it was at least mid-morning. She had never slept so long in her life. She stretched, luxuriating in the fine fur and wool blankets wrapping around her bare legs.

Teague turned to her, a smile tugging at his lips. She had thought the room fine before, but it was nothing compared to Teague's face when he smiled. She was glad she was lying down.

He straightened and a warm flush crept up her skin as she noticed scratch marks along the collar of his tunic. Grabbing another tray, he sat on the bed beside her. Instead of any sumptuous fare, this tray contained two cloths, one wet and one dry.

A knowing light gleamed in his eyes. 'You may have need for these.' When he tugged her blanket, she tugged back.

He chuckled. 'I thought we disposed of any modesty after the third time.'

'It's bright in here.' She pointed out the obvious.

'Yes, I know.' Taking the hem, he slowly pulled up the blanket and trailed his fingers along her thigh. In the dim light she could see the contrast between his skin and hers. Though she thought her body replete, desire rippled through her with his touch.

Abruptly, he released the blanket laying halfway up her thigh. Regret was etched in every plane of his face as he lifted one of the linens on the tray. 'I brought you these to soothe you.'

Breathing in shakily, he added, 'I thought myself sated enough to do the task, but I know now I'll never make it. Or if I did, I would be intensely jealous of the linen.' He laughed.

Anwen was caught in that laugh. Something was different about him; he was almost boyish.

A bubbling lightness inside her echoed his. It was as perplexing as his tenderness. But now that she knew what the linens were for, she did welcome those, just not in front of him.

'Turn your head,' she ordered.

Sighing, he went to retrieve the food and she heard the clink of dishes. She was done by the time he returned and he removed the platter with the linens, and replaced it with one laden with cheeses, fruits, cold meats and fresh bread. She was hungry, but since the fire, her stomach continually protested her eating choices. It was a reminder of their baby she carried and that she still needed to tell him.

Instead, she grabbed the bread and tore into it with her teeth.

'You eat like that and you'll not get a chance to finish.' His eyes moved to her lips before he turned his attention to the tray.

As she watched him bite into a honeyed fig, she understood what he meant. It would be so easy to delay what she needed to say, but she had delayed enough. 'I believe you,' she said.

Teague's eyes sharpened. 'What do you believe?'

Anwen took another bite and tried to steady her nerves. 'I came back for you because I believed you. On the ramparts, I was trying to find you, to tell you.'

She breathed, calmed her thoughts. She must take this slower. Have some caution when there were many obstacles between them. 'You are no traitor,' she confessed. 'I knew what Urien was, but I chose to be blind to it. He was, although he did not acknowledge it, my father. He was not family to me, but I hoped I came from some good.'

She blinked back the sting in her eyes. 'But he wasn't good. He was arrogant, selfish and cruel, and because he worsened after Gwalchdu sided with the English, I...attributed his cruelty to you, thought Brynmor suffered because of...you. But I was wrong.'

Teague looked past her shoulder, and released a breath. When he looked at her again, his lips were curved and his obsidian eyes were lit from within. 'What else do you believe?'

He was English. Greedy. It was expected.

He had told her of Urien. Rescued her from the ramparts. He had kept her safe. It was a gift she couldn't repay, but he deserved more words nonetheless. 'That you did not, by intention or by hand, cause Brynmor's fire.'

His brow furrowed. 'But it would not have happened had I not gone to Brynmor.'

She firmly shook her head. 'You couldn't control or know that such a senseless act would be committed. I understand that now you told me of Urien and of Gwalchdu. This place is important to you, you've committed your life to it. Of course you would pursue someone threatening it. You're no traitor to Brynmor...or to me.'

Teague's brow eased. 'Is that all?'

No, there was the child to talk of as well, but she didn't know how to approach that now. After all, what were his feelings for her, or for that matter, hers for him?

A baby required more than understanding. It required love, trust, protection. Could a Marcher Lord, could *Teague*, provide that? After all, Urien, a minor prince had never been able to.

'I was cold and frightened last night,' she began, 'but that wasn't why I came to your bed.'

'And stayed.' Teague's mouth curved again.

She felt her cheeks burn. 'I wouldn't have come if you had not told me of your past.'

It wasn't only his tale of Urien's betrayal, but also of his mother's death in childbirth that called to her. He had suffered much in his childhood.

'I've told you more than I've ever told another soul and yet...' He shook his head and looked away. Began to pace as if he'd been caught in a trap that he hadn't seen.

He wanted more. She should have expected it though she'd given him more than she'd ever given any man before. Not just her body, but something of herself. Despite her past and the way her father treated her and her sister. Maybe her words weren't enough.

'What more do you want?' she said.

'I want your—' He stopped and his eyes searched hers. Looked away as she did when she didn't want him seeing too much.

And he kept his back to her as he poured himself wine, as he took a sip before he turned to her again. In the light, she could not see the emotion in his dark eyes. She was again reminded how this man was both light and darkness.

'I want your trust,' he said.

Trust. He told her so much, but could she truly trust this man or any man of such power? 'I believe you…what you said. It's why I intend to—'

'Good,' he interrupted. 'Then you'll believe me when I say you must go.'

She pulled the blanket up to her chin. 'What?'

He clenched the goblet in his hand. 'The latch to the ramparts was crushed. The enemy you say I have no control over purposefully locked you out on the ramparts. Do you understand?'

A cold rush prickled her skin. Someone had locked her outside and purposefully endangered her life. The enemy who set fire to her home had tried to kill her. She understood all too well.

'Did anyone know you were going?' he asked.

'I think I told Greta.'

'Greta!' Teague frowned. 'She waited on my

mother and Ffion when they were young. I cannot think ill of her. But she should have stopped you from going.'

'I don't think I gave her a chance.' She straightened in the bed. 'Does it have to be anyone we know?'

'I can't dismiss anyone now. It's not just me, or my home. They tried to get to you, which is why you have to leave. I can give you an escort to Edward's court.'

This she didn't understand. 'If this enemy of yours is after me, it won't matter where I am.'

He slammed the goblet on the table. 'I'll not take any chances,' he said. 'When you fell from the tree, when I carried you through Gwalchdu's gates, you became my responsibility. You will go.'

Responsibility. Orders. She didn't like it. She believed he was no traitor, but she was right not to truly trust him. He was still a Marcher Lord and she wouldn't be ruled by him. 'I won't go.'

'Why change your mind now? You said this was a temporary home; that you'd leave come spring. I'm telling you to leave now.'

'But you told me of your past. The reasons for me to leave are no longer there.'

'There's every reason for you to leave.' He walked to the bedside and towered over her, and she saw clearly the grimness of his expression and his determination. 'Everything's changed. Think of the ramparts, the fact you are in danger. You will go. I won't have any weaknesses here!'

Dark. Forbidding. Arrogant. This was the man who strode into her chambers that first day. The one she feared. But she was still no coward.

And she wasn't a weakness. What would he do when he discovered she carried his child? Tie her to a cart and send her off? She wouldn't let him control her. She wouldn't let any man control her. 'Your need to protect me comes from your English need to conquer.'

'No, it comes from trying to keep my future wife safe!'

Anwen's heart skipped. 'Your wife?'

'Yes, in order for you to have my protection at Edward's court, we must marry.'

Marriage. He was demanding, conquering. As his wife she'd be nothing but his property. And poor property at that. 'I'm Welsh!'

'Have you not been listening to me? I don't give a damn that you're Welsh,' he said.

It was said in the tone of voice no one would disobey, but he was the Devil of Gwalchdu and the right hand of the English King. For someone of Teague's position, marriages were for political reasons. 'Your King would,' she pointed out.

Teague frowned at her. 'Edward worries over his wife, who is sick, but he is practical. With the death of Urien and your sister, you are the heir to Brynmor.'

'All that's left of Brynmor is ashes and dirt. And what does that matter since all Welsh land is now English?'

'But the people of Brynmor trust you and they come to you despite their living on Gwalchdu's land. You have influence here. A marriage between us may bring a true peace to this land and not one merely wrought by the sword.'

'So you marry me to bring peace?'

'I marry you to keep you safe!'

Safe. A home. He'd marry her and her child would not be a bastard. But they'd both be ruled under a Marcher Lord's fist.

But no, they wouldn't even be here at all.

'Even married, you'd send me off to Edward's court?'

'Immediately.'

Anwen wrapped the blanket around her, rolled to the other side of the bed. As quickly as she could she collected her clothes and threw them on the covers.

'Where do you think you're going?'

Tugging on her chemise, she retorted, 'I'm dressing. I'm going, isn't that what you wish?'

She had come so close to telling him of the child. She believed his past, but it wasn't enough to fix the present. He was a Marcher Lord. He once kept her prisoner. Now he dictated marriage and would force her to leave. She'd never subject her child to the will of a powerful man.

He tilted his head and studied her. 'Preparations for the wedding will be made today.'

She stabbed her feet into her hose and tied them around her waist. 'You misunderstand me, Lord of Gwalchdu. I'm leaving, but I won't marry you.'

'I will be obeyed in this.'

Pulling her gown over her head, she ignored the fierceness in his voice. 'You won't keep me prisoner this time. You have no authority over me.'

'Do you think that matters? I told you of my past, and what I did to save my home.' His lips twisted sardonically. 'I betrayed kings and countries. I make my own authority.' He walked to the door, opened it. Without looking back, he said, 'If you didn't want my protection, you shouldn't have saved me from the fire.'

Chapter Twenty-One

Anwen could not sleep, could not keep her mind on the tasks before her. A day of thinking on Teague's words, a night of tossing and turning had passed until now.

It was Martinmas, the beginning of winter. Now was the start of the Christmas season. A time of year she enjoyed for the work needing done and the festivities.

She wasn't the only one up this early. Martinmas was always a busy day at Byrnmor and so, too, it was here at Gwalchdu.

Though the sun's light barely covered the land, already the day had begun. It was the end of harvest and livestock needed to be slaughtered and hung in smokehouses. The meat would be preserved to keep them fed throughout winter.

But she didn't want to leave the keep to help with the animals and instead she went to the gardens. As she hoped, Melun was there.

'I see Edith has you busy at your task.' She knelt beside Melun. His eyes were worsening, but he had gained weight and his skin no longer looked sallow.

'Yes, confounded woman has me kneeling here every day. These flowers are taking too long in their training,' he said. 'But I suspect they'll come to hand in spring.'

She smiled. 'With you at their creance I am sure of it.'

Melun smiled. 'I told her so, but she won't leave me alone, though I tell her she's much too busy to waste time on an old man like me.'

Edith was just Melun's age, but they acted like children around each other. She watched him add more eggshells to the dirt. He was more content here than at Brynmor.

Her home was gone now. Yet she knew part of it was planted at Gwalchdu. Her people, the chaos, the flowers. Those were all the parts of her home she wanted. The parts of her home she had thought perhaps she'd be able to keep.

'Can I help?' she asked. 'You'll have to teach me.'

Melun nodded. 'I would always be glad of your help. Ffion has been teaching me.' He pulled some weeds. 'But I don't think you come here merely to help an old man.'

'I wanted you to know, I can't stay here.'

Wherever she went next, she knew some parts of her former life had to go. She'd controlled her life at Brynmor, so that she was needed. So she wouldn't be thrown away like her mother. She never realised how her need changed Alinore and Melun. She never gave courage to Alinore like Robert had done. She never suggested other tasks for Melun to help him gain his pride. He was happy again here because he had a purpose. In her next home, she wouldn't make the same mistake.

Melun stopped and looked around at his plantings. 'It's not Gwalchdu, is it?'

'No, it's Teague. He's demanded I marry him.'

Melun's eyebrows rose. 'Truly?'

She gawked at him. 'Oh, don't look so pleased. He demanded it.'

'I have every right to be pleased.' He chuckled. 'You are my daughter despite you being of Urien's seed and I rejoice to know some love comes back to you.'

'I didn't speak of love. He said it was for peace.'

'And that's why you wish to leave? A man does not marry for peace unless a king has ordered it, and I know King Edward has made no such obligation. Peace. Hah! It's for love.'

Melun beamed contentment. She couldn't change his mind. She certainly wouldn't tell him of the danger and reveal the other reason Teague demanded marriage. If she did, Melun most likely would help Teague tie her to a cart and send her to court.

Melun stuffed leaves and eggshells around a stalk and nodded to the outside bailey. 'If it's his past bothering you, know it cannot be changed. But what I've seen of his future, it seems he's trying.'

Anwen followed Melun's nod until she saw Teague sitting at a table set in the outer courtyard with a queue lined up in front. People chatted as they held ropes tied to horses, cattle, carts of chickens and grain. Some came empty-handed, but she watched Teague treat them all the same.

'There's much more to tell you. Teague is no traitor. He never was.' She told him of what the lord had done in the past and what threatened him now. When she was done, Melun crushed the shells left in his hand.

'I wish I could have killed Urien when I had the strength and eyesight of a peregrine.'

'You were his falconer, not a soldier,' she reasoned.

'I was a man and could see how he abused his daughters. That should have been enough.'

Anwen squeezed his hand. 'You did more than enough. I could not have asked for a better father than you.'

Melun released her hand to hug her. 'Are you

as sure of your feelings about Teague as you are about me?'

She laughed. 'No, for now, my sole certainty is that every morning I'm either starving or sick. Everything else seems to be confusion.' She patted his arm. 'Why do you look strangely at me? I merely jest.'

'Do you?'

She could never hide anything from Melun. 'I'm carrying his child.'

'Ah! So you are closer to him than you let on. I don't think you are confused about your feelings.'

No, she wasn't confused. She might believe his past, but he was still a Marcher Lord and she carried his child.

A baby. Anwen wanted to clench her arms around her stomach to hold it close. As much danger and indecision she was in, she could feel only joy. No matter what happened, she would keep her child safe.

But how to keep it safe? If she married Teague and was sent to Edward's court she'd be safe. But then she'd only be going from one powerful man, to yet another with even more power and control. No, it was best if she just left. She had skills; she could protect her baby.

'This baby is his, but for now, I'm keeping this our secret.'

'I wouldn't wait long. He's requesting to marry you now. Once he knows, he'll demand it.'

And that was her issue. Power. Control. Every trait she fought against with Urien.

'Even with the baby, I can't stay here.'

'Ah.' Melun nodded his head. 'You worry for the child; you worry about what kind of man he is.'

Teague's laughter startled her and she turned to watch. She noticed the different way the villagers looked at him today. Many were reserved, a few still crossed themselves, but there were more who talked to him. As if they could sense the change in him as she did since the fire.

Teague...changing. Opening his home and his coffers to her people. Would Urien have ever done such a thing? Was Teague like Urien?

Teague gave of himself, gave to King Edward his unswerving loyalty and gave help to her people. Gwalchdu's lord wasn't all darkness; there was light in him, too.

He could be fair, but there was something more. Hadn't he said he wanted to marry her, to send her away to keep her safe? Hadn't he told her to stay away from the fire? Perhaps his orders, his demands, came not from selfishness, like Urien's, but from the need to protect.

'Yes.' She did worry about what kind of man he was. But she also worried about the enemy.

Melun tucked her hair behind her ear as he used to do when she was a child and something rested just a little inside her heart. 'You're stronger than you think and so is he.'

Anwen spread her fingers wide over her stomach, willing the life inside her to feel none of her fear.

It seemed not only did Teague need to find the enemy, but if he was right about the fire, about her being trapped on the ramparts, it seemed so did she. The enemy was after her, as well. It was right for her to leave. It wasn't safe here for her baby.

Her life was immeasurably tangled with Teague's. She didn't know how the enemy knew it, but it was why she feared—

Anwen closed her eyes. Fear. She was no coward, but she'd been acting like one. Not telling Teague of the baby was a cowardly act. He deserved to know regardless of who he was and what power he held. Melun was right. Teague was trying to change. By not telling him, she wasn't giving him a chance to do what was right.

As for this enemy, when had anyone driven her away before? Even Urien's fists hadn't forced her to leave Brynmor. And the heart of Brynmor was here. Knowing the truth of the past, there was no reason to leave. She wanted to make her home among Brynmor's people and Melun. If Teague wanted to acknowledge the child or not, she would have some family. More than anything, she wanted her baby to know it was loved. She could only have that here and she wouldn't let anyone take that away from her.

Especially Teague. She knew he wanted her to leave to keep her safe. He was acting as he always did. He wasn't a traitor, or a devil, or a foe. He was a man, who for too many years stood alone. But no more. Enemy or none, he had caught her and he'd have to keep her.

She was strong enough to take his protection, but also to return it. She had saved him from the fire and she'd keep saving him. She wouldn't abandon him when he needed her the most.

He was used to controlling matters around him, but she realised now that she was used to controlling her life, as well. She wanted what was here. All of it. Gwalchdu and Teague. It was almost as if she—

'Weak! Useless!' Ffion cried, walking unsteadily into the gardens. 'Sacrilege!'

Anwen rushed to her side immediately. 'What has happened?'

'He's done it again! The Marcher Lord has let those peasants flaunt their ignorance! Only God can keep us safe and how is God to help us, if the Lord of Gwalchdu can't honour Him? See there!'

Ffion pointed to the outside bailey. In the queue several villagers waited to pay their tithes. Many of them carried a Mari Lwyd for the festivities later on.

'Those are to honour Mary on the donkey as she travels to Bethlehem,' Ffion spat. 'Those aren't to come out now with the slaughter of animals and no doubt drunkenness. It's sacrilege!'

'Peace, Sister,' Melun began. 'That's just a harmless horse skull with a bit of linen for the wassailing parade—'

'Harmless! What do you know of harmless or safe? You'll know soon enough. You'll know the harm here and so will he. He'll know what has happened here and he will pay. He will—'

'Ffion, please.' Anwen laid her hand on Ffion. It was then she noticed the hem of her gown and sleeves were streaked with blood. 'Sister, there's blood—'

The Sister swung her arm away. 'Do not touch me! You know what sacrifices have to be made on this sacred day!'

Of course, on Martinmas day they prepared the animals for winter. Still Anwen's heart didn't ease.

Ffion's eyes gleamed then. 'But you know nothing of sacredness, do you? You think you were alone in this garden? Hmm? I know what grows in your belly. I heard you. I've been watching you. Haven't been eating, have you, and all that sickness that you've been covering up? You lay with him and now God will forsake us all since we have forsaken Him!'

Anwen's mouth went dry. Ffion had been listening to her conversation and her fervency was spiralling. Teague and Rhain were animatedly talking to several villagers. They could not be disturbed.

She wouldn't leave Ffion pale and hurting like this, though. She'd seen what happened at Byrnmor and could take care of her.

'Should we go to your room?' Anwen said.

'Or perhaps we should find Greta,' Melun suggested.

'No!' Ffion gripped her wrist, her nails sunk in. 'I'll be fine. Take me into the keep, to the chapel. It is the light. There's too much light here.'

Teague was uneasy. It had been hours since he last saw Anwen. It had been a good day, a profitable day in more ways than not. Even in spite of Anwen ignoring him and rejecting his offer.

He would make her see reason. If he had to imprison her until she agreed, it would be done. He didn't care.

No, he did…too much.

An enemy who destroyed her home and killed her family was now after her. He must keep her safe.

Glancing around the courtyard for that bright golden hair, he adjusted the sword at his side.

It had been foolish to tell her of his past. His reasoning was weak, circuitous. He had severed the connection between them until she felt only animosity for him and the enemy had no need to make her a target. But because he opened up to her, she had tried to find him. And it had almost killed her.

Teague rubbed his chin. He hadn't been thinking when he'd told her. Couldn't think when faced with her animosity. Not when she told him she was leaving because she could never trust him. It hadn't sat well with him. He had *wanted* her to know the truth.

Another weakness. He had too many when it came to her. Hope. Desire. Loyalty. Trust. But he couldn't love her. Love had weakened his mother and ultimately caused her death. No, with an enemy after Anwen, he would not dare to love.

'Have you seen Anwen?' Teague turned to his brother.

Rhain shook his head. 'I haven't seen her since she took Ffion from the gardens and into the keep.'

'Ffion?'

His brother nodded. 'She didn't look well, but she was walking, so maybe it was an upset rather than an episode.'

The queue was dying down now that people were eating and drinking. There was work to do still, but maybe it could be delayed. 'I will check on them,' Teague said, standing.

Rhain stood, as well. 'If you go, so will I. If Ffion has worsened, it would be better if I'm there, as well.'

Teague nodded, already walking to the great doors. He wanted Anwen to himself, but Ffion would want Rhain.

Blood. Everywhere. It was dripping from the draperies adorning the bedposts; slithering down the walls; pooling on the stone floor.

'It's not hers.' Rhain stood just behind him in the doorframe. 'It's not hers. Teague, do you understand? Look—there in the corner are buckets from the slaughtering. It's the animals' blood.'

Teague couldn't move. His heart and breath had completely left him. A search for Ffion and Anwen in Ffion's rooms had led them to Anwen's chamber.

It was saturated with blood. He stepped inside the room as his brother followed. 'Close the door,' he ordered.

'Shouldn't we search the grounds to find Anwen?' Rhain said.

'She's with Ffion and safe. The blood is fresh; we end this now.'

He stepped through his mother's…no, Anwen's room. It was like some macabre nightmare. His nightmare with cryptic blood-drenched words written on the wall just for him.

'I will kill him,' Teague said, his words no more than the truth.

Rhain carefully stepped over a blanket on the floor. 'I'm for finding him first. There doesn't appear to be a forced entry.'

Teague brushed the tapestries aside. He didn't care how rough he was with them. Everything in the room was ruined. The bed, the walls and the tapestries were stained with blood.

Teague pointed his sword towards the wall directly across the room from the bed where Anwen slept. Rage coursed fresh through his body and he thrust a killing stroke in the air before lowering his sword. The blood on that wall was not splattered clumps, but neat concise red slashes: a message in blood.

Wronged blood covers wrong blood. Child first.

There were significant differences in this message. The previous messages had been threats against him; they had never threatened others. This one wasn't vague, it was cryptic and it was written in blood.

'Who is writing these?' Teague seethed.

Rhain crossed his arms. 'I am unclear as to

what covers wronged blood. All I could see was it covered the walls of Anwen's room.'

Teague's world shifted and he turned to his brother, a man who shared his blood, but not his resemblance. Even their mannerisms and temperament were different, but he never doubted their bond. Teague had been there the day his mother died giving birth to Rhain.

'That wall was not only Anwen's wall, but Gwalchdu's wall.' Teague's voice grew urgent as the idea took hold. 'When was the last time you visited the chapel's books?'

Rhain merely lifted an eyebrow. 'There was no need to spend my time reading them when Ffion has them so well memorised.'

'No, I do not mean God's book. I meant the chapel's logs, our family's history?'

Rhain's shrugged. 'Never. I have only been interested in making my own history.'

'The message mentions blood and blood could also be interpreted as blood *lines*. We cannot find the enemy outside Gwalchdu, so perhaps the enemy is within. There may be some meaning in our family books. This may have something to do with my past.'

Fingering his dagger, Rhain lowered his voice. 'He's a fool thinking to turn back time. Wales is ruled by England now.'

Remembering Anwen's story, Teague knew

how the past affected the present. 'But it hasn't sat well with everyone. It might be speculation; they may be simply mouldy books.'

'Maybe, but something nags at me. Like a sword about to sweep behind me.' Rhain shook his head. 'The animals must be the wronged blood, but how are they wronged?'

It was a clue, but it was also a warning.

Teague's breath froze in his lungs. A warning is for those who can heed it. Those who are alive.

Blood. Child. Bloodlines.

Teague felt his sword slip in his hands before he gripped it tight. 'When you saw Ffion, how close were you?'

'I was talking to Peter, but close enough to see the worry in Anwen's eyes.'

'And Ffion's?'

Rhain shrugged. 'They appeared focused, but they did shift.'

Teague's gut wrenched. 'Yes, like a liar's. How long ago did they leave the garden? An hour? Two?'

Rhain turned, concern etched on his face. 'What is the matter?'

'It's Ffion. All this time. We dined with the enemy.'

Rhain shook his head. 'Ffion. What are you saying?'

What was he saying? Blood pooling around his

feet. Fresh blood. 'This is our blood. Our blood-lines, but this isn't about history. This is about what is happening now.'

'Where are you going?'

Teague had already opened the door, his shoes marking the floor with every step he took. He'd been betrayed. Again, but by his mother's sister. The agony arced through him. 'Do you think I want to say this? She is family, but she is the enemy. She knows how important Anwen is to me. I cannot conceive anything else.'

'I won't believe it. Even so, what do you want me to do?'

'Go to the rooms in the outside chapel and bring men with you. If they are there, send someone to get me. I'll search the private chapel in the far tower.'

'Alone?'

Running, Teague snarled, 'She's got Anwen!'

Chapter Twenty-Two

Teague bounded up the stairs to the private chapel at the top of the tower. The door was unlocked and it slammed against stone as he shoved it open.

Ffion knelt before the small altar. Her back was to him and she made not a sound or movement to acknowledge his arrival.

Standing to his left, and close to Ffion, Anwen turned to him. Her eyes were wide with terror, with…relief? No…regret. She deliberately shook her head and slowly gestured for him to remain still.

He took in the totality of the scene before him. The afternoon sunlight scattered rays of light through the room and reflected the scene in all its horror. It was laid like a nightmare before him.

'So you have come to the rescue.' Ffion slowly removed her headdress. 'How predictable.'

Teague could do nothing but watch. Ffion knelt at the altar. Her back was to him, her black habit and headdress falling to the floor like a sweep of unbound hair. It was so like the memory of that fateful day from his childhood and now, as then, he stood helpless.

He glanced at Anwen. She was trembling, but there was fire in her eyes. His past and future lay before him in this room and he knew he would change the course of history this time.

Ffion swept away her headdress, stood and turned. Her shorn blonde hair was in contrast to the black she wore.

'What do you do with that blade, Ffion?'

'You do not ask what I do with the poison.' Ffion pushed up her sleeves so a vial, bound to her wrist, swung hypnotically. 'Your whore noticed it.'

Ffion pursed her lips. 'Of course, I had to make her notice it. She insisted on obtaining help. I threw a blade; you can see it embedded in the door behind you. But it was no deterrent to keeping her in the room. Foolish child to not fear a dagger... but she did fear the poison.'

Anwen was in the middle of the room, too far away to get to, but not too far from Ffion to be safe if she threw another blade. Anwen was trapped and so was he.

'I never thought you patient enough to hear what needs to be said.' Ffion smiled, her eyes like madness gleaming around control. 'She was not so patient.' Ffion skimmed the blade along the vial to keep it swinging. 'No, the only reason she stayed, and stayed quiet, too, is because I told her *I'd* drink this poison if she left.'

Teague clenched his sword at the hours of terror Anwen suffered before he got here. And she couldn't even cry out?

'I had to do it or she wouldn't stay.' Ffion shrugged. 'If she left the room, you wouldn't come here to hear my tale. And it's time for you to hear it because my illness is worsening and I want things in order before I go.'

This was his aunt, his family, yet she was a stranger. Was it her sickness? She'd changed since his childhood, becoming more crazed with control. With her hatred of him. 'Ffion, it isn't Anwen you want. It's always been me. Let her go.'

'I wasn't merely holding her here for you. She has her purpose, too.'

He wanted Anwen safe. 'She serves no purpose.'

'Of course she does. For you to worry. To feel out of control. You must realise I could have killed her at any moment. I may still.'

He had no blades to throw. Anwen was too far away to protect. Still his hand tightened on his sword. His training, his fear, demanded he do something.

'If you take one step towards me—' Ffion enunciated each word '—the blade I hold will swiftly end her life. You are not quick enough.'

A brutal fact. He could do nothing. Nothing, as Ffion perched on the high-backed chair underneath the window behind her. He watched the light from the window envelop his aunt briefly before she emerged again, sitting regally in her scarlet-streaked robe. 'You are right, it has always been you.'

'Then let her go,' he said. 'Let me help you.'

'Help me?' Ffion's eyes darted to the vial.

Poison in his aunt's fragile hands. Had she had an episode before this? Perhaps she was disoriented or maddened temporarily. In the past any help he offered made her angrier, but nonetheless he tried. 'It is your illness that is making you this way. Do not do this.'

'Do not talk to me of my illness!' A blade quick, unseen, but heard, skimmed past his ear and hit the wall behind him. Another was quickly in her hand. 'I know my sickness worsens. I know I must end it, but only after you know the truth.'

Then he understood. She had always intended to take the poison. It was about control. Order. Something he cloaked himself in, something his aunt had been hiding behind. Both of them suffocating. He understood that now. Anwen had given him hope. His aunt still had a chance.

'Put down the blade and the vial. God would never allow this.'

'God?' She waved her hand and the knife

glinted in the light. 'You speak to me of God? I know Him as much as I know my illness. He gave it to me; He gave me my gift, as well. I know what you do not. He has left me. Your whore is testament to that.'

He didn't dare look at Anwen. As long as he talked to Ffion, her attention was on him. 'Then tell me,' he bit out. 'Tell me this truth.'

'I loved my sister,' Ffion said. 'Love, like only the most pious person experiences. In our childhood, she saved my life many times.'

'Because of your illness,' he said, as if his heart wasn't hammering.

Ffion nodded. 'I was older when the episodes started. There weren't many at first. They would come about if there was a sudden jarring sound or someone suddenly opened shutters to let the sunlight in. If I became upset, it worsened. Elin was the only person there when it first happened. So we conspired to hide it.'

'At the time, we had a healer and Elin thought we could study under her to find a cure. Obviously that was Elin's idea. I humoured her, but knew it wasn't possible to end my affliction. Yet, I could study to protect myself. I learned how herbs harm people and I learned to throw these blades.

'By the time I turned fifteen, I could kill anyone with a blade or by a crushed flower, but I couldn't control what was happening to me. Elin was almost past marriageable age and no Welsh-man asked for her hand. I blamed myself and even more so when she was forced to marry an English bastard.'

All these years and he hadn't known. His mother and aunt had been close, but now he could see their kinship for what it was. How Elin suf-fered for her sister; how she might have feared her.

'Elin said she loved William. I sought answers at God's altar, but all I could think of was that En-glish bastard using her body for his lust. I made a plan and it included you, Gwalchdu's lord.'

'What did you do to Teague's father?' Anwen asked.

Ffion threw a blade that sliced the air near An-wen's head. 'You should keep your whore quiet.'

Teague wanted to fling his sword at his aunt. Anwen was now crying; her tears flowing un-checked, but there was fire in her eyes. This wasn't fear, he knew, but anger at her helplessness. It was costing her to be quiet and do nothing. It was cost-ing him not to protect her from Ffion. His aunt, who murdered his father.

So many years had passed, and yet he could re-member that day. Remember the discordant whis-pers of Ffion and his mother. Anwen did not know the story of his past, and yet did she guess this?

'You killed him,' he said.

Ffion waved her hand, flashing another blade. 'Elin was mine; no one could love her like I did and so I convinced her he could not be faithful. When he left to meet with Lleweyln, I gave him a potion. It was easy enough, but with his size it took too long. That's the reason he died in the forest and not at home.' She pursed her lips. 'Dead is dead, of course, and Elin never knew the truth.'

So his father had loved his mother and it had been Ffion who betrayed them. Ffion, who he kept fed, clothed and sheltered. Ffion, who hated him.

'Why?'

Ffion smiled as if savouring his question. 'I was pregnant at the same time as your mother.'

Anwen visibly started at the news. Teague couldn't move at all. Ffion pregnant? How had no one known?

'That day I killed your father I alone attended Elin at her childbirth. She was my sister, my love. I did not want our time together to be polluted by intruders and barred everyone from the room. But the birth took too long and her life was seeping away.'

'Her baby was still. Dead. By God or gift, I began my own labours. I silently welcomed the pain. Elin had suffered worse; her labour was so much longer. She never knew of mine because she was overtaken with her pain.'

'She looked like an angel when I placed my baby in her arms. By giving her Rhain at that moment, I was repaying a lifetime of her loyalty to me.' Ffion's smile changed, softened. 'When the servants came, I wrapped her dead babe in the bloodied blankets and disposed of the body.'

Teague reeled. All these years, he was right. Ffion had given peace to his mother, had made those last moments full of love. He had protected her from the Church, from Gwalchdu's villagers because of that. Yet...he never knew the truth. She was always fervently preaching against adultery, but then, maybe that made sense now. Ffion closed her eyes, eyes that were as amber as Rhain's. She was Rhain's mother and he had never seen it. Rhain was his *cousin.*

'Didn't you ever wonder about who named him?' Ffion's smile remained the same; this was a secret gift she was proud of and she had a son that made her prouder yet. 'Such a strong name, and of course I had to have some acknowledgement to my abilities.'

He'd been blind to the truth. Many great Welsh rulers were named Rhain, which meant 'spear'. It was a name that matched his aunt's ambitions.

'Tell me the rest of this story,' Teague commanded. He would not have her die on him.

'You were born, impure, from an English bastard, who gave you his family's name.' Ffion trailed the blade along the vial again. 'Made it so easy to fit in with the English King, didn't it?'

'Is that why you threatened me?'

'Your betrayal to Wales didn't surprise me. No, I simply hated your companionship with my son. Rhain was my gift to Elin. Not you. You treat him like a brother, a second-born, when, had the truth been revealed, he would be superior to you. His blood is pure and he was given from the heart. My heart.'

'Who is his father?'

'You ask this?' Ffion pursed her lips. 'Ah! That knowledge is not for you, but my son… Although, I did not wish for him to see me like this.' Her eyes darted to the vial before their amber gaze held his again. 'I'll give you a hint, though it matters not. He is gone now, as he should be. But that, too, was because of you. You, who never deserved Rhain.'

'That's not enough to tell me.'

'I just told you as much as I ever will now that she's arrived.' Ffion pointed the blade at Anwen.

'I could no longer just kill you, but her and the babe she carries.' Ffion smiled. 'Ah, yes, warrior, she breeds. She has not told you? It was not my intention to kill Gwalchdu's children, but *your* child.'

Ffion's pale skin did nothing to hide the increasing feverishness in her eyes. She tapped the blade to the vial now as if counting out the time. She intended to take that poison soon. It would end this nightmare for him and Anwen, but he couldn't have her do it. Even after everything, he couldn't.

'Ffion, you're hurting. Let Anwen go. Let her get Rhain for you. Let her—'

All three of them jumped as the door banged behind them. It was the distraction Teague needed. Launching across the room, he slammed Anwen against the wall, using his body as a shield.

Rhain raced through the door.

'My son.' Ffion tilted the vial's poisonous contents to her lips.

Rhain skidded to her side, but the poison was already taking effect. Her body now slumped in the high-backed chair.

'Who was my father?' Rhain demanded, his harsh breaths mixing with Ffion's much shallower ones. Whatever she had taken was hitting her fast and her limbs were already convulsing.

Still she must have sensed the force behind the question for she struggled to lay her hand on Rhain's cheek. 'Your father is—' Her eyes closed; her breathing became laboured. 'East... It hurts.' She laid her hand to her chest. 'Use my necklace...'

But she could convey no more. Ffion, Sister of Gwalchdu, was dead.

Chapter Twenty-Three

In the enclosure of Teague's arms, Anwen watched Rhain slowly cover Ffion with her black robes. When he stood and turned, an invisible mantle had spread across his face, hardening his golden features.

Teague spoke first. 'I couldn't find a way to stop her. If I could, for your sake—'

'No, brother.' Rhain shook his head. 'Cousin,' he corrected.

'You *knew*.'

'I was running to the chapel when Melun and Greta came out of the tower and took me to Ffion's rooms. I don't think I've ever seen her move that fast. There were papers hidden in her chest.'

'None of us knew.' Teague moved to step forward, but stopped as Rhain lifted his hand.

The two men could not be more different in colouring or temperament. Now, Anwen could see another difference. Ffion's story had eased something within Teague, but for Rhain, grief was setting in.

She squeezed Teague's arm until he looked down at her. For her, her fear and grief were changing, but into no less of a worry. So much pain was in this room.

Teague's eyes softened, and he squeezed her hand. Turning to Rhain he said, 'We'll leave you, but only for now. Understand this, you are, and will always be, my brother.'

Rhain's eyes shone with a fractured light.

Teague nodded once, then he swept her up in his arms as if he knew she was suddenly exhausted, her legs too tired to hold her up.

The room was dimly lit by a fire when Anwen awoke, but she knew she was not alone. It wasn't only the smell of sandalwood and leather, or the heat from his obsidian eyes, it was her hand cradled in Teague's.

'I fell asleep?' she asked.

'I brought you back and sat you on my bed. I left your side to open the door and order wine. When I turned around, you were already lying down with your eyes closed. I couldn't disturb you.'

She sat up. 'But I slept for hours. I wanted to—'

'You slept a day,' he interrupted. 'This is the next night.' He stood from the chair by her bed and poured wine and tore some bread. She accepted both, then stared at the bounty suddenly in her lap.

'Ffion?' she asked.

'She's gone.'

Anwen knew Ffion would be, still she must have hoped because her heart stabbed again. With every horror rushing to her memory, she handed the wine and bread back to him. 'I need to—' She nodded her head in the direction of the garderobe.

'Of course.' He stepped back.

When she returned, Teague was crouched before the hearth, the flickering light casting him in light and darkness. He looked so grave, so…alone.

'Will you forgive me?' He stabbed at the fresh logs to increase the flames. 'Upstairs, when I hurt you. I didn't think—'

'You didn't hurt me.' She didn't need to see this proud, brave man apologise. Did he think he failed her? How could he, when she was now realising it was her who failed him. 'Not once. Just feeling your arms around me was a shield from that room.'

That room. Ffion. Everything was like a nightmare she couldn't wake from. Walking to the bed, she grabbed some wine and bread, if only to hold something, and sat down.

'I had to tell the household,' he said, his voice hoarse. 'There were questions almost too difficult to answer. You probably have questions, too.'

Many, but those weren't what she wanted to talk of now. She hadn't started this nightmare, but how she handled the end was her fault. She should have waited for Greta's help. 'I'm sorry.'

He nodded his head at her words. 'I tried to talk to Rhain. To make him realise he is family. With your understanding—'

'No, Teague, that's not what I meant. Will you forgive me?'

She'd been trapped in that room, but how Ffion ended her life was entirely her fault. If she hadn't just taken control perhaps she could have seen the warning signs.

He considered her then, reading correctly what she tried to portray in her eyes. 'Don't. I must believe Ffion was lost long before you arrived. If you have even an inkling of guilt, how could I not? I, who had spent years with her?'

So she made it worse by saying something at all.

'I have not told you of the day my mother died. The facts, as I believed them all my life, have changed since Ffion's confession.' Teague stood and poked the fire as if felling enemies before he set the iron rod against the fireplace. 'I still cannot comprehend everything she said. My entire life was rewritten yesterday. But everything that happened since my mother's death had shaped me. Shaped how I have been with you. You know most of the facts, but there is more I want you to understand now.'

Anwen wanted to apologise again, but something in Teague's words stopped her. It wasn't the change of subject, it was the way he didn't face her. The way he stared into the fire so she couldn't see the desolation in his eyes, but she heard it in his voice.

'I was but five when my father left. What no one knows was I'd overheard my mother and Ffion argue. I believed, as did my pregnant mother, that he had left for another woman.'

Teague spread his hands closer to the fire, but he didn't feel the increase of the warmth, he only remembered that day. 'The shock of my father leaving caused my mother to give birth early. She knelt before me bleeding and she needed help. Except the Hall was unnaturally empty and the nearest I could find anyone was in the kitchens.'

He remembered the hard thumping of his heart as his legs struck the packed dirt. 'In the kitchens, there was freshly baked bread with jam that I had been eating just moments before.

'The bread, with the sweet berry jam, appeared out of place…wrong somehow. Things had no right to be the same. I started throwing whatever I could grab: potatoes, bread and pots just out of the fire. It was Greta who stopped me. I remember staring at her stained apron as she stood in front of me, as though she was willing me to understand and I did eventually. She had found help.

'When I returned to my mother, the blood had soaked into her skirts, streaking up into the fabric. I clutched her hand, but she was in so much pain she didn't know I was there.'

He lowered his hands, flexed his fingers and wished he had rocks to throw. Anything to keep his body moving, so he could distance himself from the memories.

'The guards and Ffion came to take her to her room. I followed, trying to recapture her dangling hand, but I never could. She needed me, but they closed the door on me. I was Gwalchdu's lord then, but I was not allowed into the birthing chamber.

'With guards at my side, I sat on the outside of that thick wooden door, and stared at my burned and blistering hands. I listened as the muffled sounds became shrieks and then screams. Screams that eventually stopped. Died, just as she did.'

He turned around. Anwen sat on his bed, clutching a goblet of wine in her lap. 'Until I discovered the truth yesterday, I knew only betrayal. My father left my mother. My aunt ignored me after her sister died. Urien tricked me with his schemes.'

Teague walked to the table and poured some wine to drink deeply.

'I have been alone a long time. I wanted nothing but this piece of rock that could not betray. So when the time came, I sent my brother away. Not wanting any reminder, I even replaced those blood-soaked stones.'

Too many emotions shone in her wide blue eyes, but she held still, listened, and he felt his hope grow. 'Until I found you in the forest, I didn't think myself capable of trust. But it is what happened. Piece by piece. I didn't want you, but couldn't stay away, and every moment I was with you, I was learning how to trust.'

Her mouth curved. 'You hardly trusted me even when I was bandaged in your bed.'

It was true. He clasped his goblet between both hands and tilted it back and forth. 'But there was something…necessary about you. Something that compelled me to help despite my past and the threats plaguing me now. It was your loyalty. To Alinore, to Melun, to Wales. Stubborn, determined, you climbed a tree, risked your life because of your devotion to the old falconer.' Teague looked deep into the goblet. 'Then…you came back for me.'

'The fire? You would have died otherwise.'

He raised a brow and set his cup aside. 'Wouldn't that have been to your advantage?'

He'd known Anwen was fearless, loyal, but though he fought his hope, he never truly believed she'd offer any such loyalty to him. Especially not when he didn't deserve it. He had never treated her fairly and yet she had not betrayed him.

'If I hadn't rescued you, where would I live?'

He heard the teasing in her voice; he also heard something else, some awareness of the importance of her actions. His hope clung to that awareness. 'You didn't have to; I didn't expect you to.'

No, he hadn't.

Anwen's hands shook and she spilled some wine. She watched the stain expand across her leg like blood and she took a shuddery breath. Her heart was breaking for Teague. How alone he must have been until Rhain returned. She realised now why Rhain remained flippant despite all the threats. He was trying to give Teague laughter, but it wasn't enough. Teague needed love.

After his mother's death, and then Urien's betrayal, Teague shut himself away and depended solely on himself. When he'd gone to Brynmor to search for an enemy, he acted as he had his entire life. As a man who fought the world on his own.

But he wasn't on his own any more.

'I could never have left you there,' she said. 'Not after that day I jumped towards you in the forest.'

'That was a very long time ago.'

A lifetime ago. 'But I trusted you even then.' She had to get the words out; she had to tell him. She didn't, *wouldn't*, waste another moment. 'But trusting that quickly scared me. Since I knew who you were, I fought it. My entire life I blamed you for what happened at Brynmor. My feelings didn't make sense.'

Setting the cup aside, she clenched her trembling hands together. 'I hadn't considered the sacrifices you made. I may have believed you when you told me your past, said that you are not a traitor, but I couldn't stop comparing you to Urien. But his cruelty had nothing to do with his power. It was just…him.

'I know now you had no power over your past. I know that even if you did, you wouldn't have wielded that power like my father did. I didn't think of you as a person, as a man, but I can think of you as nothing else now.'

Her eyes welled with tears and she brushed them away. 'All this wealth, power, even this rock, could crumble as long as you held me. I was right to trust you so quickly. I was wrong not to believe in it. But Ffion showed me what happens when there is no trust—'

'That you ever beheld such horror,' Teague interrupted, 'that I can't take it away. The debt that I now owe you, I don't think I could ever repay.'

She shook her head. 'No more debts; no more feeling like we owe each other. You paid it with your past and maybe, I hope, I have done the same.'

She waved her hand between them. 'You and I are not so different. We have both put our respective worlds on our shoulders. I turned my hatred to you for making Brynmor vulnerable. But some of our misunderstanding is my responsibility. I may not like power or control, but I wielded it, as well. I was bastard-born and didn't have a rightful place. So I ensured I was needed and took control. I didn't help Melun find new tasks to fulfil him; I just took his away. With Alinore, I didn't help her find her courage the way Robert did.'

She wiped again at her tears. 'So stubborn, so desperate to be needed, I never relinquished any control.'

She shifted, tucking her feet under her and grabbing a pillow to clench in her lap. 'I walked into the private chapel thinking to help, to control Ffion, but suddenly her hands tightened on my wrists like iron maces. I knew then I couldn't control what was to happen to me.

'Then you came for me.' Anwen gave a ghost of a smile.

Teague took a step towards her, his eyes never leaving hers. 'Say it,' he commanded.

Always too stubborn, too proud, she had never surrendered herself to anyone, until Teague. She'd surrendered. Fallen. Right into his arms.

'I love you, Teague of Gwalchdu.'

He took the remaining steps towards her and

crouched at her feet. 'I never knew how much I wanted to hear those words until you. I never knew how much I wanted to say them until now.'

'Teague?'

'Yes, my love. I love you. Even before Ffion's confession, I knew I loved you.' It was his turn to smile, taking her hands and kissing them. 'You're necessary, remember? I was a fool not to tell you before.'

He rubbed his thumbs along her hands and she felt every roughened callus, every tender emotion in each caress. 'It wasn't only your loyalty that captured me. You took my heart when you came back for me in the fire. I didn't know what you had done. It was why I couldn't refuse you that night. I felt how alone you were. Already I cared too deeply.'

She thought of the night of the fire, how she sought comfort from him, how he gave it. 'I'm sorry, about Alinore, about my words,' she said.

He squeezed her hands. 'No, I deserved them. Deserved your reservation, as well. I hadn't fully trusted my feelings. I ignored the knowledge that what I felt was stronger than loyalty.

'But I couldn't deny it was love when I swung the axe to release you from the storm. You were barred from me, just as my mother had been. Everything I had been holding back splintered through me just like that door.'

Teague bowed his head and looked at their hands, so she squeezed his and saw the gentle curve to his lips before he looked back up.

'Can you imagine the demons I fought when you were outside in the storm?' he said. 'I was terrified of what I'd find on the other side of the door. When you jumped into my arms and wrapped around me I felt I didn't have any skin to protect my soul. I was raw, left open. At that point, it wasn't my body you clutched, but my heart.'

Her heart hurt with joy, and she squeezed his hands even tighter. His lips curved even more.

'There was a part of me that still believed...' he said, brushing his thumbs along her fingers. 'I thought love weakened my mother and she died. There was still an enemy to fight so I denied any love. How could I be weak, when I needed to protect my home, protect you? It's why I ordered you away. It's why I tried to stay away from you. When I saw you trapped in the chapel, I realised love was strengthening me. I could not have faced Ffion's confession without you by my side.'

Untangling a hand, she pressed it to her stomach. 'We will always be by your side.'

'It's true? Another hope of mine I hadn't dared believe true.' He placed his hand over hers. 'So you'll stay and marry me now.'

It was a statement, a command, and one she

understood. 'Yes.' She laughed. 'And you call me stubborn.'

Teague rested his head against the pillow in her lap. She ran her fingers through his dark locks, feeling fiercely protective of this man who gave her so much.

'It's not over,' he said. 'I explained Ffion's death so that she will be buried in consecrated ground. She was mad, but I'll not put her soul in hell.'

Anwen brushed his hair. 'Your mother and Rhain would like that.'

He turned his head. 'My brother...'

His anguished voice twisted her heart.

'In a sense he has lost his mother twice and now he thinks his brother, too.'

'He hasn't lost me,' he said fiercely.

'But he hasn't fully comprehended that. I suspect he'll seek his own answers now.'

'You talk of how your world changed when I told you of Urien's past deeds; now I feel my world is upside down.' Teague half-laughed, but there was grief behind the sound.

'There was only one other time of my life that I was helpless,' he said. 'I vowed then I'd never feel that way again. But I broke that vow so many times since I first saw you in that tree. I swear I haven't felt anything but helpless since.'

'You are not helpless, nor alone in this.'

'At what cost will Rhain pay for his answers?'

Here was a lesson she had learned: to let others find their own strength. 'That is not for you to decide. The responsibility is his own, not yours. It is time for you to let go.'

Teague sat up to face her. Gently, he cradled her temple in his large hand, his thumb tracing the scar. 'There have been so many times I could have lost you. I may keep you locked in this room for our lifetimes.'

'Only if I let you.' Anwen pressed her hand to his lips. 'I want no more thoughts that we can control everything and everyone around us. I want no more debts we feel we have to pay. I want only love and trust.'

Teague slowly kissed her hand before clasping it in both of his. 'And hope, like you've given me since that day in the forest.'

'Hope?'

'Hope and trust and love. When you fell from that tree, I didn't catch you for nothing. I want it all.'

She gave him a mock frown. 'You're showing that interminable English greed again.'

'Yes, I'm showing greed and you the stubborn Welsh heart.'

He pulled her in for a kiss that she willingly gave. Oh, she wanted this, wanted this man, wanted their life together. When he shuddered, she felt her own body shiver in response. When Teague pulled away, she gave a sound of protest.

'Soon,' he whispered against her lips. 'Every time we are together there is some danger. I want it to be only us.'

There was only them. Everything wasn't resolved, but they were here, together, their love encompassing them, and it was so very good. They had paid their debts and now she wanted the rewards.

'Now.' She twined her hands behind his nape and pulled his lips back to hers.

Drawing her closer until his heart pressed to hers, he answered, 'How could I refuse?'

* * * * *

If you enjoyed this story, you won't want to miss these other great reads in Nicole Locke's
LOVERS AND LEGENDS *mini-series:*

THE KNIGHT'S BROKEN PROMISE
HER ENEMY HIGHLANDER
THE HIGHLAND LAIRD'S BRIDE

MILLS & BOON®

&HISTORICAL

AWAKEN THE ROMANCE OF THE PAST

MILLS & BOON®

EXCLUSIVE EXTRACT

Wealthy gentleman Benjamin Lovell has his
eyes on the prize of the season. First, though, he
must contend with her fiercely protective sister,
Lady Amelia Summoner!

Read on for a sneak preview of
THE WEDDING GAME
by Christine Merrill

'I merely think that you are ordinary. My sister will
require the extraordinary.'

The last word touched him like a finger drawn down
his spine. His mind argued that she was right. There was
nothing the least bit exceptional about him. If she learned
the truth, she would think him common as muck and
far beneath her notice. But then, he remembered just
how far a man could rise with diligence and the help of
a beautiful woman. He leaned in to her, offering his
most seductive smile. 'Then I shall simply have to be
extraordinary for you.'

For Arabella.

That was what he had meant to say. He was supposed
to be winning the princess, not flirting with the gate-
keeper. But he had looked into those eyes again and had
lost his way.

She showed no sign of noticing his mistake. Or had
her cheeks gone pink? It was not much of a blush, just

the barest hint of colour to imply that she might wish him to be as wonderful as he claimed.

In turn, he felt a growing need to impress her, to see the glow kindle into warm approval. Would her eyes soften when she smiled, or would they sparkle? And what would they do if he kissed her?

He blinked. It did not matter. His words had been a simple mistake and such thoughts were an even bigger one. They had not been discussing her at all. And now her dog was tugging on his trousers again, as if to remind him that he should not, even for an instant, forget the prize he had fixed his sights on from the first.

She shook her head, as if she, too, needed to remember the object of the conversation. 'If you must try to be extraordinary, Mr Lovell, then you have failed already. You either are, or you aren't.'

Don't miss
THE WEDDING GAME
by Christine Merrill

Available January 2017
www.millsandboon.co.uk

MILLS & BOON®

Why shop at millsandboon.co.uk?

Each year, thousands of romance readers find their perfect read at millsandboon.co.uk. That's because we're passionate about bringing you the very best romantic fiction. Here are some of the advantages of shopping at www.millsandboon.co.uk:

* **Get new books first**—you'll be able to buy your favourite books one month before they hit the shops

* **Get exclusive discounts**—you'll also be able to buy our specially created monthly collections, with up to 50% off the RRP

* **Find your favourite authors**—latest news, interviews and new releases for all your favourite authors and series on our website, plus ideas for what to try next

* **Join in**—once you've bought your favourite books, don't forget to register with us to rate, review and join in the discussions

Visit **www.millsandboon.co.uk**
for all this and more today!